"A charming start to the new Bookmobile Cat series. Librarian Minnie Hamilton is kindhearted, loyal, and resourceful. And her furry sidekick, Eddie, is equal parts charm and cat-titude."

—*New York Times* bestselling author Sofie Kelly

"*Lending a Paw* is a pleasurable, funny read. Minnie is a delight as a heroine, and Eddie could make even a staunch dog lover more of a cat fan."

—*RT Book Reviews*

"This first in the series charms with a likable heroine, feisty and opinionated cat, and multidimensional small-town characters." —Kings River Life Magazine

"[A] nice introduction for a new mystery series titled the Bookmobile Cat Mysteries." —Gumshoe

Also by Laurie Cass

Lending a Paw

Tailing a Tabby

A BOOKMOBILE CAT MYSTERY

Laurie Cass

AN OBSIDIAN BOOK

OBSIDIAN
Published by the Penguin Group
Penguin Group (USA) LLC, 375 Hudson Street,
New York, New York 10014

USA | Canada | UK | Ireland | Australia | New Zealand | India | South Africa | China
penguin.com
A Penguin Random House Company

First published by Obsidian, an imprint of New American Library,
a division of Penguin Group (USA) LLC

First Printing, July 2014

ISBN 978-0-451-41547-9

Printed in the United States of America
10   9   8   7   6   5   4   3   2   1

To Jon.

Always.

Chapter 1

Once upon a time, I'd imagined my adulthood would include a bright purple bicycle, a daily dish of ice cream, hair that would do whatever I wanted it to, and lots of books.

Fast-forward to my present age of thirty-three. These days, my bicycle was a silvery green, my ice cream had turned into fruits and vegetables, and my black curly hair still refused to obey any command I gave it.

I glanced into the small round mirror above the windshield and grinned at what I saw behind me. At least I'd gotten the books part right.

"Hey, Minnie, did I tell you that if I ever get a tattoo, it'll be a cherry blossom?"

Of course, my childhood vision of a bookish future hadn't taken into account that the books would be on a bookmobile, that I'd be driving said bookmobile, that I'd be accompanied by a teenage volunteer, or that my—

"Mrr."

—that my recently acquired cat, Eddie, would have become a fixture on the bookmobile. "There is no way,"

I told him, "that you're getting a tattoo. Thessie can do whatever she wants, assuming her parents approve."

Eddie didn't respond, but Thessie did. "I still don't get why you haven't told your boss about the Edster. He's the sweetest, most adorable cat ever." She leaned forward and stretched her long fingers into the cat carrier resting under her feet.

Though he'd originally been a bookmobile stowaway, Eddie had been an instant hit with the patrons. It had quickly become obvious that he was going to be a permanent addition to the bookmobile, so I'd bought a proper carrier and retired the picnic basket I'd first used for cat transportation. Eddie had acclimated to the change with an ill grace that had been eliminated with an offering of his favorite cat treats.

"Yes, you are," Thessie cooed, scratching the side of his face, "you're sweet and purry and so very furry."

"Exactly," I muttered. My boss, Stephen Rangel, the director of the Chilson District Library, was a stickler for rules, cleanliness, and propriety. And not necessarily in that order. "If Stephen finds out about Eddie, he'll use cat dander as an excuse to end the program."

From the moment I'd dreamed up the idea of a bookmobile, Stephen had done his best to shoot it down. Homebound patrons could download e-books from the library's Web site, he'd said. There was no reason to spend the money on something so outrageously expensive. It just wasn't needed, he'd said.

Thanks to a donation from a wealthy—and now sadly deceased—library patron, the bookmobile's cost, outfitting, and first year of operational expenses weren't a matter of concern for the library's board of directors.

Unfortunately, a source for the second year of expenses hadn't yet materialized.

In the financial fantasy world that I visited occasionally, I'd find a solid revenue stream that would support operations perpetually. When I took even wilder flights of fancy, I'd find enough money to hire a part-time bookmobile assistant. Thessie was going back to her senior year of high school in a few more weeks, and it would be far easier to hire a replacement than to find another reliable volunteer.

"What are you thinking about?" Thessie asked. "Your face is going all squinchy."

I thought about telling her my monetary concerns. After all, she was considering library science as a college major. Maybe I should tell her about the harsh realities of library life. About fiscal woes and endless meetings and the occasional twenty-three boxes of *National Geographic* magazine left on the doorstep like twenty-three foundlings. Then again, this intelligent and attractive young woman was thinking about going into library science. Who was I to discourage her?

"Dinner," I said. "There's nothing but some sad-looking lettuce in the fridge."

Thessie gave Eddie's chin one more scratch and sat up, her long, dark hair sliding back over her shoulders. "You were not thinking about dinner. You were still thinking about your boss and the bookmobile."

And someday her intelligence was going to get her into trouble.

"What I don't get," she went on, "is why Mr. Rangel hasn't changed his mind. I mean, we're doing great out here!" She flung out her arms at the rolling countryside.

"Every week we're getting more people to come to the bookmobile and they're checking out more and more books. Plus, people are signing up for library cards, like, every day, and soon we're going to start the contest."

Her cheeks flushed pink. The contest had been her idea from top to bottom, including the ultimate prize of the bookmobile stopping at the winner's house. The idea was brilliant, and I was glad to give her full credit. "Why doesn't he see how cool this is?" she asked.

"Because he's a . . ." Just in time I stopped myself from saying an unkind word. "Because he's the library director. Because he's thinking about repairs and maintenance and breakdowns and the cost of replacing the vehicle."

Thessie laughed. "Replacing? It's brand-new!"

Indeed it was, but it had also cost an amazing amount of money and, if a future library board ever wanted to replace the bookmobile, we had to start saving now. Where that money was going to come from, I had no idea, but it was too nice a day to worry about it.

"Well, I think he's dumb not to see how sweet this bookmobile is." Thessie turned around and looked at the shelves. "Three thousand books, right?"

A few more than that, since I'd shoved more books onto the shelves than I should have, but she was close.

"And we have what no other bookmobile has." She tapped the cat carrier with the toes of her flip-flops. "We have an Eddie."

"How lucky can we get?" I asked dryly.

"Mrr."

Thessie peered through the slots of the plastic carrier. "He's looking at you. I think you hurt his little kitty feelings."

I doubted it. The three months I'd spent with Eddie had taught me many things, and the top two items were (1) A Cat's Purr Makes Everything Okay and (2) The Cat Always Wins. Eddie was my little buddy and I loved him dearly, but he could make Machiavelli's advice to the Medicis look like kindergarten lessons.

Take the day of the bookmobile's maiden voyage, for instance. Unwilling to be left behind, he'd snuck out and followed me on my walk through town, then bounded aboard when my back was turned. I hadn't known he was there until it was too late to take him home. The patrons loved him, but with Stephen's certain disapproval looming, I hadn't taken Eddie out for any additional trips until Brynn, a five-year-old girl in remission from leukemia, asked to pet the bookmobile cat.

I'd been strong in my resistance to her request for perhaps three seconds, which was how long it took for her lower lip to start trembling. As a result, Eddie was now as much a part of the bookmobile as I was. More, perhaps. Everyone knew Eddie's name. I was "the Bookmobile Lady." But as long as the patrons were happy and as long as Stephen didn't find out about Eddie, all was well with my world.

Thessie looked at me sideways. "Aren't you afraid that someone's going to tell Mr. Rangel about Eddie?"

Of course I was. "Not really," I said. "Stephen says that since the bookmobile was my idea, I should take care of everything about it. If people as much as even say the word 'bookmobile' to him, he sends them in my direction."

"I don't know," Thessie said doubtfully. "Seems like you should just tell him. I mean, he's going to find out one of these days, right? Wouldn't it be better if you told him yourself instead of someone else telling him?"

Life advice from a seventeen-year-old. Advice that was correct, no less. I gave her a crooked smile. "Yep."

She giggled. "Minnie, are you scared of your boss?"

As if. While the rest of the library staff was, in fact, intimidated by the curt and abrupt Stephen, I had an inherent advantage—I was short. Really short. As in five feet tall if I stood with perfect posture. I'd spent my entire life smaller than the majority of the world, and as a self-defense mechanism, I'd learned not to be intimidated by people.

"No, I'm not scared," I told Thessie. "I'm waiting for the right time to tell him, that's all." The afternoon before the world ended would be perfect. Lawsuit-minded, allergy-sensitive Stephen would never allow a cat on the bookmobile, and I couldn't disappoint Brynn and all the other Eddie fans. I'd backed myself into a conundrum of a corner and there was no way out.

"Uh-huh." Thessie settled back into her seat. "Well, let me know when you figure out the right time. I'd really like to be there."

"What, so you can get it on your smartphone and upload it to the Internet?"

She gave me a hurt look that was completely fake. "Would I do something like that?"

"In a heartbeat." I studied the road ahead. "Hang on, kiddo. We're about to hit the roughest stretch of road in Tonedagana County."

My adopted county was in the hilly, lake-laden, and summer-tourist-packed countryside of northwestern lower Michigan. (In mitten-speak, the ring finger's first knuckle.) Though I'd grown up in the Detroit area, I'd spent many youthful summers with my aunt Frances, my dad's sister, up in Chilson, a small town that overlooked both the sparkling blue Janay Lake and the majestic Lake Michigan. The happy fact that I'd landed a wonderful job in my favorite place in the world was a piece of good fortune for which I was grateful every single day.

The condition of some of the back roads, however, wasn't anything the area chambers of commerce were likely to talk up.

I slowed, steered around the largest of the potholes, gritted my teeth, and hoped that I wasn't doing any permanent damage to the bookmobile. We bounced and rattled and, after approximately an eternity, made it through the worst of the holes without unshelving a single book.

Thessie leaned forward to check on the only creature in the vehicle who wasn't wearing a seat belt. "Hey, Eddie, are you okay?"

"MrrRRRrr!"

"Sorry about the bumpy ride, pal," I said. "We'll go home a different way."

Thessie gave me a look. "You talk to him like he really knows what you're saying."

Most hours of most days I knew it was impossible that my furry little friend could understand human speech. Every once in a while, though, he'd react to something I said in such a way that made me wonder.

"I live by myself," I told Thessie. "Since there's no one else around, I guess I've gotten into the habit of talking to him like he's a person."

She looked at the cat carrier, looked at me, then looked back at the carrier. "Does he ever talk back?"

"Mrr," Eddie said.

I laughed at the startled expression on Thessie's face and flicked the left turn signal. The bookmobile's first stop of the afternoon was the parking lot of a long-shuttered restaurant. At first, the owner hadn't been thrilled with the idea of becoming a bookmobile stop, but when I'd casually mentioned the increase in traffic the property would inevitably get, he'd agreed and a bright new FOR SALE sign had appeared in the restaurant's front window the next day.

We bumped into the parking lot and I headed for the shade of a large maple tree. When we came to a complete stop, I said, "The Eddie has landed."

Thessie unbuckled her seat belt and popped open the cat carrier. "That sounds familiar. Is it a movie quote?"

I thought about having a teaching moment regarding the Apollo moon landing, but we didn't have time. "Not exactly. Can you please pop the vents?" Thessie, at five foot eight, could easily reach up to the ceiling to open the vents. Being undertall has its advantages, but ceiling-reach ability isn't one of them.

"Is there anything wrong with the air-conditioning?" Thessie asked.

"Nothing." But I'd heard enough stories about generator problems from fellow bookmobile librarians to want to avoid running ours as much as possible. "We'll be fine here in the shade."

There was a knock on the back door. "Hey! Are you in there?" a loud male voice called. "Hey!"

As I hurried down the aisle to open the door, making sure my shirt was completely tucked into my cropped pants, a wave of unease washed over me. The man's fist pounded on the door and I was suddenly very aware that Thessie and I were two females alone out in the middle of nowhere.

I shook my head at myself. We'd be fine. For the last few weeks I'd been taking an intense series of self-defense classes, Thessie had a smartphone practically embedded into her skin, and we had Eddie who, if he was awake, could potentially function as a deterrent to crime via howling and hissing and the use of his claws. Plus, I'd always had the vague feeling that bookmobile librarians generated a protective shield. Heck, maybe the books themselves created the shield.

My fanciful thoughts must have been making me smile, because when I opened the door, the gray-haired gentleman standing outside barked out, "What's so funny?"

His face was sour with a grimacing frown, as if he was trying to put a bad face on a bad face. My smile stayed determinedly on. "It's a beautiful day, isn't it? Welcome to the bookmobile." I lowered the outside steps. "Come on in. We're glad to have you."

"I'm here for my wife," he growled as he thumped up the stairs. "She ordered some books, but she's got a doctor's appointment, so she asked me to pick up her holds. What did she order this time, more bodice rippers?"

The sneer in his voice made me want to defend the romance genre, but I swallowed down my reaction and stayed the helpful professional I'd trained to be. Four years of undergraduate work followed by almost three years of graduate study had given me a wide range of knowledge. The subsequent years during which I'd been a librarian had supplied me with the know-how to apply that knowledge. And then there were the lessons my mother had tried to instill in me, starting with "Be nice to people, Minnie."

I continued to smile, asked for his wife's name, and handed him the small pile of books she'd requested.

"Is there anything else?" I asked.

He didn't look up and didn't look around. "No," he said shortly. "There's nothing here for me."

I almost recommended *Beyond Anger: a Guide for Men*, but I held back and he stomped out as loudly as he'd stomped in.

"Hey," Thessie said. "That guy didn't check out those books!"

"Discretion is the better part of valor."

"What?"

"I can do it another way." I started up the computer at the rear desk. When the system came online, I matched the name from the slip of paper I'd removed from the pile of books and pulled up the woman's library card number. In practically no time, I'd changed her hold books to being checked out.

Thessie watched me from the front, where she was setting up the other computer. Eddie watched me from his favorite bookmobile perch—the top of the passenger's seat headrest. Thessie looked unhappy. Eddie looked almost asleep.

"I can't believe you didn't make him check out those books," Thessie said. "That's against the library rules."

One of the things I'd learned in the six weeks the bookmobile had been on the road was that a bookmobile is not quite like a library. It's a different creature altogether and, subsequently, the types of behaviors for both patrons and staff are different.

I wasn't sure how to explain this to Thessie. She was young enough to still be seeing the world in black and white.

"Did you hear him?" she continued. "'There's nothing here for me,' he said, in front of all these books!" She pointed at the shelves. "And even worse"—she whipped around to face Eddie—"he ignored you completely. You're sitting right there, looking all regal, and he doesn't say a thing. What kind of person can ignore a cat?"

I knew how she felt, but professionalism dictated that I keep my opinions about patrons to myself. It would be best if I didn't have any opinions at all, but since I was still living and breathing, I didn't see that happening.

The sound of multiple pairs of footsteps came across the parking lot. Even before the feet reached the stairs, a woman's voice called up, "Is Eddie here?"

"He sure is," Thessie said.

The middle-aged woman, followed by another middle-aged woman, a grandmotherly type, and two preadolescent girls, bounded aboard the bookmobile. "Hello, Bookmobile Lady," the first woman said, grinning. "And good morning, Bookmobile Girl. We're going to need a bunch of books, but first we need our Eddie fix."

All five brushed past us on their way to Eddie's perch. He graciously allowed their petting, and even lifted his chin while the youngest girl scratched him.

Thessie elbowed me. "Look at that. A month ago, that first lady brought her sister to see Eddie, remember? Then they brought their daughters, and now they brought their mother. Eddie is increasing circulation. Tell that to Mr. Rangel."

I reached out, picked an Eddie hair off a bookshelf, and handed it to her.

"Well, sure," she said, putting it in her pocket, "there's a little bit of a downside."

I stooped, picked another Eddie hair off the floor, and handed that to her, too.

"Um, Bookmobile Lady?" The grandmotherly woman was poised at my elbow. "Can you help me find a good book?"

"Anything in particular?" Historical novels, I guessed. Maybe a romance.

"Something scary," she said with relish. "*Silence of the Lambs*, *The Shining*, you know the kind. What do you have that'll scare the pants off me?"

I smiled. I loved being a librarian. Absolutely loved it.

After I showed her the bookmobile's small horror section, I helped her elder daughter find the biographies and the granddaughters find the Amish fiction. While I showed the other daughter where the mysteries lived, I overheard Thessie greet a new arrival. I listened to a male request for anything on the Civil War with half an ear, Thessie's directional response, and his subsequent request a few minutes later, which was to borrow two books even though he didn't have a library card.

"What do you mean?" he asked Thessie. "The guy I saw in the parking lot said he didn't have to use a card to check out his wife's stuff. Why do I need one?"

The granddaughters came up to me, their arms piled high with books to be checked out. I didn't hear Thessie's response, but whatever she said resulted in the guy heaving a loud sigh and walking out with heavy, dragging feet.

At the end of the forty-five minutes, when they'd all

left, I shut the door and Thessie flopped herself onto the carpeted step that served as both seating and as a step stool to access the higher books.

"Wow, what was with these first two guys?" she asked. "It must be crabby day for men, or something. And that younger one, the guy about your age who wanted to check out books without a library card, did you see? He was wearing socks with sandals." She gave a fake shudder. "That's, like, the worst."

I'd been busy with the Friends of Eddie and hadn't seen anything but the back of the man's head. "Oh, I don't know. He could have been barefoot and tracked in cow manure."

Thessie snorted a laugh. "Gross. You're right, that would have been worse."

"Close the vents, will you?" I asked. "We need to get moving if I'm going to get you back on time."

Fifteen minutes later, I dropped Thessie off at her car. She was spending a large chunk of the summer with her grandparents at their home on Five Mile Lake, which was cleverly named for its length. Owing to the narrow and twisting nature of her grandparents' driveway, she'd made arrangements to leave her car in the township hall's parking lot, a lovely space with two entrances, the best possible kind of parking lot for bookmobile maneuvering.

When we'd come to a halt, I said, "Don't worry about those two men today. One bad bookmobile day does not a summer make. It'll be better on Tuesday."

She scrunched up her face into something only a mother could love. "I sure hope so. If Tuesday isn't better, I might have to quit."

Quit? I knew she was joking, but I didn't see much humor in it. "I'll make some arrangements. How about a barbershop quartet at lunchtime?"

She laughed, air-kissed Eddie, told me to say hello to my hot new boyfriend for her, and went out into the afternoon sunshine, her long hair bouncing off her back.

"Which way do you want to go home?" I asked Eddie. "We can take the highway, which is the most direct route, or we can take the lake road, which is longer but a lot prettier."

Whatever Eddie had intended to say got caught in the middle of his yawn, so his response came out something like "Rrrooorr."

"That's right," I said, nodding. "They repaved the lake road earlier this summer, didn't they?" The extra miles were worth it to avoid the potholes of the two-lane county highway. "Thanks for reminding me."

The lake road, officially named Tonedagana County Road 350, curled through glacier-carved hills, first offering up stupendous views of the hilly countryside, then descending to the shores of Five Mile Lake. Water, water everywhere, and not a drop of it fronted real estate that was affordable for mere mortals.

But knowing that I'd never be able to own a lakeside home didn't take away the pleasure I got from seeing the deep blue waters of the many lakes that graced Tonedagana County. Besides Five Mile Lake, the great Lake Michigan, and the large Janay Lake, we had Lake Mitchell, Dooley Lake, Spear Lake, Rock Lake, Peck Lake, and half a dozen other lakes of various shapes and sizes that provided our county with stunning scenic beauty and a healthy tax base.

"Too bad the library doesn't get a bigger share," I told Eddie, but if his closed eyes were any indication, he wasn't paying attention to my ramblings.

And he was right. On this gorgeous July day, I shouldn't be thinking about millages and taxable values and operational expenses or anything at all. I should be enjoying the sunshine and the view.

"There are lots of reasons," I said to my uncaring cat, "that this part of the state is the playground for the downstate folks." Of which I'd been one, not too long ago, but I didn't like to be reminded of that fact. "Lots of Chicago people come up here and I bet half the Detroit area has either a family cottage or a hunting cabin in the area." I paused. Did some quick mental math. "And two-thirds of Dearborn."

To be fair, the majority of the properties hadn't been purchased by the nouveau riche. Many cottages had been handed down from generation to generation with hardly an improvement made. Sure, some had been winterized and suburbanized, but many looked just as they had eighty years earlier, one bathroom, three small bedrooms, and a kitchen with no cabinets, only shelves.

Through the flickering sunlight that filtered down through the maple, cedar, and white birch trees, I could see glimpses of water sparkling with bright diamonds. "Too bad you're a cat," I told Eddie. "If you weren't stuck in that cat carrier, you could be up here with me, enjoying the view."

I heard a sound that might have been, and probably was, a snore.

I glanced over. Eddie was sleeping with one side of his face smushed against the front of the carrier. Tufts of black and white hair stuck out between the squares of wire, as did the tip of one ear.

"You are such a dork," I said, but I said it quietly and with affection. Eddie was a doofus, but he was my doofus, and I loved him. "You're lucky I didn't name you Alonzo." I had first encountered Eddie in a cemetery, next to the grave site of one Alonzo Tillotson, born 1847, died 1926.

I'd assumed the tabby cat had a home and tried to shoo him away, but he'd followed me all the way down the hill and into Chilson, where he'd done that figure eight thing, purring and turning and twisting around my ankles. If he'd been trying to charm me, it had worked just fine.

Dr. Joe, the vet, had checked him out and told me he was around two years old. I'd tempted fate by running a notice in the newspaper for a lost cat, but even though I'd virtuously run a normal-sized advertisement instead of the tiny one I'd considered, no one had called. Eddie and I had been together ever since.

"Not inseparable, though," I said. "That would be weird. I mean, I like you a lot, but there's no need for you to come into the bathroom with me."

Eddie opened his eyes to narrow slits, then closed them again.

"Or the shower." I tried to think of other zones that should be Eddie-free. The kitchen counter, certainly. Though I'd never seen him up there, there was pawprint evidence that he'd made the jump. And my closet. Maybe I needed to get a different latch for the door. What he found attractive about curling up on my shoes, I had no idea, but it wasn't unusual for me to come home and find him sleeping on the floor of my tiny closet. For two weeks he'd preferred my blue flip-flops, but he'd switched to my running shoes. "Hope the flip-flops don't get lonely," I told him.

"Mrr."

"Tell me about it," I said. "Depressed flip-flops are the worst. No flip, no flop, nothing but Eddie hair on them. It's a—"

"Mrrr!"

I took my gaze off the road for a scant second. "You okay, pal?" He'd sounded a little frantic and I hoped his stomach had settled completely from his lunch of dry cat food and water.

"*MRR!*" He sprang to his feet. "*MRRRR!*"

"Okay, bud, okay." I checked the road for a place to pull over. Nothing but curving asphalt, narrow shoulders, even narrower driveways, and trees. "Hang on a minute, there's bound to be a spot past this curve. Then we'll pull over and see what's up, okay?"

The road was curving sharply and the fact that I'd already started bringing the bookmobile to a stop was the only thing that kept me from hitting the woman who was running into the middle of the road, waving her arms over her head, and shouting.

Chapter 2

Vehicles that are thirty-one feet long and weigh twenty-three thousand pounds loaded do not stop on a dime, but even so, I was surprised at how quickly the air brakes brought us to a halt.

Faster than thought, I unbuckled myself and reached to unlatch the door of the cat carrier. "Eddie? You all right? Sorry about that hard screeching stop."

He glared at me from the farthest and darkest possible corner of the carrier and didn't reply. I'd rigged up a way to strap the carrier down, but even so the hard braking would have caused him to slide around inside the carrier.

Since he didn't look as if he was in dire shape, I left him to his sulk and opened the bookmobile door. I hurried down the steps and ran back to the woman. "Ma'am? Are you okay?"

As we drew closer to each other, I could see that the woman was wheezing with exertion. Her brown graying hair was falling out of its ponytail, and while her cheeks were red with the effort from running, the rest of her face was pale.

"It's my husband," she panted.

A black-and-white blur made of one hundred percent Eddie streaked past us, galloped down the road, then made a hard right down a driveway.

The woman paid no attention. "It's my husband, down at our house. He's having a stroke, I'm sure of it, and I need to get him to the hospital." Tears coated her cheeks. "We don't have a landline. I tried to call nine-one-one on my cell, but I dropped it. The back fell off and the battery popped out, it takes forever to cycle on again, and I couldn't find my husband's phone, so I just ran up here. I need help to get him into my car and please, oh, please . . ."

She grabbed my hands and suddenly no more words needed to be said. I wanted to chase after Eddie, but this came first. I didn't know much about medicine, but I knew that getting stroke victims to the hospital as soon as possible was critical. It would take an ambulance half an hour to get to this part of the county. Add another half hour to get to the hospital, and that was . . . way too much time.

I cast aside all of Stephen's warnings about waivers and insurance papers for anyone who rode along on the bookmobile. "Let's go," I said, her sense of urgency infecting me. "No." I grabbed her sleeve when she turned around. "I'll drive. It'll be faster."

Both of us running, we returned to the bookmobile. I had the door shut and the vehicle in drive faster than I should have, but not fast enough, not nearly fast enough. "How far?"

The woman was banging her thighs with clenched fists. "A little farther," she whispered, looking out the front window. "One more driveway . . . there!"

"Got it." I made a hard right and stomped on the gas pedal.

The narrow gravel driveway was tree-lined and not made for a vehicle the size of the bookmobile. Tree branches scraped our sides and the roof. I spared a single thought for the damage the mysterious equipment that lived up there could be sustaining, another for what the chances of insurance coverage might be, then stopped thinking about it.

"It's such a long driveway," the woman murmured. "We're so far away from everyone . . . How could we be so stupid?" She pounded her thighs again. "Can't you go any faster?"

I didn't reply. Couldn't, really, because it was taking all my concentration to fly us through the winding curves that were taking us inexorably downhill to the shores of a small lake, visible now through the trees.

"Faster," she breathed. "Please . . ."

I pressed the gas pedal down a little farther. We rounded a sharp corner where the drive turned from gravel to asphalt, hurtled down a last small hill, and burst into a clearing with a large Mission-style house on the far side and a blessedly large turnaround area.

Eddie sat on the porch, licking one paw and looking as if he'd been there for half an hour.

The woman was up out of her seat while we were still moving. She thumped the door with her fist, but its safety feature wouldn't let the lock release until we came to a stop. When I could finally unlock it, she shoved it open and ran. "This way," she shouted over her shoulder. "He's in his office."

I hurried after her, fixing Eddie with a steely glare. "Don't you go anywhere," I told him as I ran past.

The woman had left the front door, a heavy wooden thing held together with wrought iron, wide open. Not a simple rectangle, the door had a curved top, something that had to be expensive. This fact had barely registered when I was through the entrance, into the house, and into a low-ceilinged, oak-floored foyer that led to hallways and doorways and a switchback stairway. I stopped, trying to figure out which way to go.

Eddie streaked past. "Mrr," he called, and I followed him.

I don't know if it was a cat-born instinct or some keen sense of hearing that he'd never bothered to demonstrate before, but Eddie arrowed straight through the rough-plastered entrance to a hallway lined with framed paintings of moonlit water. Real paintings, painted with real paint, and they looked vaguely familiar. I put the assumption in my head that they were from a local artist and hurried past.

"In here!" the woman called.

At the end of the hall were three doorways that led in three different directions. Through one I saw a black-and-white tile floor and white porcelain bathroom fixtures. Through another I saw shelves and shelves of books. Eddie trotted through the third, and if cats had heels, I was right on his.

The woman was kneeling on the thick carpet, her back to a stone fireplace. A man lay sprawled on the floor, his entire left side limp and lifeless. The woman held her husband's good hand to her cheek. "Honey, I brought help. We'll get you to a hospital in no time." She looked up to me, her eyes asking the question.

I nodded. "We can take him in the bookmobile. It'll be easiest." Although how we were going to get him into it, I wasn't quite sure. The man, who looked to be in his mid-fifties, also looked to be heavy. And big. Or at least a lot bigger than five-foot-nothing Minnie. His wife had a few inches on me, but the two of us dragging this ill man through the hallway, down the front steps, and into the bookmobile was going to be imposs—

No. There had to be a way. All I had to do was find it. "Think, Minnie, think," I muttered. What was the good of taking all those first aid classes last winter in preparation for bookmobile emergencies if I couldn't remember what to do when an emergency happened? There must have been something I'd learned about transporting an injured person.

I unclenched my fists. Yes. There had been. "We need a heavy blanket. Or a rug."

The woman nodded across the room. "The sofa."

I looked over and saw Eddie sitting on the back of a brass-studded leather couch. "Move it, pal," I said, and he did as I crossed the room and snatched the blanket. A pure wool Hudson Bay blanket imported from England, if I was any judge.

"We need to get him on his side." I dropped to my knees and tried to remember the techniques I'd been taught. Using care not to hurt the man, but with speed enough to move things along, I moved his right arm straight above his head, arranged his left across his body, laid his right leg straight, propped his left leg up, gently put my hands on his left hip and knee, and pushed. With almost no effort on my part, the man rolled onto his side.

"Hot dog," I murmured. "It worked."

"What's that?" the woman asked.

"Hold him in place while I get the blanket set, okay?" In seconds, I'd laid one end of the blanket on the floor just south of his hips and flopped the far end past his head. "Okay, let him down."

The woman gently rolled her husband onto the blanket. "We're going to move you, honey, okay? We'll be as gentle as we can."

He made a guttural noise that I took for assent. I stood and stooped to pick up the loose end of the blanket. "I can try to move him by myself, but—"

She was already on her feet. "I'll take one corner."

We walked backward, grunting with the effort of pulling the stricken man out of the study, down the hall, into the foyer, and over the small bump of the threshold with Eddie on solemn parade near the man's feet.

I looked at the front steps. "Do you have a piece of plywood in your garage? I don't want him to get hurt." Wooden steps I might have risked, but these were hard slate. "Something for a ramp."

The woman's gaze darted to the detached garage. "No, no plywood." She made a small, panicked-animal noise. "No wood scraps, nothing like—"

She stopped, laid the corner of the blanket on the floor, and ran back into the house. I dragged the man closer to the steps and was almost there when she returned carrying a wide plank about eighteen inches wide and five feet long. A table leaf. Perfect.

She dropped it onto the steps where it instantly became a sturdy ramp, and we eased her husband down it, across the drive, and next to the back end of the bookmobile.

"How . . . ?" The woman looked up at the tall rear door, her face pale.

"Hang on." I hurried into the bookmobile and quickly had the electric-powered handicap ramp moving toward the ground. I ran outside, flipped the metal base unit down, and the two of us slid the woman's husband onto the ramp. "Keep him in position, okay? I'll get him at the top."

No words had been necessary; she was already doing what needed to be done. I ran back inside, followed by Eddie, and powered the ramp back upstairs. Moments later, the woman and I got him safely onto the bookmobile's floor.

I shut the doors and hurried to the driver's seat. When I buckled my seat belt, I looked back. The woman was lying next to her husband, caressing his face, and murmuring, "It won't be long now, sweetheart. Not long at all."

There was no way I was going to insist that she follow standard operating procedure and buckle up, so I started the engine. Eddie jumped onto the passenger's seat and sat, looking straight ahead. Since I didn't want to take the time to shove a reluctant cat into the carrier, I murmured a short prayer for a safe trip and dropped the transmission into gear.

Turning the vehicle around was usually a slow business; I'd turn on the video camera that had a spectacular view of the rear bumper and inch my way backward and forward, backward and forward, until I'd made a twenty-eight-point turn.

This time, I glanced in the side mirrors, cranked the steering wheel around, pressed my foot firmly on the gas pedal, and roared back. A hard stomp on the brake, then back to the gas pedal as I spun the wheel in the opposite direction, and off we went up the hill we'd come down—I eyed the dashboard clock—not even ten minutes ago.

We roared up the hill and when we reached the asphalt of the county road, I took a look over my shoulder. The woman was still on the floor next to her husband, cradling his head in her arms, protecting him from the bounces of the bookmobile.

"The hospital in Charlevoix is the closest," I called back. "Or I can take you to Petoskey or . . . ?"

She didn't look up. "Whatever is fastest."

Charlevoix, then. It would take half an hour to get us there, which was probably far too long for a stroke victim, but it was the best I could do.

No. There was one other thing.

I broke another bookmobile rule and took one hand off the wheel. My backpack lay on the console between the seats and I dug through it for my cell phone.

Please let there be coverage, I thought as I turned it on. *Please.*

I glanced at the screen. Cell phone reception was tricky in this part of the county; its hills and valleys had a way of creating dead zones that was extremely annoying, not to say frustrating. But for now there was a signal. I scrolled through the listing, found the name that I wanted, and pushed. One ring, and someone picked up. "Charlevoix Area Hospital, how may I direct your call?"

"Emergency room, please."

"One moment."

I tried to keep my concentration in front of us, scanning the road, shoulders, and forest edges. Now would be a truly bad time for a deer to wander into our path.

"Emergency, how may I help you?"

"I'm bringing in a stroke victim," I said. "We'll be there in half an hour or less."

"Can you hold, please?" There was a short pause; then another voice came on the line. "This is Rita. I'm the ER nurse today. You said you're bringing in a stroke victim?"

Rita? Who was Rita? "Yes," I said. "He lives out on the lake road and his wife flagged me down. I figured it was better to get him there as fast as possible than to wait for an ambulance."

I'd hoped for an assurance that I'd done the right thing, but instead she asked, "How long ago was the stroke?"

"Hang on." Keeping my gaze on the road, I turned my head and called back the question.

"I . . . don't know," the woman said. "What time is it?" After I told her, she said, "It couldn't have been more than half an hour. Maybe less."

I relayed the information into the phone.

"Okay," Rita said. "How old is the patient? Does he have any medical issues? Diabetes, high blood pressure, high cholesterol, history of cancer?"

More information was exchanged inside the bookmobile. "He's fifty-six," I told Rita. "The only health problem he has is osteoarthritis."

"Medications?" Rita asked.

"Just multivitamins and ibuprofen for the arthritis every once in a while."

"And what is the patient's name?"

I almost laughed. I'd been in this guy's house, touched parts of him (through clothes) that were typically reserved for family and close friends, dragged him across his driveway, and was using the bookmobile to get him to emergency care, but I had no idea what his name was.

"Just a second," I told Rita. "One more question," I said to the rear of the bookmobile. "The hospital needs to know his name."

"Yes," the woman said quietly. "I suppose they do, don't they?"

At this odd response, I turned my head halfway around, but I couldn't see her face; she had her back to me as she tended to her husband. "His name is Russell McCade," she finally said.

I faced front. Russell McCade. Why was that name familiar? I would have sworn on a stack of Nancy Drews that I'd never met either him or his wife before, so why did I know the name?

"Ma'am?" Rita asked. "The name?"

"Russell McCade," I said.

"Sorry?" she asked. "You're breaking up out there. Can you repeat that?"

I spoke louder. "Russell. McCade." And that's when the name suddenly made sense to me.

Rita's voice started cutting out. "Okay, his first— Russell. What—name?"

"McCade," I said forcefully. "McCade! And tell Tucker that it's Minnie bringing him in."

The line went dead and I had no idea if she'd heard me or not. Mechanically, I put the phone back in my backpack as my mind ran around in tiny, panicked circles. Russell McCade. Russell McCade was in the bookmobile, suffering from a stroke. Russell McCade, who went by the name Cade, who was one of the country's best-known and most successful artists.

It was all making sense. The paintings in the hallway

were early works, created before he'd established his trademark style that I'd heard described as impressionism meets postmodernism. While I had no idea what that meant, I knew that I'd loved his paintings for years, and even more so since I'd seen an original hanging in a local art gallery.

Cade had a magical ability to appeal to consumers and critics alike. Sure, some critics dismissed his work as sentimental schlock, but most agreed that it was quality schlock, and the prices on his works had long ago reached the point where owning one was considered an investment.

Though I'd heard he had a place up here, I'd had no idea where it was. Easy enough to shield ownership of property by setting up a limited liability company that would purchase your home for you. And easy enough to avoid talking to neighbors if you didn't have any close by.

I flicked another glance back. Easy enough to do all that if you wanted to avoid gawkers and stalkers and unwanted intrusions, but it sounded like a lonely existence.

"How much farther?" Cade's wife asked, her voice cracking.

"Not far," I said. Maybe this guy was internationally famous and fabulously wealthy, but right now he was a suffering man with a wife who was worried sick about him. I pressed a little harder on the gas pedal and we rocketed down the road.

We sped down the highway, over the Charlevoix drawbridge, through the side streets of town, and, accompanied by the massive bulk of Lake Michigan that lay west of the hospital, we pulled into the emergency entrance.

Half the ER staff was waiting for us. As soon as we stopped, two ER workers were up the bookmobile steps and inside with a gurney. They hefted Cade with a calm competence that was reassuring.

Dr. Tucker Kleinow, the good-looking blond, and tall, but not too tall, ER doctor who was scheduled to work that day, waited outside. "Minnie. Are you all right?" He grabbed my hand and squeezed it.

"Sure. Did . . ." I didn't want to ask, but I had to. "Did I do the right thing? Bringing him here myself instead of waiting for an ambulance?"

"Absolutely." My love interest of less than a month squeezed my hand again. "Time is a crucial element for stroke victims." The gurney came down the steps and Tucker left my side. "All right, guys," he said. "Let's get him in."

Cade's wife was clutching the side of the gurney. "I'm going with him. I'm his wife."

Tucker made a come-along gesture and the small group started to move away fast toward the white lights of the ER.

I trotted after them. From my back pocket I pulled out a small rectangular piece of cardstock. "Here," I said, sliding my business card into the woman's hand. "Let me know how he is, okay? And I won't . . . I won't tell anyone anything."

She flashed me a short smile and glanced at the card. "Thank you, Minnie. Thank you so much for everything."

I fell back. Everyone else went through the hospital doors and was gone.

For a long moment I stood there, watching the doors and seeing nothing, hearing nothing except my own heart beating too fast. I'd done what I could, and now . . . what? Tucker and the rest of the ER staff would take it from here. There was nothing left for me to do.

"Mrr." Eddie bonked the back of my leg with his head, purring loud enough for me to feel it in my knees.

"What's that?" I asked, scooping him up. "You're saying of course there's something to do, because there's always an Eddie to pet?"

He bonked my forehead. "Mrr."

I smiled into his fur and suddenly wanted to cry. "Yeah, 'Mrr' to you, too, pal."

Chapter 3

I whiled away the evening by attending the annual Post–Fourth of July Party my left-hand neighbors had been throwing ever since they bought their boat and found a summer berth at Uncle Chip's Marina in Chilson.

The Axfords played big band music, hauled in tubs of fresh oysters, and handed out plastic champagne flutes to hold the freely flowing beverage. They were wizards at making sure their guests had a good time, and I wasn't surprised when I felt Louisa Axford's firm hand on my shoulder as I stood at their boat's bow, looking out over the dark waters of Janay Lake. The sun had gone down half an hour earlier and the last remnants of daylight still glowed on the horizon.

"Minnie, is anything wrong?" she asked. "Don't tell me that Chris finally managed to offend you."

I could hear the smile in her voice, but I knew she was studying me closely. I made a laugh. "The day he offends me is the day I go online and order up a new sense of humor."

Chris Ballou was the manager of Uncle Chip's Marina, and was the most politically incorrect human on the planet. Taking him seriously would be as sensible as thinking Eddie could actually understand what I said to him.

Louisa patted my shoulder. "Good. I heard him call you Minner Dinner the other day. That seemed a little over-the-top."

Chris found my name a great source of amusement, and within minutes of our first meeting, he'd started playing rhyming games with it. Min-Tin-Tin was one of his favorites, but he also favored Min-Bin and, of course, Minnie-Ha-Ha.

I reached around to give her a quick hug. "I don't get mad," I said. "I get even."

Louisa threw back her head and laughed, the ends of her white hair curling onto her shoulders. "You are my role model," she said. "Let's go on back to the party. Now, I know you're dating that nice Dr. Kleinow, but I'd appreciate it if you could spend a few minutes with that startlingly handsome young man over there. He's new to town and could use some advice on Chilson's social scene."

Though I let her take me back to the festivities, my thoughts remained where they'd been, back at the hospital with Russell McCade and his wife.

Sunday I dawdled away by sleeping late, exchanging text messages with Tucker that reassured him I was fine after being a temporary ambulance driver, reading the newspaper, hauling dirty clothes to the marina's coin laundry, doing all the other household chores that had piled up on my little houseboat during the week, hanging out with my best friend, Kristen, at her restaurant and telling her about Saturday's events.

I wanted to ask Tucker about Cade but knew I couldn't. I wouldn't want him to violate the privacy laws and I certainly didn't want to put him in the position of having to tell me he couldn't tell me anything.

"Maybe Cade's wife will call," I told Eddie, who was on the dining table, basking in a square of sunshine. "By the way, you know you're not supposed to be up there. At least not when I'm home."

His eyes, which had been open to small slits, closed completely. It was too much work, apparently, for him to say, "Mrr."

On Monday morning, the air was thick with fog. My walk through the streets of downtown Chilson, normally a journey I enjoyed for the sheer pleasure of looking at the oddly cohesive blend of old and new architecture, was instead a damp passage through a gray world. The fog was so thick it was impossible to make out the wording on the store's signs.

If I hadn't known better, the Round Table, a diner extraordinaire, might have been Bound Town, Thorington Jewelry could have been Tonedagana Jodhpurs, and if you squinted a little, Tom's Bakery turned into Tim's Eatery.

The exercise of renaming the downtown businesses amused me, and I was in a fine mood as I settled myself in my office and got to work. After all, the fog would clear off soon, the sky would turn blue, and surely Cade would make a full recovery. No doubt about it. I nodded to myself, turned on the computer, and lost myself in spreadsheets.

"Minnie."

A chill froze my perkiness. "Hey, Stephen." I looked up from the half-completed fall activities schedule. "How are you this fine morning?"

He frowned. "There's a thick fog."

That was Stephen, always one to find the dark lining in a silver cloud. I gave him a quick scan, trying to find a clue to his mood. Dour countenance, snugged-up tie, buttoned shirt cuffs. Though I couldn't see, his pants were most likely ironed to sharp creases and it was certain that his shoes were shined. All normal. At least for Stephen.

Here in the land we called Up North, the only men who wore neckties on a regular basis were attorneys, and even then their ties only came out on court days. Most men were glad to foreswear the nooselike encumbrances, but Stephen wasn't most men.

While I thought my typical summer library wear of unconstructed jacket, dress pants, and loafers was an excellent display of Up North professionalism, Stephen would, no doubt, have preferred that I wore low-heeled pumps, nylons, and skirt suits of navy blue and black. Wasn't going to happen. Ever.

"A fog, yes," I said, pointing at the ceiling, "but the sun is above, doing its best to shine through." He looked puzzled, so I gave up my attempt to humanize him. "What can I do for you?"

The puzzlement retreated and was replaced by a much more familiar expression, that of displeasure. "We have a problem, Minnie, a serious problem."

"We do?" To the best of my knowledge, the library

had been problem free for days, if not weeks. Well, if you didn't count that minor episode in the children's section with the three-year-old and the scissors, and that had ended easily enough with a time-out and a check to replace the damaged books. "What's up?" I asked.

"Mitchell Koyne." Stephen put his forefinger on the edge of my desk. "He's been spending far too much time in this library. He's keeping the staff from their duties with his endless questions and it must stop."

"Ah." Mitchell was indeed a fixture in the library. A large one. He was one of the tallest men I'd ever met, though he didn't seem to know it, and it was hard to overlook his presence. From what I'd heard, Mitchell had various seasonal jobs—construction, snowplowing, ski lift operator—but he had more employment gaps than employment and none of us knew how he managed to feed and clothe himself. Not that his wardrobe of jeans, T-shirts, flannel shirts, and baseball caps could cost a tremendous amount, but still, you had to wonder.

Actually there were a lot of things about Mitchell that I wondered about, the first one of which was his true level of intelligence. At times he came across as one of the dumbest people you'd ever met, but at other times he'd say something that made you think he was one of the smartest people you'd ever met. Sometimes both would happen in the same conversation.

Plus, conversations with Mitchell tended to go on for five minutes longer than you wanted them to, and Mitchell seemed completely clueless that the library staff had job functions that didn't include answering his questions, which could range from "What's the longest suspension bridge in the world?" to "What's mascarpone?"

On the plus side, I'd never seen Mitchell appear in the library before noon. Mornings were the most productive times for us, by far. The man had an odd charm, but a little bit of Mitchell went a long way.

I looked at Stephen's finger, which was curving backward with the pressure he was exerting on it. "Well," I said, "I'm not sure what we can do about it. This is a public institution. Mitchell has as much right to be here as anyone."

"Of course he does," Stephen said. "But he can't be interfering with the duties of our staff."

"He isn't, not really." I watched Stephen's eyebrows go up. "I mean, maybe he talks a lot, but he's not keeping anyone from doing their job." Not for long, anyway. We'd all become experts at sliding out of the Mitchell zone.

Stephen stood up straight and folded his arms. "You think so? You'd know better if you paid more attention to the running of this library. You're spending too much time on that bookmobile and not enough time doing what I hired you to do."

I started to protest, but he ran right over me.

"And what did I hire you to do? To take care of the details. To take care of the day-to-day operations so I could be free to deal with the bigger issues. I did not expect to get mired down in the muck of daily minutiae at this point in my career and I resent being required to do so."

He smoothed his tie. "Now, Minnie"—his voice dropped into that grating patronizing tone—"I know you're trying to do your best. All I ask is that you exert a little more effort regarding your main function here. You are the assistant library director, remember?"

"Sure, but—"

"Mitchell Koyne," Stephen said. "Take care of it." He spun around, marched out the door, and soon I heard his leather-soled shoes go up the stairs to his office aerie on the second floor.

Most days it was easy enough to balance between placating Stephen and maintaining a sense of pride. "Not today," I murmured. But if I was off my game, it could mean only one thing: time for more coffee.

I picked up my mug and aimed myself at the break room. Though I hadn't checked the time, it must have been about ten o'clock. Josh, our IT guy, was at the vending machine shoving dollar bills in one end and taking diet sodas out of the other. Holly, a part-time clerk, was stirring creamer and sugar into her mug emblazoned with the logo of the American Library Association.

They both looked up when I came in, then exchanged a glance.

"What?" I grabbed the coffeepot and filled up.

"Um . . ." Holly continued to stir. "Nothing."

Josh snorted and popped open one of his freshly delivered cans. "Stephen's been talking to you, hasn't he?"

I leaned against the counter. "What makes you say that?"

Holly cast her eyes heavenward. "Well, let's see. You didn't say good morning, you didn't say what a beautiful day it is in northern lower Michigan, and you didn't ask how our weekends went."

Josh stuffed cans into the side pockets of his cargo pants and continued the list of clues. "You're drinking coffee that Kelsey brewed without making a face and you haven't said anything about Saturday's bookmobile run." He took a slug of soda. "There's only one thing that could do all that to you."

"It's that obvious?" I eyed the coffee in my mug. Kelsey was my most recent hire. Well, sort of. She'd been a library employee in the past but had left to have two children. Now that the children were older, she was pleased enough to drop them at her mother's for a few hours while she skipped off to the library. She was excited to be a part of the library staff again, so excited that she'd taken over the task of making coffee. I'd told her that not everyone liked coffee strong enough to stand up and salute, but she'd just laughed at what she thought was a joke.

"Sweetie," Holly said, "we all know what it feels like to have Stephen yell at us."

"All of us who have worked here longer than three years, anyway." Josh toasted me. "Now that you're here, he just yells at you. Thanks, Min." He grinned.

"Glad I could be of service." As I took another sip of coffee, I considered telling Holly and Josh about the Mitchell Problem but decided not to. Stephen was right. I was the assistant director, and it wouldn't be right to put any of the job's weight on them. Maybe I'd ask for ideas, but the responsibility to find a solution was mine.

"You know what?" Holly asked, laughing. "Stephen reminds me of this algebra teacher I had in high school. He scared the crap out of everyone and whenever Stephen starts in on me, all I can think about is the Pythagorean theorem."

And, just like that, my sour mood vanished. Because even though I was going to have to come up with a method of managing the previously unmanageable

Mitchell, and even though I needed to tread carefully if I was to keep the bookmobile on the road, I had friends, I could always brew my own coffee, and Stephen obviously didn't know about the bookmobile's trip to the hospital.

I quirked up a smile. Most important of all, he still didn't know about Eddie. Life wasn't so bad. Matter of fact, it was pretty darn good.

"So," I said. "How were your weekends?"

The rest of the library day passed uneventfully. Minor issues were resolved with small dosages of tact and large helpings of humor. Both were needed to pacify Mrs. Tolliver, an elderly, straight-spined summer resident from Wisconsin. Mrs. Tolliver insisted that the Nancy Drew mysteries in the library were substandard and far below the writing quality of the originals and she didn't want her granddaughter to read anything but the best. She'd been mollified when I said I tracked down as many originals as I could through interlibrary loan, and the exchange had silently been declared a draw.

I unlocked the door to my houseboat. "Hey, Eddie, do I have a story for you! Would you believe that Stephen—" I stopped midsentence, because I'd seen the evidence of what the cat Thessie insisted on calling adorable had been doing in my absence.

"Nice, Eddie." What had been a pristine roll of paper towels on the kitchen counter the day before was now on the floor in the form of a shredded mass of pulp.

Mr. Adorable looked up from his current favorite napping spot—the dining table's bench seat—and opened and closed his mouth without saying a word.

"Yeah, yeah," I said. "The mess is my fault for leaving you alone for so long. My fault for not finding a friend for you to play with. My fault for not buying you the proper cat toys, whatever those might be."

Since Eddie already knew that, he went back to nap mode. But since he'd likely been sleeping all day, I kept talking to him. If I didn't keep him awake, he'd sleep all evening and then, at two in the morning, he'd want to play cat games with my hair.

"I suppose," I said, "I should be grateful it's only paper towels that you're shredding and not furniture. Or the houseboat itself. This poor thing has enough problems as it is."

My summer place of residence was the cutest little houseboat imaginable. Made of wood long ago in a Chilson backyard, it was smaller than my first apartment. It boasted one bedroom with two bunks, a tiny bathroom, and a small kitchen with dining area. The only generous thing about it was the view I got when I sat on the outside deck. It was the sheer pleasure of being able to see Janay Lake on my doorstep morning, noon, or night, in fair weather or foul, that more than made up for the cranky neighbors that lay to the right.

Every so often, I untied from the dock and puttered around the lake, but I had no desire to venture out through the channel and into Lake Michigan. That lake was far too big for my top-heavy little houseboat, and if I sank the poor thing, I'd be homeless next summer.

October through April, I lived with Aunt Frances, my dad's widowed sister, the aunt with whom I'd stayed during my childhood summers. Come warmer weather, however, I shooed myself out the front door to make way for her summer boarders. Every spring, she said I could stay, but I loved my houseboat, the camaraderie of Uncle Chip's Marina, most of my neighbors, and all of the many moods of Janay Lake.

During a dinner of chicken stir-fry (for me) and dry cat food (Eddie), I told Eddie that Stephen had asked me to de-Mitchell-ize the library. My uninterested cat offered no advice, but he did jump up on the bench next to me and purr, so he was helpful in a different way.

After dinner the two of us wandered out to the boat's deck, skirting my one flowerpot and the metal bucket I'd been filling with skipping stones. Eddie trotted out in front and claimed the chaise longue to the left, so I took the remaining one, the one that needed sanding and painting. I'd covered both with flowery cushions, and you could hardly see the maintenance that needed doing, but still.

"How do you do that?" I asked my feline friend. "Okay, sure, cats deserve the best, but shouldn't that apply only to cat-oriented things, not people things?"

Eddie sat in the middle of the chaise's cushion and licked his hind leg.

"Cats," I muttered, and flopped down.

For a moment, I just lay there, listening to the sounds of water and wind and summer, smelling lake and from somewhere, fresh-cut grass, feeling the sun on my face, enjoying the warmth on my skin, enjoying the freedom that comes from outside temperatures that allowed you to wear shorts and T-shirt and not be a single bit cold.

"Mrr."

I jerked out of a light doze, fluttering the newspaper I held in my hand. "Right," I said. "What do you want first? Front section or sports?" Eddie gave me the are-you-an-idiot-or-what? glance. "Silly me. I forget how you need to have things read to you in order."

The last couple of weeks, I'd fallen into the habit of reading the newspaper to Eddie. Reading out loud to a cat may be an extremely strange thing to do, but I found Eddie's reactions entertaining. "Here's one," I said, and Eddie flopped down into his listening position. To non–cat owners, it might look as if he was sleeping, but I could tell from the way his ears twitched that he was paying attention.

In synopsis form, I read him an account of a local township board meeting. "Looks like they're fighting over lake access again in Williams Township. Same old same old." I scanned the article. "Yep. Adjacent property owners want it closed. Everyone else wants it open."

Eddie slapped his tail against the cushion.

"Yeah, I know, all lake access points should be used only by cats." I looked at him over the top of the paper. "But would you ever use one?"

He fixed his gaze on the horizon. *Slap, slap, slap.*

I almost started to argue with him but realized just in time that I would lose. "Fine. Next up is . . ." The rest of the front page was taken up with nothing Eddie would care about. The opening of a new movie theater, a local student winning a scholarship. I turned the page.

"Hey, how about this one?" I asked. "You know that TV cooking show, *Trock's Troubles*? The one that's filmed up here a few times each summer?" Actually Eddie didn't know since the houseboat didn't have a television. Come October it would be different, because Aunt Frances was a devoted fan.

Trock Farrand, the bumbling host of the long-running show, owned a summer home not far from Chilson and he'd persuaded the show's producers to film the show at various area locations from Trock's home kitchen to his patio to farm markets to the occasional restaurant. My best friend, Kristen, owner of the Three Seasons Restaurant, was on a short list and she was torn between excitement and anxiety.

Eddie's ears had pricked at the name of the show, so I went on. "This says Trock was out on his bicycle yesterday and was almost run over by a car. He was out on that road that runs right next to Lake Michigan, and he fell halfway down the bluff."

I paused, thinking. Farrand had been lucky to escape with the scrapes and bruises the article described. Tumbling down that steep hillside covered with scrub trees, briars, and who knew what else, he could easily have had a serious injury.

Eddie jumped down from his seat and up onto mine. He bumped the back of the paper with his head.

"Right. Sorry." I read through the rest of the article. "He says it was a black SUV with tinted windows that ran him off the road."

"Mrr." Eddie turned around twice and, finally facing the water, settled himself onto my legs.

"Yeah, doesn't narrow things down much, does it? That's what probably half the summer people drive."

"Mrr."

I started to pet him. "No, I'm not going to get a black SUV with tinted windows just because you want one. Think of how your cat hair would look on black upholstery."

He turned his head around to look at me.

"Fine. When I get a black SUV, which is unlikely unless I win the lottery, which is unlikely unless I start playing it, we'll get leather seats." Although that would be problematic in a different way since Eddie still had all his claws.

But my nonsensical capitulation must have satisfied Mr. Ed, because he started purring. Clearly, he was done with the newspaper.

Smiling, I closed it. "If you're done, I'm done, pal."

"Mrr."

Chapter 4

Early the next morning, I woke to the unmistakable noise of a cat doing something that he shouldn't.

"Eddie, whatever you're up to, stop it."

He, of course, ignored me and went on making odd noises out in the kitchen area.

Growling to myself about cats and mornings and alarm clocks, I rolled out of bed, and padded down the short hallway and up the three steps in my bare feet and jammies. At the top of the stairs, I stood over him, hands on my hips. "Although it's more what you're *down* to, isn't it?"

He looked up at me with an expression that could only be saying, "Who, me?"

"Yes, you." I kicked at the newspaper he'd pulled off the top of the recyclables pile and dragged to the middle of the floor. "What is it with you and paper products? Paper towels, newspapers. And last month it was stuff out of the printer. What are you going to attack next week?" I almost said toilet paper but kept my suggestion to myself and crouched down to gather up his minor mess.

"I suppose I should be grateful you hadn't started shredding this stuff. Having to pick up tiny pieces of newsprint first thing in the morning would be truly annoying." I tried to arrange the papers in a neat pile by shoving them around. Didn't get very far.

Eddie appeared to be finding my efforts interesting to the point that he was stretching out with his front paw to tap the paper. "Oh, quit. This isn't a cat toy, okay?" I looked at the date. "This is yesterday's paper and . . ." My voice faded away as I caught sight of an article I hadn't noticed the night before.

"Check this out, Eddie. A boat exploded out on Lake Michigan."

My furry friend edged closer, his paw still extended. I moved the paper up out of his reach. His easy reach, anyway. "The boat's owner was blown clear and picked up by a nearby boat. Marine experts are investigating the cause."

The short paragraph hadn't told me—the owner of a boat—nearly enough. Had the guy been hurt? Had the boat sunk? What had caused the explosion? Every good boat owner knew that you had to air an inboard engine before you started it in case noxious gases had collected in the engine well, but that boat had been out on the lake. Of course, maybe he'd—

Eddie's white paw darted under the bottom of the newspaper and pulled. The print ripped cleanly from south to north. I jumped to my feet.

"Cut that out! This is not, I repeat not, a cat toy."

Eddie gave me a sour look, obviously thinking that if I balled up a sheet and tossed it down to the bedroom, it would be.

"No," I said. "This is headed for the outside recycle

bin. We live on a houseboat, a small one, and organized tidiness is key." I gathered up the paper, an empty glass jar, and the flattened can that last night had held chicken broth. "Tidiness, from here on out," I said, slipping into the sandals I'd kicked off near the door.

"Mrr," Eddie said.

I opened the door and pointed at him with a librarian's index finger. "Tidiness," I told him, and shut the door before he could get in the last word.

That was a bookmobile day, which was happily free of any unpleasant incidents or medical emergencies, and the next day was a library day that was crowded from open to close with a multitude of patrons needing assistance, a children's author reading, a Friends of the Library meeting, and a delivery of brand-new books.

I slept like a rock that night. The next morning, my morning off from the library, I pulled on dress pants and a dressy T-shirt and drove up to the Charlevoix Hospital.

When I explained to the receptionist that I'd been the one to bring Mr. McCade in, she said he'd been asking about me and let me straight through.

"Hello?" I knocked on the doorframe of Russell McCade's hospital room. In my hand were flowers from Oleson's, a local grocery store. "Mr. McCade? Mrs. McCade?"

The man sitting up in the hospital bed and the woman in the chair next to him looked up at me. I remembered the woman's just-shy-of-heavyset build and shoulder-length graying brown hair, but it was the first time I'd had a chance to really look at Russell McCade.

Despite the stroke-induced sagging of his left side, I

could see that he had those craggy features that many women found attractive: bushy eyebrows, wide forehead and mouth, and a cleft chin. Sitting, he had a small belly, but that might disappear if he stood and sucked in. His hair was similar to his wife's, half brown and half gray, and though their features didn't look that similar, they gave off a sense of fitting together like a right hand in a left.

"Yes?" Mrs. McCade looked at me with a polite, yet distant smile. "May I help you?"

Rats. They didn't recognize me. Not a huge surprise, but how exactly do you introduce yourself in a case like this without embarrassing everyone involved? "Um . . ." I proffered the flowers. "I brought these for—"

She let out a half squeal, half shout. "It's Minnie!" She leapt to her feet and ran to me. The momentum of her hug sent me staggering a step backward. "Oh, my dear, I'm so glad you stopped by, so very glad." She squeezed me hard enough that my eyes popped a little. "Cade, this is your bookmobile angel." She grabbed my hand and tugged me to the bedside.

"There is nothing that I can possibly do," Mr. McCade said, the words slow and slurred but clear enough, "to repay you for what you did. Barb and I are in your debt forever."

I wanted to squirm. Did, just a little. "Anybody would have done the same thing."

"What most people would have done," he said, "is call nine-one-one and keep driving. You went far and above the call of kindness. Thank you, my dear. Thank you very much."

He reached out for my hand and patted it. I could

feel a slight heat on my cheeks and knew I was blushing. "You're welcome," I said. "Glad I was there at the right time."

His wife relieved me of my small burden ("Let me take care of those flowers") and put it on the windowsill while she extracted a promise from me to call them Barb and Cade. "Minnie, can you stay for a few minutes?" she asked. "Please do."

"For a little while," I said. "But I can't stay too long. I have to work this afternoon."

"Is that why you don't have your furry friend with you?" She smiled. "What fun to have a bookmobile cat."

"Is this afternoon another bookmobile trip?" Cade asked.

I pulled up a chair and perched on its edge, explaining my split roles of assistant library director and bookmobile driver. Halfway through the explanation I stumbled a little, because I suddenly realized why I was taking such a fast liking to this man I barely knew. He looked like and had a personality similar to my first-ever boss, the library director in Dearborn, the town where I'd grown up. Mr. Herrington had given me a summer job and he'd even kept me on part-time my senior year of high school.

Then I stumbled over my words a little more, because Mr. Herrington had passed away when my parents and I were in Florida over Christmas break, visiting my older brother. Mr. Herrington had died of a sudden heart attack in the library, during the hours I would have been there working, and I'd never quite forgiven myself for not being there to help him.

I blinked a time or two and stumbled back to my

current narrative. If either McCade had noticed my fal-
terings, they were both too polite to say so.

"Well," Barb said, "I'm glad the Chilson Library has
a bookmobile. If it didn't, Cade here might not be making such a fast recovery."

"Long way to go." Cade looked down at his left side.
"Pity I'm left-handed."

"You're . . . left-handed?" My mouth went dry. "But . . ."

"Don't worry about his painting," Barb said. "He's
such a nut to paint that he'll learn how to do it right-
handed if he has to."

Cade lifted his right hand and flexed it. "Learning
new techniques is what keeps me young. Well, that and
learning how to use Facebook."

Barb snorted. "Waste of time," she said. "I know, I
know, your agent thinks it's giving you a better connection to your legions of fans, but it's so artificial. How
can typing two sentences to a stranger mean anything?"

"Better to use social media than have to tour," her
husband said. "Pick your poison, my dear."

"Scotch," she said promptly. "On the rocks."

"Gin and tonic for me." He chuckled. "We're quite a
pair, aren't we, Mrs. McCade?"

She held his hand, the hand closest to her, his left
hand, his weak hand, and kissed it. "Indeed we are, Mr.
McCade."

Cade's eyes faded shut. "Indeed."

The moment was rich with love and comfort and
security. With all my heart, I hoped that my marriage
would be as strong as this one. When I got married,
that is. Not that I was thinking about weddings or anything.

"Minnie," Barb said, watching her husband. "Is that your full name?"

"Nope." I didn't say anything else, and she chuckled.

"When I get out of here," Cade said, opening his eyes, "when I'm better, Barb and I are going to treat you to a night on the town. Dinner, drinks, dessert." A smile curved up one side of his face. "All the best *D*'s possible. Dancing, if you want it."

I grinned. "Disco?"

"Done."

"Do-si-do?"

"Indubitably."

Barb looked at him askance. "That's not a *D* word."

"No, but it feels like one. Say it out loud and you'll see."

So there we were, saying the word "indubitably" over and over again and getting a serious case of the giggles. Since it was a hospital, we tried to keep the noise down, but that made my stomach start to cramp. "Don't," I panted, "it hurts. Don't."

"*D* word," Barb managed to get out, and we were off again.

A male voice intruded. "As I thought. It's Minnie Hamilton, out and about and making trouble."

"Tucker!" I jumped to my feet and went to him for a quick hug. Not a big one, because he was in doctor mode, but even a little one felt good.

Barb looked from me to Tucker and back. "Our bookmobile angel and our emergency room doctor hero are an item?" She clapped her hands. "Oh, how perfect this is. How absolutely perfect!"

"Stop her," Cade said, "or she'll be making calls for your wedding caterer."

"We've only been dating a few weeks," I said, my face once again going warm.

"Good weeks, though, right?" Tucker kissed the top of my head. "Good to see you're doing well, Mr. McCade."

"Thank you again, Dr. Kleinow," Barb said. "Thank you so very much."

He smiled. "Just doing my job, ma'am." He nodded a good-bye, gave me a quick hug, and left.

"I should get going, too." I stood. "I'm glad you're doing so well, Cade."

Barb stood, too. "I'll walk you out, Minnie." She leaned forward. "Go to sleep, my sweet. I'll be back before you know it."

"Mmm." Cade's eyes were already closed. By the time Barb and I reached the door, he was snoring.

Out in the carpeted hallway, Barb stopped. "Minnie . . ." But whatever words she wanted to say got lost somewhere and she just stood there, looking at me with eyes full of emotion.

My throat clogged up a little. "You don't need to say anything, okay? I'm glad I was there to help. Truly."

"You're a lovely girl." Barb laid her hand on my cheek for a brief moment. "Your parents must be very proud."

I wasn't so sure about that, but hey, maybe she was right.

"I'll call you," she said. "We'll set a date for a nice lunch. I should have called before, but I've been a little . . ." She looked back down the hall.

"Busy," I supplied. "Don't worry about it. My cell number's on my card. Call whenever you want."

"Thank you, Minnie." She gave me a hard hug. "So very much."

I watched her walk back down the hall to her husband's room, sniffled a little, and felt a sudden urge to talk to my aunt Frances.

"Minnie, my sweet. How are you?"

Even though I wasn't feeling bad, not really, hearing my aunt's voice made me feel better. She had a knack for making people feel not just better, but happier. And beyond that, more comfortable with themselves and who they could be.

It was a mild push from Aunt Frances that had gotten my friend Kristen thinking about opening a restaurant, and it was an Aunt Frances suggestion that motivated a neighbor of hers to make the move from composing music for friends and family to selling it over the Internet and eventually to making a mint writing movie sound tracks.

I glanced through my office doorway. No one in sight. "Just wondering about breakfast on Saturday. And how things are, you know, going." Because Aunt Frances ran more than a summer boardinghouse and she did more than amateur career coaching; she was a secret matchmaker.

My aunt sighed. It was an uncharacteristic sound from my permanently cheerful relative. "There are what you might call issues."

Every spring Aunt Frances took careful stock of the boardinghouse applicants for the upcoming summer. Though she didn't have a Web site or even a Facebook page, she did have years upon years of happy boarders who referred friends and family and near strangers. The stack of letters and e-mails from people asking to stay was thicker than the phone book for the entire county.

Aunt Frances studied each letter carefully, and if a candidate looked at all probable, an intense series of letters and phone calls followed. To explain the unusual setup at the boardinghouse, Aunt Frances would say, and go on to explain that the summer's fee included a daily breakfast, with one catch. On Saturday, a boarder cooked for everyone else. The daunting task of cooking for the six boarders, Aunt Frances, and often her librarian niece had made more than one applicant back away.

The cooking of breakfast, however, was a requirement Aunt Frances would never change. Because the real reason she took so much time studying the applicants was that the entire summer was a secret matchmaking setup, pairing boarder with boarder.

"There's no better way to get a person's measure than to see him or her working in the kitchen," she'd said to me privately. And she had a gift for pairing up her boarders. In all the years she'd been running the boardinghouse, which had been ever since her husband died so young that I barely remembered him, she'd never once missed. Until now.

She sighed again. "It's a downright mess."

"Do you want to talk about it?"

There was a pause. "Not really." Then she spoke in a lighter tone. "It'll work out. I'm sure of it."

Because this year, early on, her carefully selected summer pairs had mismatched completely. The lovely twenty-six-year-old Deena and the fifty-year-old Quincy had taken to each other with a liking that seemed far more than friendship. This had pushed fifty-three-year-old

Paulette, Quincy's theoretical match, into the companionship of sixty-five-year-old Leo, which left twenty-three-year-old Harris, Deena's supposed match, to spend a lot of time with Zofia, a grandmother who wore clothes of many colors and a baker's dozen of rings. But Zofia had been matched with Leo. It was a problem and my match-making aunt was ready to pull out her hair.

"Well," I said, "there's always breakfast to look forward to. And that's one of the reasons I called. Tucker and I both have the day off and I was wondering if it would be okay to bring him."

"Oh, honey." Aunt Frances laughed. "Of all the Saturdays to bring your young man to breakfast, you pick this one."

"What's up?"

"Harris," she said succinctly. "He's been making a mess of the kitchen all week, working on a culinary creation of his own."

"Not good?"

"Horrible. I can't count the number of eggs he's gone through, and I have to tell you, the smell of burning maple syrup isn't something I'd wish on my worst enemy."

"You don't have an enemy in the world."

"I'll have a houseful if I don't have a backup plan for breakfast this Saturday. Do you have any ideas where I could hide a few boxes of cereal?"

I suggested the trunk of her car, thanked her for the warning about breakfast, and went back to work.

Saturday morning, the first Saturday I'd had off in weeks, started off with a dawn so bright and shiny that the world felt brand-new.

I'd taken my aunt's warnings to heart and had asked Tucker to come by the houseboat later that morning, but I found some courage, took a deep breath, and headed up to the boardinghouse.

"Good morning, favorite niece," Aunt Frances greeted me on the front porch. She had a mug of steaming coffee in her hand. "Would you like a cup? It'll be the best thing about breakfast."

Since I was her only niece, I didn't let the favorite comment go to my head. "Is it going to be that bad?"

She sipped her coffee. "You be the judge. But you know the rules."

"No making fun of the food and always compliment the cook."

She smiled. "A credit to the family, that's what you are."

I glanced at the front door. "So, how are things going in there? Apart from the breakfast, I mean."

Her smile fell away. "Horrible. Simply horrible."

It disturbed me to see my normally cheerful aunt look so morose. "I'll be the judge of that," I said, and opened the wooden screen door for her. We passed through the spacious living room, oak floorboards creaking, past the end tables and coffee tables built from driftwood, past the maps thumbtacked to the walls and the fieldstone fireplace, and entered the dining room.

I exchanged morning greetings with five of the six boarders, and within five minutes, I understood what my aunt had meant. The young, funny, intelligent, beautiful Deena was pouring coffee for the middle-aged and balding Quincy. She added sugar and a little cream, stirred it, then handed it to him and watched anxiously until he sipped it and nodded. Her resulting smile was bright and happy and I didn't dare look at Aunt Frances.

My favorite boarder of the summer, Zofia, stood at the window, smiling at the view of the bird- and tree-filled backyard. Zofia had a tendency to wear flowing skirts and dangling earrings, clothing to match her Gypsy-sounding name. She hadn't been able to wear that type of thing when her husband was ladder-climbing for a major car manufacturer, but after his death she'd spread her wings.

The white-haired Leo was sitting at the table with Paulette at his side. Paulette, tawny-haired and comfortably plump, had been matched with Quincy, but she'd shown no interest in him whatsoever once the dapper Leo appeared on the scene.

My aunt's plan had been to match Zofia with Leo, but Zofia seemed to be comfortable with her single status and hadn't shown a hint of interest in the man.

Unless something changed fast, this was going to be Aunt Frances's first matchmaking failure ever. Well, not a complete failure, because four of the six boarders would be matched up, even if not according to plan, but that would leave two of them alone, and that would just about kill Aunt Frances.

"Breakfast!" Harris called. "Morning, Minnie. Could you ring the bell?"

"Sure." I went out to the screened porch that lay adjacent to the dining room, and pulled on the rope that went from the porch to the top end of a bell. Years ago, the bell had been taken from an old train engine and installed in the branches of a maple tree for this very purpose. The bell dinged once, twice, and three times, summoning one and all to the breakfast table. Everyone was there already, but ringing the bell was a tradition that dared not be broken.

We sat down to toast, orange juice, and a breakfast casserole made of . . . well, I wasn't quite sure what. Eggs, certainly. Bacon? Green peppers? And was that . . . it couldn't be pineapple, could it? A few silent minutes went by while eight people chewed, seven of whom were searching for something complimentary to say. Harris, who had recently graduated from college, and who had been matched with Deena, didn't seem to care about his romantic loss. What he seemed most concerned about was our reaction to the food.

"Harris, dear," Zofia said, "the coffee is outstanding this morning."

"Absolutely." Leo held up his mug. "Never better, young man."

Aunt Frances cleared her throat. "It takes ingenuity to create your own recipe, young man. You've shown great courage."

"You bet," Deena said quickly. "I would never have dreamed of making up something. Not ever."

"Interesting combinations," I said. "I'll have to tell Kristen."

"Just think," Paulette added, "maybe Kristen will name a new entrée after you."

Quincy said, "And they're still filming that cooking show up here, aren't they? Maybe you could get on that."

Harris laughed and visibly relaxed. "Oh, come on, it's not that good. Not *Trock's Troubles* good."

We all protested. I hoped Harris wouldn't catch on to the fact that it was a token effort.

With the compliments done, Aunt Frances moved on to the next item on her agenda. "Quincy," she said heartily. "Did you see the creation Paulette made the other day? She's a knitting magician, don't you think?"

It was obvious that Quincy cared far less about Paulette's needleworking skills than he did about staring into Deena's eyes. "Sure," he said vaguely, most of his attention still on Deena. "Nice work, Paulette. Real nice socks you made."

Paulette stared at him. "They were mittens."

But Quincy had already turned back to Deena.

Aunt Frances sent me a despairing look. "So, Zofia," she said, reaching for a piece of toast. "Did you hear that Leo ran ten miles yesterday? Nice to see people our age take such an interest in fitness, don't you think?"

Zofia slathered butter on her own piece of toast, then added a large dollop of orange marmalade. "Hard on the joints, running is. Don't want knee replacement surgery myself."

I watched Aunt Frances bite her lower lip. Something had to be done, and done fast.

"Say," I said. "Did I tell you what Eddie did the other day?"

Everyone, Aunt Frances included, turned to me, smiles already forming on their faces. They were all familiar with Eddie stories and I'd been told—in a friendly way—not to show up to breakfast if I didn't have a new one.

I launched into his most recent escapade, one that involved a marina neighbor's eighty-pound black Labrador retriever, a bit of bread fallen from who knew where, and a short cat vs. dog tussle over said bread. Soon everyone was laughing and I breathed a small internal sigh of relief that Aunt Frances was joining in.

Eddie to the rescue. The world was indeed a mysterious place.

"Good morning, Minnie." My left-hand neighbor, Louisa, pulled her long white hair into a ponytail and tied it with a scarf. "The weather forecasters have been at it again, did you see? Wish I could have had a job that let me make so many mistakes."

"Last I checked," I said, looking at the blue sky, "they were saying mostly sunny and mid-seventies."

"You poor dear," she said sympathetically. "On your Saturday off, no less. Now they're saying seventy percent chance of rain and high sixties." She turned and pointed to the west.

I looked where her index finger was aiming. A solid line of clouds was low on the horizon and inching our way. "Maybe it'll blow apart." But the line was dark and thick and heavy. I tried another possibility. "Or maybe it'll stay out on Lake Michigan. That happens, sometimes."

Louisa studied the incoming weather, an educated gaze born from years of Great Lakes boating. She pursed her lips, deepening the small vertical lines around her mouth, and shook her head. "Not today. It's going to start raining around eleven and it's not going to quit for hours."

"Little Miss Sunshine, you are not," I said wryly. "Tucker and I were going to go out on Janay Lake today." So much for the picnic I was going to make. So much for the route I'd laid out, and so much for the bottle of wine Kristen had recommended.

"Hmm." Louisa put her hand to her forehead and frowned mightily. "You and that fine-looking young doctor? My, my. What could two young, single people possibly do on a rainy day?"

I tried not to laugh. "How do you know I'm that kind of girl?"

"If the circumstances are right, we're *all* that kind of girl." She waggled her eyebrows. "Have a nice day, dear."

This time I did laugh.

While I waited for Tucker to show up, I came up with numerous alternative plans for the day that ranged from sitting around the boat and hoping Louisa was wrong about the weather to driving to Traverse City and trying every brewpub in town, to driving back and forth across the Mackinac Bridge hoping to watch a thousand-foot freighter cruise underneath us.

I stood at the boat's cockpit, trying not to frown at the incoming weather. "We're not going to let a little rain stop us from having fun," I said out loud. "We're just not."

Eddie, who was lying on the back of the dining area's bench seat, opened one eye, then closed it again just as Tucker came to the door.

"Knock, knock," he said through the screen.

"Hey there." I felt a happy smile on my face and saw an answering one on his. "Come on in. Welcome to my humble abode."

He stepped inside, and while the houseboat had always seemed just the right size for me, it suddenly seemed far too small with the addition of a five-foot-ten, broad-shouldered man.

"This is really great." He looked out the front window and ran his hand along the cockpit's dashboard. "When you get tired of people, you just untie your house and go for a boat ride."

It was a common reaction for first-time visitors. I decided not to tell him about the utilitarian technicalities involved in detaching. Let the boy keep his illusions.

"And this galley." He grinned at the miniature kitchen. "What more do you need?"

"Mrr."

Tucker spun around. Eddie was now standing up on the back of the seat and stretching his head high. The furry face and the human face weren't exactly eye to eye, but it was pretty close.

"Ah." Tucker lifted a hesitant hand. "This must be Eddie." He looked at me. "Is it okay if I pet him?"

"As long as you don't mind getting cat hair all over you."

Tucker looked at his clothes. Dark red polo shirt over khaki shorts. "It'll come off, won't it?"

Eventually. "You didn't have cats growing up, did you?"

He shook his head and gave Eddie a tentative rub. Eddie immediately pushed against the pat, putting his weight into it, which was enough force that Tucker's weight was shifted. He took half a step backward. "Cat's got some strength, doesn't he?"

"You should smell his breath."

Tucker eyed Eddie. "Um . . ."

I laughed. "Joking. His breath isn't that bad." Most

of the time. I watched Eddie watching Tucker. My little pal was being as tentative with my boyfriend as my boyfriend was being with my cat. For a brief second I considered telling Tucker that Eddie liked being talked to, but I ran the conversation through my head and gave it a pass.

"So," I said, "what do you want to—"

Ka-bam!

A clap of thunder buffeted the air, so intense it was almost too loud to be heard. On its heels came a sizzle of lightning that made the hairs on my arms stand up.

"Mrr," Eddie said.

I wasn't sure if he was protesting the storm or the way Tucker was petting him. "So," I tried again. "What do you want to—"

Rain fell from the sky in large, loud drops. I looked at my watch. Louisa had been all of ten minutes off.

I glanced out through the front window, out to the driving rain. If this rain kept up, neither driving down to Traverse City nor going up to the Mackinac Bridge would be very sensible, or very relaxing.

"So," I said, hoping I wasn't starting an infinite loop. "What do you want to—"

Tucker help up his index finger and bent his head to his shoulder. "Ah . . . ah . . . *choo!*" He rubbed his face, still holding up his index finger, and sneezed two more deep sneezes.

"Are you getting sick?" I asked.

"I work in a hospital. You wouldn't believe what walks in the door."

It was hard not to edge away. "Oh."

He smiled. "No, honestly, I feel fine. There's probably just a lot of stuff in the air right now, with that storm coming in."

I wasn't sure that made a lot of sense, but hey, he was the doctor. On the other hand, wasn't it a truism that doctors couldn't make their own diagnoses?

"So, what do you want to do today?" he asked. "I assume boating is out."

Yes, the signs were there. Slightly reddened eyes, slightly running nose, and a slight sag to his normally straight shoulders. Maybe it was just fatigue. He worked far too many weird hours, and that could do a number on anyone's immune system. But the last thing I wanted to do was drag him out to expend more energy and make things worse.

On the other hand, what were we going to do all day? I kept my thoughts firmly averted from Louisa's suggestion. We barely knew each other, after all.

Tucker hooked his finger under Eddie's chin. "Hey, he's purring!" He grinned. "I'm not sure I ever made a cat purr before."

"Mrr," Eddie said, and pushed up against Tucker's rubbing.

An idea popped into my head. "What do you think about going to the movies?"

Both Eddie and Tucker turned to look at me. Eddie didn't say anything, but Tucker sneezed and said, "Hot buttered popcorn, Sno-Caps, a vat of soda, and I'm happy for hours."

"You are so not alone."

"Any kind of movie you don't like?"

"No horror."

He grinned. "I don't do movies with subtitles. Too much work."

"I doubt the multiplex in Petoskey is showing any foreign films today."

He held out his hand to me, palm up, inviting me to take it. "Then I say we have a plan."

The Saturday movie marathon was a great success. We chose movies based on nothing whatsoever, picked out snacks based on what the people ahead of us bought, and after the credits rolled, we ventured out to the lobby to check the weather. If it was still raining, we went back for another round of movie and snacks. Since on that particular day it rained for twelve hours straight, we saw a lot of movies. And had a lot of snacks.

"How many movies did you watch?" Kristen had asked on Sunday afternoon. "You were really in there all day?"

And a good chunk of the night. I tallied up the films on my fingers. "There was the new Pixar movie at noon, then that romantic comedy with what's her name around two, then a really funny vampire movie at four thirty, then that end-of-the-world movie at seven, and last was the big new thriller at nine."

Kristen was counting along with me. "You watched five movies?"

"It was almost six. They were having a midnight showing of the first *Star Wars* movie, but Tucker had to be at the hospital early this morning."

"Sounds fun," she said halfheartedly.

For us, it had been. During the intervals between the movies, we discussed the plots and characters of the movie we'd just watched, learning a little more about each other in the process.

I was telling Kristen all about it when my cell phone

rang. "Do you mind?" I asked and, when she shrugged, took the call. It was a short conversation, and when it was over, I hung up, smiling.

"Looks like I'm going to lunch tomorrow at the one restaurant in town that's more expensive than yours," I said.

Kristen's eyebrows went up. "Tucker's taking you to Seven Street? Must be true love."

"Seven Street, yes," I said. "But it's not Tucker. It's a woman."

My best friend's eyebrows went up even farther. "Does Tucker know about this?"

I grinned. "He's met her."

Barb McCade was already seated when I walked into the restaurant. I'd eaten at Seven Street once before, so I knew my typical library attire wouldn't fit in. That morning I'd chosen a soft dress and covered it with a jacket that almost matched. Stephen had nodded at me approvingly over his coffee mug. I didn't have the heart to tell him it was a onetime deal.

"I'm so glad you could come," Barb said. "I thought about Three Seasons, but I thought this would be more special."

Part of our conversation at the hospital had included the facts that Three Seasons was one of the McCades' favorite restaurants and that the owner of said restaurant was a good friend of mine.

"No apology necessary," I told her. "Matter of fact, there might be a law about that. No apologies required for any behavior incurred during times of extreme emergency."

She laughed. "Aren't you a sweetheart? But as I said

before, I should have called right away to thank you for all you did."

"Oh. Well." I shifted around in my seat, trying to find a comfortable way to accept undeserved praise. In a weird way, I felt as if I'd finally been able to help Mr. Herrington, my old boss. It didn't make sense, but that was the way I felt and I would never share that feeling, ever. "Anyone would have done the same thing. I was just the first person to come along, that's all."

"Actually you were the fourth." Her tone went a little flat.

I winced, then nodded at a passing waitress. "But Cade's still doing well?"

"Much." The happiness was back. "He's been transferred out of the hospital and into Lakeview for a few weeks of rehabilitation therapy."

"That's wonderful!" The Lakeview Medical Care Facility in Chilson was not only a nursing home, but also a long-term and rehabilitation care provider. "So . . ." I hesitated. "Is he . . . I mean . . ."

Barb was willing to voice the frightening question that I was dancing around. "Is he going to recover enough to paint again? The doctors say yes, with time. Cade figures that means a month at most." She laughed.

"Five weeks," I said confidently, and waved at a pair of not-quite-elderly ladies on their way to be seated.

She laughed. "Minnie Hamilton, you are just what the doctor ordered. Anytime you want to stop by and see Cade at Lakeview, you go right ahead. He's in a restricted-access room, but I'll make sure your name is on the visitor list."

A warmth spread through me. "If you think he'd like to see me, I'd be happy to stop by."

"Minnie, he wants to *paint* you."

Ack. "Then there's no way I'll stop and see him."

She laughed again. "That's the third time you've made me laugh in five minutes. I'm not sure I've laughed since the stroke except when you're around. Forget Cade, stop by and see me."

"With the bookmobile or without?" I asked, then stood to say hello to the cane-carrying Mr. Goodwin.

"Minnie," Barb said, when I sat down. "Do you know everyone in this town?"

I smiled. "Only the ones who have a library card."

The most elegant woman I'd ever met in my life paused at our table. "Good afternoon, Barb. And, Minnie, how are you?"

Once again, I stood. "Mrs. Grice, it's nice to see you again."

The very wealthy and widowed Caroline Grice smiled. "It wasn't long ago that you were calling me Caroline. How is it that we've regressed so far?"

"Well, because I'm not that smart. Really I'm not." Because if I'd had half a brain I would have guessed that Caroline, primary sponsor of Chilson's Lakeview Art Gallery, would know the McCades.

Barb laughed. "Don't believe a word of it, Caroline. Minnie here is one of the brightest young women I've met in ages." The two women exchanged a few more pleasantries; then Caroline moved on.

"You can't tell me," Barb said, "that Caroline Grice has a library card."

"Well, no." She had recently made a nice donation to the library, though.

"Then you do know everyone in town." When I

started shaking my head, she covertly pointed to the front of the room. "How about her?"

I glanced at the hostess. "Cheryl Stone. She and her sister are trying to start a sheep farm north of town. I don't know her sister's name, though."

"Still counts. And him?" She gestured to a man at the table nearest to us.

"One of the county commissioners."

Barb solemnly held up her water glass. "To Minnie, the person to call if I ever need an introduction to anyone in town."

I snorted out an unladylike noise and tinked my glass to hers. "To Barb, who is far too easily impressed."

We both laughed, and I got the comfortable feeling that we were going to be friends for a long, long time.

Twice that week, I went over to Lakeview Medical Care Facility, but both times I stopped by, Cade was sleeping. Both times I wrote out a short note that said I'd stop again, and ended the note with a bad sketch of Eddie.

Then, late on Friday night, or rather, early on Saturday morning, my cell phone rang. As I'd placed it on the small dresser next to my bed, the ringtone made Eddie jump as high as I did.

I fumbled for the ON button and managed to say hello.

"Minnie? It's Barb. I'm so sorry to wake you, but I didn't know who else to call. You were so helpful when Cade had his stroke, and you know everyone around here and . . . oh, God, I'm so sorry. I must sound like an idiot. Go back to sleep and forget I ever—"

"Barb," I said calmly. Or as calmly as I could after being jerked awake in the wee hours of the morning. "Talk to me. How can I help?"

"Oh, Minnie, you are a blessing." She pulled in a small breath. "Do you know a good lawyer? A criminal lawyer? Because the sheriff is about to arrest Cade. For . . ." She stopped for another life-sustaining gasp of air. "For murder."

Chapter 5

I threw back the covers and jumped out of bed. Eddie voiced his displeasure, but for once I didn't explain anything to him.

"I'll make some phone calls," I told Barb. "Don't worry. I'll find somebody."

"Oh, Minnie . . ."

"No crying," I said firmly. "Not until later, anyway."

Amazingly, she laughed. A small laugh, but still. "You're right. No crying until later. Minnie, how did you get so smart while so young?"

"It's not me," I said. "It's the Brontë sisters and Charles Dickens. Plus lots of Roald Dahl when I was young and impressionable." I told her I'd be there as soon as I could and thumbed off the phone.

Through a yawn, Eddie squeaked out a "Mrr."

"Sorry, pal, but I have to go." I yanked off my sleeping shorts and pulled on what I knew to be clean and relatively free of cat hair. Though the county sheriff's office was more formal than the much smaller city police department, considering the hour, jeans and a polo shirt would have to suffice.

I snatched up the phone and started pushing buttons as I hunted for a pair of shoes. "Hey, Kristen. Sorry to call at this hour, but I need your help and I don't have time to answer any questions. Do you know any criminal attorneys?"

My best friend showed her true colors. "What'd you do, kill someone? Let me guess. You finally tipped over the edge and took out that Stephen—"

"Kristen!"

There was a short pause. "Okay, sorry. You'll fill me in later. I know lots of lawyers, but they're all municipal and family types. I can't think of criminal guys. I could make some calls in the morning, if you want."

"That might be too late," I said tightly. "I needed one half an hour ago." I kind of listened to what I'd just said and jumped in before she could ask the question. "No, it's not for me. A . . . a friend needs one."

Kristen said she'd think some more, and I started scrolling through my list of phone numbers. By this time I'd slipped on a pair of sandals and was in the kitchen looking for my purse. The light breeze that had cooled us earlier was gone, and the night was warm and sticky and still.

I dialed again. "Rafe? Minnie. Sorry to call at this hour, and please don't ask any questions because I don't have time, but do you know any criminal lawyers?"

Rafe Niswander gave a happy laugh. "You need a lawyer? Hot dog! What'd you do? Come on, tell me. Vandalism, I bet. Did you climb up the water tower to paint your name? Five bucks says you got caught before you got to the letter *N*."

Rafe and I often made five-dollar bets about everything from song titles to the top recorded speed of a cheetah, but not tonight. "Rafe, please."

"Yeah, I wasn't supposed to ask questions, was I? Criminal lawyer, you said. I know the prosecuting attorney. Does that help?"

"Wrong side."

"Gotcha. Well."

I could almost see him scratching his head.

"I could make some calls for you, but it's three in the morning, Minnie. Do you really need a lawyer right now?"

"It's not for me." Despair was starting to lap at my toes. "Thanks, anyway. Talk to you later, okay?"

We hung up and I went back to scrolling through names. Why didn't I have any friends who got into trouble?

"Mrr." Eddie jumped up onto the dining table and butted the phone.

"Not now, pal." I gently elbowed him out of the way. "I need to find an attorney for Cade. There's no way he did what they're saying he did. I'm sure it's all a mix-up. I mean, how could Russell McCade do . . . do that? But he'll still need a good lawyer to get him out of this mess."

"Ah, Minnie?"

I went still. Gunnar Olson. What was he doing up at this hour, and even more so, what was he doing talking to me? I looked up. The big man was standing on the dock between our boats and holding a smoldering cigar.

"Uh, hello," I said. Every window in my houseboat was open and Gunnar and I were maybe ten feet apart. One of the hazards of marina life was that if you weren't careful, everyone heard everything.

Gunnar held the cigar to his lips and inhaled, making the dark orange coal burn bright. "You're looking for a criminal attorney, I heard."

For a second I couldn't breathe. "I am. Yes."

"And not for you."

"No."

He held out the cigar and studied its glowing end. "For Russell McCade. Also known as Cade."

I could see where this was going and I didn't like it one single bit. "Cade is completely innocent. I'm sure of it. It's just a mix-up and if you breathe one word of this to anyone I'll find an attorney of my own and see that you're sued for slander and—"

"Hold on, missy, just hold on. I know you don't like me and the feeling is mutual, but I'm a big fan of Cade's work."

"You . . . are?" I gave Eddie an absentminded pat, picked up my purse, and went out to the dock.

"First original art I ever bought was one of his early moonrises and it has appreciated in value ten times over."

Now, that figured. Gunnar's worldview was dollars and cents and—

"But I'd never sell it," he said. "Not if it was my last possession on earth. I love that painting. Makes me feel young again. And I'd be honored to provide a little help to the man who painted it."

I rearranged my open mouth to the shut position. "Right now he needs an experienced criminal lawyer."

"Here." He reached into his pocket for his cell phone. "You're going to be talking to Daniel Markakis. He works in the Detroit area, but he's got a summer place up here. I golfed with him yesterday, so I know he's around." He stabbed at the phone's screen a few times and handed it over.

"I can call him at this time of night?" I asked.

Gunnar glanced at me. "He's used to it. Tell him I gave you his number. Just leave the phone on the dock. I'll get it later." He turned to go, then stopped. "And don't worry. I won't say anything about this. McCade's got a right to privacy, same as anybody else."

"Hey, Gunnar?" I called softly. "Thanks."

He gave a shrugging nod and waved, the cigar sketching a wide orange arc in the darkness, and headed down the dock to his boat.

I watched my cranky neighbor walk away. Truly, every human being was a mystery and we should never assume we know anything about anyone.

Then I turned my attention to the phone. "Mr. Markakis? I'm sorry to bother you at this hour, but Gunnar Olson lent me his phone and . . ."

When I opened the door to the small waiting room, Barb didn't even glance up but continued to stare at the wall, barely breathing, hardly blinking. The day she'd flagged down the bookmobile, she'd worn the tight look of fear. Now she looked . . . empty, as if all her emotions had been played out and there was nothing left to feel.

"Barb?" I asked softly.

She came to life with a jerking start. "Minnie." She stood, swayed a little, then came toward me. "So good of you to come," she said, and enveloped me in a hug that I was glad to return.

When I felt her arms start to release me, I patted her shoulder and stepped back. "I found an attorney," I said.

"He should be here in fifteen minutes." Or less, if he drove as fast as he'd vowed he would. It seemed wrong for a criminal attorney to promise to break speed limit laws, but I wasn't going to tell him not to hurry.

"Oh, Minnie." Barb put her hand to her mouth. She started to sway again and I guided her back to the chair in which she'd been sitting.

I sat next to her. "Now, I've never met this guy before, but a neighbor of mine recommended him." I suddenly wondered why Gunnar happened to know a criminal attorney. I knew Gunnar was a loudmouthed, arrogant boor, but . . . I pushed the thought away. None of my business. And there were all sorts of ways they could know each other. Maybe they were cousins. Or worked in the same building. No reason to suspect that Gunnar had ever needed the services of a criminal attorney.

"What's his name?" Barb asked.

"Markakis."

Her eyes went wide. "Daniel Markakis?"

I nodded. "That's it. Do you know him?"

"He was the lead attorney in that big murder case last winter. You remember."

Kind of, sort of, but not really. I watched very little television, and local newspapers didn't cover downstate news with much fervor.

"Daniel Markakis." Barb shook her head and crumpled a little. "Hard to believe we need to hire a man like that."

I spoke as gently as I could. "What happened?"

She got a faraway look. "I really don't know. Cade's been at Lakeview since Monday. Wait. I told you that at lunch." She put her hands to her forehead. "I'm losing it," she whispered. "I'm not sure how much more I can take."

I hitched my chair closer to her and put my arm around her shoulders. "You're doing fine," I said. "Maybe you don't feel at the top of your game, but you're not sitting in the corner, curled into the fetal position and going catatonic."

She snorted something that might have been a laugh. It probably wasn't, but at least it wasn't a sob. "Maybe when I get home."

"Okay, then." I gave her a one-armed hug. "Markakis is going to be here soon. I don't know if he'll want to talk to you or Cade first, but maybe it'll help if you talk through what happened, just to get it straight in your head."

"Yes. That's a good idea." She sat up a little straighter. "My phone rang about an hour ago. It was Cade, saying that he'd been taken into police custody."

Her hands gripped each other so hard that the skin pushed up into tall wrinkles. "He'd left Lakeview," she said. "Walked away in the middle of the night without telling anyone, without anyone knowing."

I opened my mouth to ask how that could have happened, but managed to keep quiet. If it was important, I'd learn soon enough.

"Cade left Lakeview," she went on, "and went to a house, a duplex. The police showed up on an anonymous nine-one-one call and found him over the body of a thirty-nine-year-old woman. She'd been killed by a blow to her head." Barb put her hand to the back of her own head. "Cade was there. To the police it seemed obvious that he killed her, so they brought him here."

She looked around the small bland room. "I'm in a

police station at three thirty in the morning because my husband has been arrested for murder." She choked out a laugh, but I sensed that it could turn into hysterical laughter in a heartbeat.

"But why was he there in the first place?" I asked.

Barb tipped her head back and closed her eyes. "I have no idea. Absolutely none."

I swallowed. This wasn't good. This really, truly wasn't good. A zillion questions bounced around in my brain, but Barb wasn't likely to have any of the answers. And even if she did, I didn't want to trouble her by asking them. I was here to help, to be a friend, and that's what I would stick to.

The waiting room door swung open so fast and so far that it banged against the wall. Two men strode in, one on the heels of the other. I assumed one was Daniel Markakis but had no clue who the other guy might be.

Both of them were fiftyish, both walked with confidence, and both wore expressions that said they had all the answers and would dole them out to us if we asked politely and were willing to pay.

They even looked the same with their slightly too long hair, rumpled pants, dress shoes with no socks, polo shirts, and dark jackets. Maybe they'd gone to the same college and taken the same course. How to Dress When a Client Calls You in the Middle of the Night. The only real difference between them was that one carried a briefcase.

Barb stood and walked to the man on the right with her hand outstretched.

"Dr. Carpenter," she said. "Thank you so much for coming." She looked at the other man. "And you must be Daniel Markakis. I'm Barb McCade."

Before either man said a word, the door opened again and a police officer poked his head in.

"Ma'am? Oh, uh . . ." He looked at the newcomers. "One of you is the lawyer?"

Markakis nodded. "I need to see my client. Right now."

The doctor spoke up. "And I need to see my patient. He had a stroke less than two weeks ago. Before anything else happens, I need to make a determination that he's physically able to withstand questioning."

The deputy looked from one man to the other. I could almost see visions of lawsuits dancing in his head. Then he did what any sensible young officer would do. "I'll be right back," he said, and withdrew.

Markakis wheeled to face Barb. "Mrs. McCade, glad to meet you." He held out his hand. "Before we go any further, I have an agreement that needs signing." He laid his briefcase on a chair and, from it, withdrew a pen and a multipage document. Using the pen as a pointer, he gave Barb a fifteen-second contract synopsis. "If that's agreeable, please sign here. Then all we'll need is a monetary exchange and I'll get started."

Barb halted, midsignature. "But I don't have any money with me." Her eyes went wide again. "I don't have any—"

"Here." I handed Barb the money I'd started pulling from my wallet as soon as I saw the briefcase open. It was a five, which was what I always had handy for bets with Rafe.

"Minnie, I can't—"

"Take it." I forced it into her hand. "Pay me back later."

The bill dangled from her fingers. Markakis deftly

reached out. "Thank you, Mrs. McCade. You can provide the rest of the retainer at your convenience. The end of the day tomorrow?" He smiled. "Excellent. Now I need to talk with my client."

The door opened and the young officer looked in. "Uh, the sheriff says you can meet in the conference room down the hall."

In short order, we were all sitting in hard plastic chairs around a laminate table that looked older than I was. A limping Cade was ushered in by a uniformed man with a shorn head and biceps, which wanted to burst out of his shirtsleeves. Barb was sitting next to me and I felt her entire body twitch at the sight of the handcuffs around his wrists.

The officer more or less dropped Cade into a chair. His gaze skated over the rest of us; then he left. He'd made no acknowledgment whatsoever of our presence, and that, more than anything, made me realize where we were.

"Barb, honey." Cade's voice was raspy and twisted. "This is all a huge mistake. I never, ever would have killed anyone."

"Of course not." Barb slid her chair closer to her husband and reached out to him. She was sitting to his left, next to the side affected by the stroke, next to the side of his face that sagged, next to the arm that didn't have the strength to lift itself, and she cupped her hand to his drooping face. "I know you wouldn't. Not ever."

Dr. Carpenter went to Cade's other side and began taking his pulse. He asked a few questions, about lightheadedness, headache, etc., then stepped back, frowning. "You'll do for now, but this had better not take long."

"Right." Markakis clicked his pen. "Let's get going. Russell McCade, I'm Daniel Markakis. What I need first and fast is a quick summary of tonight's events. Are we ready?"

Cade, listing slightly to the left, looked at his new lawyer. "Daniel Markakis. You're the guy who—"

"That's right. Now, unless you'd like to be billed hundreds of dollars an hour to discuss something you can read in old newspapers, let's get on with it."

Barb bristled, but Cade gave a lopsided grin. "We'll find out in a minute if you're worth that kind of money."

The pen Markakis held stopped making notes. "How's that?"

Cade sat back a little. "Just before midnight, I received a phone call. It was a man, and he spoke in a low, whispering voice."

A tingle crawled up the back of my neck. Whispery male voices? Phone calls don't get much creepier than that.

"He told me," Cade was saying, "that he was holding my wife hostage, and that I needed to come right away to discuss a ransom, that if I called the police, he'd"—his words caught—"he'd kill her."

Barb made a faint and pain-filled cry.

"Keep going." Markakis scribbled furiously.

Cade coughed and continued. "The man gave me an address and said to get there as soon as I could. I found my aide and told her there was a family emergency. She talked to the nurse on duty and they found someone to give me a ride."

Markakis looked up. "Not a taxi?" Then he must have realized what he'd said. "Never mind. We're Up

North. The closest twenty-four-hour taxi service is probably a hundred miles away. Go on."

We waited. Cade sat quietly, staring at the wall; then finally he looked at Barb, smiled, and started talking again. "The driver they'd found for me was a custodian. He dropped me off at the address, telling me to call if I needed a ride back, and left. It was a duplex. I could see a light on inside, so I walked to the front door."

He swallowed. "The door was open a few inches and I went inside. A woman was lying facedown on the floor. Her hair . . . there was blood all over it, and her . . . her head was the wrong shape. I assumed it was Barb. I shouted her name, ran to her. I turned her over and saw that it wasn't Barb at all, but Carissa. Carissa Radle." He closed his eyes and dipped his chin to his chest. "I checked her pulse, but she was dead," he whispered.

"And who is Carissa Radle?" Markakis asked.

Cade looked at him. "You know what I do for a living?" The attorney nodded briefly. "Carissa was a big fan of my work," Cade said. "We'd had lunch two or three times."

"Alone?"

Barb started to say something but stopped when Cade shook his head. "No, in a restaurant, with my wife at my side."

Markakis made another note. "I suppose you've told all this to the police?"

Cade nodded. "I just wanted to clear up what is obviously a misunderstanding. Before tonight I had no idea where Carissa lived. I only got truly concerned when I told them about the phone call and they seemed not to believe me at all. That's when I told them I wanted an attorney."

The door opened and a man walked in. He was tall and thin, basically shaped like the letter *I*, which was how, not that long ago, I'd learned to remember his last name. Detective Inwood glanced around the table, slowed when he saw Markakis, slowed again when he saw me, then finished up with Cade. "We've made some accommodations for your ill health," he said, "but it's time to finish up the interview."

"Has my client been Mirandized?" Markakis demanded.

"Yes, sir, he has. We're just trying to get some—"

"Has he been charged?"

"Not at this time," Detective Inwood said. "However, we're waiting for—"

"If my client hasn't been charged, then he's free to go."

The detective leaned against the doorjamb, his hands in his pockets. "Now, Mr. Markakis, you know that we can hold him for twenty-four hours with reasonable cause, and in this situation, it's pretty reasonable. Yes, Mr. McCade had a stroke on his left side, but it appears that the victim was killed with a large Petoskey stone by someone using his or her right hand."

Killed by a Petoskey? That was just so wrong. The gray stones of fossilized coral were found only in northern Michigan. Sometimes you could find little ones on the beach, but big ones were typically expensive and sold by dealers. To have one of those prized stones be a murder weapon was just . . . wrong.

"Situation? What situation is that?" Markakis stabbed his legal pad with his pen. "That you're holding this man for no good reason? What's going to happen when the public finds out that—"

"That a sick man is being held by the police when he should be in a hospital?" Dr. Carpenter was on his feet. "Look at him. He can barely keep his head up. Not even two weeks from a stroke and you're saying he killed someone? He lacks the strength, man. He doesn't have it in him."

Detective Inwood studied Cade. "Yet this sick man managed to make his way from Lakeview to the victim's home."

"Because he thought his wife's life was in danger," Markakis said. "Let's discuss some realities. The true killer used an object to bludgeon the poor woman to death. What are the chances that this man, who can't even hold up his left arm without support, who is dragging his left leg, what are the chances that this weakened man could have committed a brutal murder?"

I squinted at him. That had the ring of a courtroom argument. Did that kind of stuff come naturally after a couple of decades of defending clients, or did he have to work hard at it?

"I'm not that weak," Cade protested, but his wife, his doctor, and his attorney all glared at him. His chin started to jut forward when there was a knock on the door.

"Detective Inwood?" A young uniformed woman handed him a sheet of paper.

Inwood scanned the sheet. Frowned. Scanned it again. He grunted and left the room with the woman trailing in his wake.

The five of us looked at one another for a beat, and then we all started talking at once.

"That was weird," I said.

"Cade, what's going on?" Barb held on tight to her husband's arm.

"This is ridiculous," Dr. Carpenter said. "Cade should have been back in Lakeview long ago. This stress is going to set back his recovery dramatically."

"Barb, don't worry." Cade made a move to hold his wife's hand, but since he was still in handcuffs, the effort fell short in a metallic sort of way. "It'll be fine."

Markakis smiled, checked to make sure his pen was closed, and clipped it to the placket of his polo shirt. "I predict you'll be released in less than an hour."

I'm not sure if everyone else's jaw dropped, but mine certainly did.

Barb leaned across the table, stretching her hands out to him, so obviously wanting to believe his words that it almost hurt to watch her. "How do you know?" she asked.

His smile widened to include an element of condescension. "I don't charge five hundred dollars an hour just because I can." He looked thoughtful for a moment, then went on. "What that lovely young officer handed the detective was most likely the medical examiner's preliminary findings. Judging from his expression, it wasn't what he wanted to see, and that means it's good news for us."

"You mean whatever's in that report will prove his innocence?" Barb asked.

"Proving innocence is the job of the court system." Markakis leaned back in his chair. "The police want enough evidence to prove guilt. If they can't get enough, the county prosecutor won't take the case."

Barb sent Cade a quick look. "So even if they let him go, some people might think he still did it?"

"Probably." Markakis shrugged. "Unless they find and convict someone else for the murder."

Barb frowned and Cade looked troubled. Which didn't make sense to me, because if Markakis was right, the police had no case against Cade and he wouldn't be prosecuted. What else could matter?

We sat in a silence broken by nothing except the occasional rattle of Cade's handcuffs. After a short eternity, the door opened again and Detective Inwood returned.

He stood over Cade, studying him carefully. It wasn't a look that Cade, the successful artist, could possibly be accustomed to, because this was full of suspicion and speculation. The detective took a small key from his pants pocket and unlocked the handcuffs. "You're free to go," he said.

"What?" Markakis, still leaning back, raised his eyebrows. "No explanation?"

Detective Inwood gave the eminent attorney almost the same look he'd given Cade. "I am not required—"

"Oh, come on, Detective." Markakis crossed one ankle over the opposite knee. "You know I'll find out, one way or another. Let's save us both some time, and these good people some money."

Inwood shrugged. "The medical examiner's preliminary findings indicate that the victim was killed between nine p.m. and midnight, a time when Mr. McCade was reported to be in bed by the staff at Lakeview."

"But—"

Markakis rode over Cade's protest. "Thank you very much, Detective. I appreciate your courtesy. Perhaps I can return the favor someday."

"Perhaps." Inwood's smile didn't reach his eyes. It

barely reached his lips. "Mr. McCade, Mr. Markakis, please keep in mind that preliminary findings aren't final findings. I'm sure we will be talking to you again soon." He gave our small group one more look-over, nodded briefly at me, then left.

"Minnie?" Barb asked. "Do you know him?"

I stood. "Not really. Let's get Cade back to Lakeview, okay?"

The doctor left us as soon as Cade was safely in his room, in his pajamas, and sitting on the edge of his bed. "I'll be in tomorrow," Dr. Carpenter said. "Can't have my favorite artist backsliding in his recovery. You have a lot more paintings in you, and I want at least one."

As soon as he was gone, Cade closed his eyes and shrank at least a full size. Maybe two.

"I knew it," Barb muttered. With the familiarity and ease of long-marrieds, Barb turned Cade and lifted his legs onto the bed. "I knew it," she said again. "That strong act was just an act. I could see how exhausted you were, I knew you were about to keel over, but did you say anything? No, of course not, you had to be strong."

"And stupid," he said in a whispery voice. "Don't forget stupid."

"I won't." She pulled the covers up over him. "Go to sleep and I'll be back first thing in the morning."

"Barb?" he asked faintly.

"What?" She continued to tuck him in.

"I'm glad it wasn't you who was dead."

She froze in place. Pulled in a deep, shuddering breath and took hold of his hand. "Thank you, my sweet, for coming to my rescue, even though it wasn't me."

He smiled his uneven smile. "Beautiful Barb," he said sleepily. "You're my beautiful . . ." But he fell asleep before he could finish the sentence.

Barb kissed his forehead. "And you're my handsome husband," she whispered. "Sleep tight, my prince."

I walked Barb to the entrance. "What a night," she said, her words weighed down with fatigue. "And I doubt we've seen the end of it."

Since I'd been getting the same feeling, all I did was nod.

"Once again you've come to our rescue," Barb said.

I wasn't so sure about that. The police would have released Cade if Markakis had been there or not. All I'd really done was saddle the McCades with what would undoubtedly be a massive attorney's bill.

"What was Carissa like?" I asked as we pushed open the door and exited into the still-dark morning.

Barb sighed. "That poor young woman. She was one of Cade's followers. A superfan. He has a number of them, if you can believe it. We'd had lunch together a few times. I even took a picture of the two of them and posted it on Cade's Facebook page. His agent loves that kind of stuff," she said, shrugging.

After a pause, she went on. "Carissa was one of those happy people, all light and laughter. Nice enough, but I'm not sure there was much depth to her, if you know what I mean. Still, she was pleasant to be around. I enjoyed the time we spent with her. Such a shame that she's dead."

I looked at her in the dim light. Something hadn't sounded quite right. Then again, I shouldn't be surprised if Barb was saying things that didn't sound right on a night that her sick husband had almost been arrested for murder.

"At least the police released him," she said. "I don't even want to think about the media attention if Cade was arrested. And I don't think the police even know who he is, which is a blessing."

I wasn't so sure she was right on that account, so I didn't say anything. Not that long ago, I'd made a serious error in judgment about Detective Inwood and his partner, Detective Devereaux.

This time, I wasn't going to assume anything.

Chapter 6

B y the time I got home it was practically time to get up, but I crawled into bed anyway. Eddie, who'd been sleeping in the exact center of the bed, murmured an objection, then rearranged himself at the small of my back. I was sound asleep in seconds.

Too soon, the alarm clock went off. I smacked the snooze button and went back to sleep. The fourth time the alarm rang, I realized it was going to keep waking me up every six minutes until I either got up or turned the thing off altogether.

Yawning, I slid out of bed and headed for the shower. Halfway there, my brain woke up and panic set in. It was Saturday. A bookmobile day.

"Eddie!" I shrieked. "We're going to be late!"

My startled cat scrambled off the bed and leapt to the floor. Side by side, we raced up the short hallway, me on the way to the shower, Eddie on the way to the door, where he sat, voicing criticisms, until we were ready to go.

*   *   *

In an amazingly short period of time, we were in the bookmobile and driving down the road. "I know I forgot something," I said.

Thessie reached through the wires of the cat carrier door to scratch Eddie's face. "You? Forget something? Doubt it."

"*D* word," I murmured.

"Sorry?"

"Did you ever think how many fun words there are that start with the letter *D*?" I asked.

"You mean like death, destruction, and dystopia?" She said the last word with relish, rolling it around in her mouth and enunciating the consonants cleanly and clearly.

There couldn't be many seventeen-year-old girls who knew what that meant. "Dystopia?"

"You know what it means, right?" Thessie asked. "It's, like, a world where everything is horrible, so bad that it can't get any worse."

"A world without books," I said.

Thessie grinned. "Or a world with only e-books that your reader won't open."

I laughed. What was I going to do when Thessie went back to school in September? She was the perfect bookmobile companion. Smart, funny, and, as a volunteer, not on the library's payroll. The odds of finding anyone close to her caliber were nil to none. But since I didn't have to worry about that for a few weeks, I decided not to. Why ruin the present with worry about the future?

"This contest is going to be so much fun," Thessie said. "That was so nice of your friend Kristen to donate the candies."

In reflex, I almost looked back at our latest acquisition, which was safely bungee-corded on a bookshelf. The road, however, was winding and narrow and I kept my gaze forward.

"It's really too bad I can't enter the contest," Thessie was saying.

"Sure is," I said cheerfully. "Anyone connected to the library is out of luck. Besides, you know how many candies are in there. You helped me count."

I didn't remember the number, but then I didn't have to because I had that information in the spreadsheet I was using to track the names of the entrants and their guesses. We had blank slips to write down guesses for the number of candies in the jar, and the guess that was closest would win the candies, the jar, and the ultimate prize of the bookmobile coming to her or his house. Everyone would get one slip per visit and may the best guess win. The local paper had agreed to write up the contest-winning personal bookmobile stop and I was already planning to have the bookmobile's carpet steam-cleaned of all Eddie hair before any reporter set foot inside.

"Maybe I forgot?"

Unlikely. Thessie's sharp brain wouldn't forget anything it didn't want to, let alone the number of Kristen-made maple-flavored hard candies, individually wrapped and placed in a large, clear, thick plastic jar I'd found in my aunt's attic.

"You know," I said, "even if nobody's close to guessing right, you still won't get it."

"Not even if everyone's *really* far off?" she asked hopefully.

"If everyone is that far off, I'll suspect someone was priming them with wrong numbers."

"Hey!" she protested. "I wouldn't do that!" But she turned back to look at the jar with a contemplative look on her face.

Shaking my head, I flicked on the blinker and made a wide-sweeping right turn into the parking lot of a former gas station, now a gardening supply store. By the time we were set up, half a dozen people were milling about, waiting for someone to open the door.

"Good morning," I said, smiling wide. "Welcome to the Chilson District Library Bookmobile. Come on—"

But they were already up the stairs and in, no further invitation necessary. And there, kicking up dust as she walked across the gravel parking lot, was the exact person I'd hoped to see at this stop.

"Good morning, Faye," I said as she came up the steps. "Did you remember to bring those cookbooks?"

Her face, which had been smiling, instantly transformed into a horrified—and very guilty—look. She tucked her short graying hair behind her ears with hands that held no books, not even the overdue cookbooks that I'd found for her through the interlibrary loan system. "Oh, wow, Minnie. I forgot all about them. They're at home, but . . ." She glanced over her shoulder. "But you'd be gone by the time I got back. Um . . ."

I crossed my arms, put on my firm librarian face, and looked her in the eye. Which was only possible because she was standing one step down. "You know the library's policy is to refuse lending privileges until any and all overdue books are returned."

She hung her head and sighed. "I know. It's my own fault." With drooping shoulders, she retreated down the stairs.

Uh-oh. I must have carried the Firm Librarian Face a little too far. "Faye!" I called. "Come on back. I know how much you were looking forward to reading the new Nicholas Sparks. It'd be unusual punishment to make you wait."

"You mean . . . ?"

"We'll bend the rules just this once." I put my finger to my lips and looked left and right. "Don't tell anyone, okay?"

She nodded toward the front of the bookmobile where a black-and-white feline was perched on the headrest of the passenger's seat. "Not even Eddie?"

"Especially Eddie." I rolled my eyes. "Cats are horrible gossips, didn't you know?"

Laughing, she headed straight for the Special Orders shelf.

"Um, Minnie?" Thessie stood at my elbow. "We have a little problem. You know how the guessing game was supposed to be for kids? Well . . ." She held out six slips of folded paper.

At this particular moment, the youngest human on the bookmobile was Thessie. I glanced at our patrons, all of whom had their noses deep in books, just as it should be. "Didn't you tell them it was for kids only?"

"By the time I noticed, it was too late. They'd made their guesses."

Yet another thing no one had taught me while I was getting my library science degree. Clearly, there should have been at least one lecture on how to run contests.

A white-haired gentleman approached. "Here you go, Minnie. May the best guess win, eh?" Smiling, he held out a slip of paper. "Winning a jar of candy from the Three Seasons would be a nice treat, but I can't pass

up a chance to have the bookmobile come to my very
own house. Brilliant marketing, by the way."

What choice did I have? I took his guess. "Thanks,"
I said faintly. Thessie, a smirk on her face, started to say
something. "Not a word, Thess," I told her. "Not one
word."

"Dystopia," she said, grinning.

I crossed my eyes at her and went to help a patron
find the perfect beach read.

My early-morning activities eventually took their toll.
At lunchtime, I made an unplanned stop at a convenience store and bought a large bottle of caffeinated
soda. Near the end of the day, I wished I'd bought two.

"See you on Tuesday," I said when I dropped Thessie off at her car.

"What's that?" she asked. "I couldn't hear you through
that yawn."

I snapped my jaw shut and gave her a mock glare.
"When did the youth of today get so smart-alecky?"

She put on an air of deep thought. "I'd guess it was
when the first teenagers were born." She looked at me.
"Um, are you okay? To drive, I mean? You look really
tired."

I smiled. "Thanks, but I'll be fine."

"Mrr!"

Thessie laughed. "I guess Eddie will keep you awake."

She left and I looked at my feline companion. "Please
don't listen to her," I told him. "The last thing I need is
you howling all the way home."

"Mrr," he said quietly.

"Thank you." I pointed the bookmobile in the direction of Chilson. "She's right, though. I am tired. But I'm not going to think about it. If I do, I'll just get more tired and that's no good, not on such a beautiful day."

And a beautiful day it was, one of those perfect summer days that northern Michigan seemed to specialize in. Temperatures in the high seventies, a light breeze, low humidity, and a few fluffy clouds dotting the sky. No wonder this area was such a tourist draw.

"Speaking of drawing," I said, "I wonder how Cade's doing. Last night couldn't have been good for him."

Actually there were a lot of things I was wondering. Having a murder in my happy little town was hard enough to wrap my head around, and I was bothered by the fact that I knew nothing about the victim.

I didn't know if Carissa Radle had been blond or brunette or redheaded. Didn't know if she'd been short or tall or pretty or athletic or funny. Didn't know who was left behind to mourn her. Didn't know anything about this woman whose life had so unexpectedly intersected Cade's and now, in a diagonal sideways sort of way, mine.

Those thoughts kept me awake all the way to Chilson. They kept me mostly awake while I tucked the bookmobile in for the night, and they sort of kept me awake as I kept an eye out for Stephen while I moved Eddie into my car and then drove home.

"Yo, Miniver!"

I was halfway between the marina's parking lot and my houseboat. I had Eddie in his carrier in one hand and my backpack in the other. My longed-for nap was less than a hundred feet away. I slowed but didn't come to a complete stop. "Hey, Chris. Nice day."

Chris Ballou, the marina's manager, squinted at the sky, his weathered skin crinkling. "Yeah. Should stay this way for a while."

Back before I knew better, I would have thought he was using his years of experience of living next to the water to make such a prediction. "Is that the Weather Channel's forecast or NOAA's?"

He took a toothpick out of his shirt pocket and stuck it in his mouth. "Got something I want to talk about. Come on down to the office a second, will ya?"

I hefted Eddie's carrier. "I'm kind of busy." And sleep-deprived. Really, really sleep-deprived.

"Ah, it'll just take a minute."

Two sentences ago, it had been a second. Then again, Chris rarely asked me for anything, and he was giving me a discount for renting the slip next to Gunnar Olson. "Let me put Eddie in the houseboat and I'll be right down."

Chris grinned around the toothpick. "Nah. Let's bring him with. Bet he fits right in with the guys." He took the carrier out of my hand and sauntered off, his long and skinny legs covering ground fast. I had to half trot to keep up and I was very glad when the short walk was over.

"Look what we got here, boys." Chris carefully placed Eddie's carrier on the shop counter. The four men lounging on ancient canvas director's chairs and drinking beer turned to look.

Skeeter, a summer boater about my age, went to the effort of lifting two fingers off his beer can in a sort of salute. "Minnie."

Rafe Niswander grinned. "Hey, it's an Eddie." Rafe was my nearest on-land neighbor and a good friend.

September through mid-June, Rafe was the principal of the local middle school. Mid-June through August, however, he did as little as possible and played the bumbling Up North hick role to the hilt. "What do you say, Eddie, my man?"

Thanks to Rafe's tendency of being accident-prone, he was the reason I'd met Tucker, so I could forgive him much, but it was thanks to his propensity for procrastination that the electrical repairs on my boat were behind schedule.

"Mrr."

The third and fourth guys laughed. Number three had a shaved head and looked to be in his mid-fifties; number four had light brown hair and was in his mid-forties. I'd never seen either one of them before.

"I think he said quit asking such stupid questions," the older one said. "How you doing?" He stood, and turned into a very tall man. He held out his hand, and I realized he was a very tall man with very large hands.

We shook and, since no one else was doing the honors, I introduced myself. "Minnie Hamilton. Are you renting a boat slip?"

"Greg Plassey," he said. "Need to buy a boat first. And this is my bud Brett Karringer. He does something with computers that I don't understand and plays some really bad golf."

I nodded at Brett. There was a beat of silence. Rafe held his hand out, palm up, to Chris. "Hand it over."

"Come on, Min," Chris pleaded. "Tell me you know who Greg Plassey is. I got five bucks on this."

"Sorry." I smiled at Plassey. "No offense, but I've never heard of you. Should I have?"

Chris groaned and dug out his wallet.

Rafe laughed. "Told you. This girl don't know jack about baseball."

Or pretty much any other professional sport; I was more the toss-around-a-Frisbee-on-the-beach type of person. In short order, I learned that I'd just dissed a Major League Baseball pitching star. Sure, he'd been retired for more than fifteen years, but the human males in the room were still astounded that I didn't recognize the name of the guy who'd helped pitch the Detroit Tigers to two American League championships.

I shrugged. "How can you gentlemen not know who won the Newbery Award last year?"

Skeeter lowered his beer. "That a new hockey trophy? No, wait. Golf."

"Golf?" Chris slapped Greg on the shoulder. "Too bad you're not as good a golfer as a pitcher."

Greg grinned. "Doesn't hurt any worse than a line drive."

I stared at him. "You were hit by a golf ball?"

"By a ball his buddy there smacked," Rafe said.

Brett Karringer nodded sheepishly. "Hit it off a tree and it caromed into the back of his head."

"You got to work on your aim," Skeeter said. "Next time see if you can get him right between the eyes."

For some reason, the men found that hilarious. When the laughter faded, I turned to Greg. "Did you go to the hospital?" I asked. "Head injuries aren't anything to mess around with."

"Being hit with one more ball isn't going to do me any damage." Greg smiled. "I'm fine."

I wasn't sure how he could be so sure, but it was hard enough to get my male friends to take care of themselves, let alone practical strangers, so I let it go. I looked at Chris. "You wanted to talk about something?"

"Oh, yeah." He reached into the carrier to scratch Eddie's chin. "You know our other marina, the one at the east end of Janay Lake? It's full up this year and I'm looking to keep them happy enough to come back. So I was wondering if you could talk your boss into getting the bookmobile to make a stop out there."

My boss? Maybe someday I'd get used to being underestimated. But I doubted it. "I'll see what I can do," I said dryly.

"Yeah?" Chris smiled, his teeth showing white against the leathered skin. "Cool. Thanks, Min-Tin-Tin. You're all right, for a girl."

If I'd been more awake, I'd have come back with a snappy rejoinder, but fatigue was turning my brain into mush. "And you're . . . not so horrible for a boy." Lame, so very lame. I nodded at the other boys, slid the cat carrier off the counter, and headed home for a long afternoon's nap.

"Hang on, Min, I'll walk out with you." Rafe got up and took the carrier from me. "I'd like to stay, guys, but there's a house that needs working on."

Rafe owned what you would call, if you were being kind, a fixer-upper. When he was done redoing the siding, wiring, HVAC, and plumbing of the century-old house, it would be a showpiece, but for now it was more a blot on the landscape.

"How's your cut healing?" I'd taken him to the Charlevoix Hospital after an accident with a reciprocating saw.

"Never better," he said promptly. "You should quit

worrying so much. If you're not careful, you're going to grow up into a regular old girl."

"I can think of worse things to grow into," I said mildly.

"Five bucks says you can't come up with ten by the time we get to your dock."

I immediately started counting on my fingers. "A person who doesn't read. A narrow-minded person. Someone who doesn't understand the necessity of an occasional day off. Someone who doesn't know how to laugh at herself. Someone who doesn't like chocolate. That's five. Someone with no sense of humor. With no appreciation for architecture. With no appreciation for art. Or with no love of beauty. Or someone who cares so much about a single issue that they forget about everything else in their life. Ten."

Rafe handed me the five-dollar bill he'd so recently won from Chris, but I wasn't done. "I'd rather be a girl than someone who doesn't like girls, or someone who thinks girls are useless. And I'd rather be a girl than—"

"You won, already," Rafe said. "See you later, Minnie." He handed me Eddie's carrier and headed off, shaking his head.

"And," I told Eddie, "I'd much rather be a regular old girl than someone who doesn't like cats."

Eddie didn't say anything, but I'm sure he was pleased.

On Saturday evening I walked up to Kristen's restaurant. Kristen Jurek and I had met on Chilson's city beach at the age of twelve. Though Kristen was a born and bred local, she'd committed the unusual act of taking a summer kid under her wing. I'd never forgotten her kindness, and every time I said so, she rolled her eyes and said I'd paid her back a zillion times over and to forget about it, okay?

I would reply that offhand suggestions I'd made three years ago about what to name her restaurant hardly counted in the grand scheme of things, and she'd say that karma was karma, no matter who did what, and to shut up about it or she'd stop making crème brûlée for me every Sunday night.

That was a threat I didn't want to risk, so I kept quiet. At least for a little while.

I said, "Hey, guys," through the kitchen's screen door and went on in. Even late on a Saturday night, the staff was hard at work. Cutting, chopping, cooking, baking, all those things I rarely did and made a mess of when I tried. The one time Kristen had tried to explain the importance of presentation was two hours of my life I could have spent reading. I still regretted the time lost.

A fortyish woman in a tall white hat and a white jacket glanced up at me, her face sharpening at the sight of a stranger in her midst. But the sous-chef, his assistant, and one of the summer interns all nodded to me and/or said, "Hey, Minnie," and the woman's face relaxed.

"Hi," I said to her. "I'm Minnie Hamilton. Is Kristen in her office?"

"Misty Overbaugh," she said in a gravelly voice. "And I'd be careful if I were you. She's wrestling with the menu for next week."

My eyebrows went up. Kristen never waited until the last minute to work up a menu. Never.

"Somebody called with a special deal on chicken

breasts," Misty explained. "She said she couldn't pass it up."

I grinned. That was Kristen. "Nice meeting you," I said, and headed back to the office. I navigated the maze of short hallways and storage rooms that were a direct result of Kristen's insistence during the remodeling phase that the kitchen be the best possible kitchen, forget the expense, full speed ahead.

What had once been a massive summer cottage was now one of the finest restaurants in Tonedagana County. Diners ate food grown and produced in the region while seated in the rooms where wealthy summer people had formerly spent their leisure hours. Nothing served in the restaurant was frozen, and nothing edible was shipped in from outside the state of Michigan. Well, she did make an exception for spices, but there wasn't much she could do about that and it was noted on the menu.

I stood in the doorway, looking fondly at my fair friend. Kristen, at nearly six feet tall and Scandinavian blond, was the reverse image of five-foot, curly-black-haired me. "I hear chicken nuggets are popular," I said.

She looked up at me with bleary eyes. "Why didn't you stop me from ordering all that chicken?"

"Because I like to see you suffer." I dropped into the rickety wooden contraption that served as the guest chair. "That, and even if I'd been here you wouldn't have listened to me."

"I would, too, have."

"You think?"

She pushed herself away from the computer and stretched. "No. I would have said what makes you think you know anything about running a restaurant when you can't even pop microwave popcorn without burning it."

"My skills are more in the peanut butter and jelly range."

"It's good to know your strengths." She picked up her phone. "Harvey, can you . . ." She gave me a thumbs-up and grinned. "You're the best, kid," she said, then hung up. "Two crème brûlée desserts being prepped right now."

"Have I ever told you how much I like having a restaurant owner for a best friend?"

"Only almost every Sunday evening, May through November."

Kristen's restaurant was named the Three Seasons because it was only open for three seasons. Come winter she closed everything down and hied herself to Key West, where she tended bar on the weekends and did absolutely nothing during the week.

"Sure, but tonight is Saturday."

She flicked her index finger at me. "Only because I have to drive down to Cadillac tomorrow for my grandmother's birthday party. For you and me, this is Sunday."

"How's the new chef coming along?" I asked. "Misty, right?"

"So far, so good."

Harvey knocked and bustled in with a tray of dessert, decaf coffee, cream, and silverware. He unloaded it all on the small table in the corner, asked if we needed anything else, and bustled away.

"Have you heard if the restaurant is going to make it onto *Trock's Troubles*?" I asked.

"No, and every time I think about it I start to hyper-

ventilate, so let's change the subject, yes? Yes." Kristen
pushed the latest newspaper over to me. "Did you hear
about this?" Since I'd already read the article she was
pointing at, I didn't reach to pick it up. But even from
five feet away, I could easily read the main headline,
blaring its bad news in big black type: LOCAL WOMAN
MURDERED.

"The weird thing?" Kristen asked. "I knew her."

"You . . . did?" While our circles of friends didn't completely overlap, I'd thought I was familiar with all their
names.

"Sort of. She came in to apply for a waitressing job
when I first opened." Kristen pulled the newspaper
back toward her and stared at the article. "It's weird
knowing someone who was murdered."

"Yes," I said quietly, "it is." We sat for a moment,
thinking our own thoughts. Then I asked, "What was
she like? Do you remember?"

She smiled a little. "Most of the time I don't remember the ones I don't hire, but she was different. It was
too bad she didn't have a lick of waitressing experience. If she had, I'd have hired her in a flash, but I had
to have people who knew what they were doing. I
didn't have time to train a complete newbie." A strand
of hair had escaped Kristen's ponytail, and she brushed
at it impatiently. "Makes me wonder. If I'd hired her,
would things have turned out differently for her?
Would she have been killed?"

Kristen was starting down a path that shouldn't be
taken. Diversionary tactics were required, stat. "Why
did you want to hire her if she didn't have any experience?" I asked.

"Personality," my personality-loaded friend said.

"Beyond the basic waitstaff skills, personality is what makes a waiter memorable. Carissa was loaded with it. Funny, smart, charming." Kristen sighed. "And gorgeous, too. I should have hated her, but I couldn't find a way."

Someone had, but the fact was too obvious, and too painful, to say out loud.

"What other jobs were on her résumé?" I asked, but Kristen didn't remember.

I wanted to talk about Cade, about my run to the police station, about Detective Inwood and Daniel Markakis and Barb and the letter *D*. But I didn't want to share that information without Cade's permission. Though I didn't like keeping secrets from Kristen, this wasn't my secret to tell.

"Let's eat," I said. "Our crème brûlée's going to go stale."

Kristen frowned. "Are you trying to distract me from dark and depressing thoughts?"

I grinned. She was getting in some good *D* words and I hadn't even told her about the game. Maybe it was time to set up rules. "Is it working?"

She picked up her spoon and cracked the sugar. "Getting there."

"Maybe it'll help if I tell you how the bookmobile's candy guessing game is turning into a debacle."

"Now you're talking."

So I did, and soon the sadness that had been filling the room flowed out and away.

"You got quite a mess down here, Minnie." It was Sunday morning and Rafe's head and upper body were deep into the houseboat's engine compartment.

"Tell me something I don't know," I said gloomily. It would have been nice if I could have afforded the fees the marina charged for boat repairs, but without going into serious credit card debt, something I sincerely hoped to avoid, paying Rafe the peanuts he'd charge me was my best option. "Please tell me you'll have it finished before you go back to school."

"Oh, sure, not a problem."

Hope sang in my heart. "You mean it won't take very long?"

His habitual humming wafted up into the clear morning air. "I bet it'll take almost exactly as long as it'll take you to develop a new after-school reading program."

"A what?"

"Of course, it might take me longer to fix this mess, but we'll call it even up."

"Call what even?" I asked.

He lifted his head and peered at me over his shoulder through black hair that he wouldn't get cut until the day before classes started. "After. School. Reading. Program. You got a problem with English?"

Rafe often spoke in badly constructed sentences just to annoy me. From my perch on the end of the chaise longue, I laughed and kicked him lightly in his backside. "Stop that." As my foot touched the seat of Rafe's jeans, I heard footsteps on the dock. I turned to see Tucker staring at me with an odd expression.

"Tucker!" I stood up and brushed my hands for no good reason. "What are you doing here?"

Rafe looked around. "Hey, Doc. What's happening? Don't tell me you're making boat calls. Besides, I'm healing great." Rafe held out a very dirty arm. He glanced at it. "Well, maybe you can't see it through the grease and all, but it's fine." He sat up, frowning at the small gadget he held. "Say, Minnie, my voltmeter is running out of juice. You got any spare triple A's?"

"Sure," I said absently. "In the same place. Remember where?"

"Bedroom, top shelf in the back corner. Gotcha." Rafe clambered to his feet. "Be right back."

Tucker's odd expression went a little odder.

I frowned. "Are you okay?"

"Well," he said, "I'm just wondering why—" The phone in his pants pocket rang loud and long. "Hang on, it's the hospital." He answered it and I watched his face go still. "I'll be right there." As he slipped the phone back into his pocket, he said, "Sorry, but I have to go."

"Sure. I understand." What I didn't understand was why he was looking at me like that. "Is everything okay?"

"Just another hospital emergency. I'll call you later." He waved and headed off.

I watched him go, thinking that I hadn't been asking if the hospital was okay; I'd been asking if *we* were okay.

"The doc gone already?" Rafe asked, letting the houseboat's screen door slam behind him. "He just got here."

"Hospital called," I said shortly. Tucker hadn't kissed me good-bye. Or even hugged me. Maybe I wasn't looking my best this morning, but I wasn't so ugly that the neighbor's dog would bark at me. Was I?

"Yeah, suppose that happens." Rafe got down on his hands and knees. "That's the beauty of being a school principal. No emergency calls in the summer."

I sat down on the chaise longue again. I'd talk to Tucker later and find out what was going on. No need to worry about that right now. Now, in fact, was the time to continue the conversation Rafe had started. "Let's get back to that reading program you were talking about. What, who, when, and where?"

He put his head deeper into the engine compartment. "We have too many kids who don't have anything to do between the end of school and when their mom or dad gets home from work. I have a line on a volunteer and there's a small grant available from the local foundation that's the perfect target for buying some books. All I need is some direction."

"Don't you have English teachers who could do this?" I asked.

"It would have to go to a committee," he said darkly. "And why mess with that if I can get you to do it?"

Why indeed? We instantly started a conversation about reading levels, the amount of fiction versus nonfiction, whether it made more sense to buy paperbacks or e-books, and what the plot of the next *Diary of a Wimpy Kid* book might be.

At some point I realized that Rafe hadn't picked up a tool in fifteen minutes and that I hadn't touched any of the windows I'd planned to wash. The windows could wait, but the repairs couldn't. Maybe I'd take a walk up to Lakeview and see how Cade was doing.

I stood. "Okay, I'll do it. And wipe that smirk off your face." His grin was there because we both knew that I'd spend twice the time on the reading program that he would on my boat. "Let me know how much you spend on parts, but I'm not feeding you."

"Not even pizza?"

"Well . . ." He was doing the boat just for me, and I'd be trying to encourage kids into a love of reading. "Maybe once."

"Sweet! Any day I don't have to cook is a good one."

I eyed him. Every summer, away from easy access to the school's cafeteria, he ended up skinnier than the skinniest rail. Even I wasn't that bad about cooking. "What you really need is a wife," I said.

He gave me a horrified look. "Bite your tongue, woman." He grabbed a pair of pliers and dove back into the engine compartment. "A wife would try to take care of me," his voice echoed up.

"Talk about thankless tasks."

"What? Sorry—can't hear you."

He'd heard me; he just didn't have a quick response. "I'll see you later," I said, and left him to his labors.

I stood in the open doorway of Cade's room.

He sat in a chair facing the television, but he wasn't watching the black-and-white movie on the screen. He also wasn't reading the book flopped open on his lap. Instead he was staring out the window. What he was seeing, I had no idea, because I would have thought the pleasant view of an interior courtyard landscaped with flowers, bench, and a fountain would have been reason to smile, not to look as if the world was about to end.

I knocked on the doorframe. "Hey there."

The bleak expression on his face disappeared instantly. "Minnie! What a treat. Sit down, young lady, sit down."

As I dragged a chair over to him, the librarian in me sneaked a look at the book he wasn't reading.

He caught my glance. "Can you believe I've never

read the Harry Potter books? The day after I was moved here, my agent sent me the entire series. Told me it might be the perfect time to think about moving my work in a different direction."

That made sense. Sort of. "How will reading fantasy books set in England do that?"

"No idea," he said. "I think she just wants me to read them so I'll stop saying I never have."

I nodded at the book, whose bookmark was maybe fifty pages in. "Is that the first one?"

He sighed. "Did you know they get longer the further in the series you go?"

"Did you know you can get them in audio version?"

He blinked at me. "Genius. Sheer genius." He used his weak hand to flip the book shut and used both hands to toss it onto the bed. "I've never been much of a reader," he said in a stage whisper. "No offense to the librarians in the room."

"And I've never had a broad appreciation for art," I said in the same level of whisper. "No offense to any nearby artists. Though I do love your pictures."

He smiled. But then a big fat silence filled the room, broken only by the muted footsteps of people walking down the hallway and canned laughter from a television in the adjacent room.

This was, I realized, the first time I'd ever been alone with Cade. It was also the first time we'd been in the same room without an ongoing major life experience.

"How," he asked, "did you manage to find me the most successful defense attorney in the state?"

"It was kind of an accident," I said, passing on the opportunity to note that defense was an excellent *D* word.

He laughed. "Accidents happen." He used his good hand to put his weak one in his lap. "There are accidents everywhere, every day. It was an accident that I started painting. A huge mysterious accident that I ever became successful. It was an accident that we bought a house up here. It was an accident that we ever met Carissa. And—" He stopped, then shook his head and went back to looking out the window.

I didn't like it. Though I didn't know Cade very well, when he'd been at the hospital, he seemed different. Cheerful, in spite of the stroke. Now he seemed to be sliding downward. No, I didn't like it one bit. But I supposed that finding a dead body and then falling under suspicion for murder could do that to a person.

"How did you meet Carissa?" I asked.

"At the art gallery here in town. Barb and I were talking to the manager about displaying some of my paintings and Carissa walked in the door. We got to talking, and since it was close to lunchtime, we moved on to a nearby restaurant."

"But you didn't know her all that well."

He shook his head. "I truly don't understand why anyone would want to frame me for her murder."

"Well, the police will figure it out, I'm sure."

Cade's left hand—the weak hand—started to twitch. He laced his fingers together and looked at me. "Has anyone ever told you that reputation is everything?"

"Yes." My mother had, on and off for years when I was growing up, and a dear friend, not that long ago.

"It's true. And it's even more true when you're talking about the creative world." He edged forward in his chair. "My art, such as it is, isn't just about the art. People buy it because of reputation. My artistic reputation is squeaky clean. Long-term marriage, three successful grown children, quiet life, no parties, no drugs, not much alcohol, just me and the canvas and the paint."

I had no idea where he was going with this. "So . . ."

"So if I become a serious suspect in a murder investigation, the reputation I've enjoyed for thirty years will disappear instantly and never return. I'll be given a new one, but it won't be the same."

Nope. I still didn't get it. "Um . . ."

"Don't you see?" He perched on the edge of the chair. "If my reputation as the cleanest-cut popular artist in a generation is destroyed, the value of my paintings will drop substantially."

Now I got it.

"All the people who have scraped and saved to buy a painting, not just because they love it, but also and probably primarily for investment purposes, all those people will be out of luck. Their hard-earned dollars will vanish."

I squinted at him. "Any chance you're exaggerating?"

He rattled off three names I'd never heard before. "Look them up, Minnie. All were rising stars in the art world. None of them are painting now, and why? They lost their reputations. Plus, there's one more thing."

"What's that?"

He half smiled. "I really, really don't like the idea of ending up in prison. There's not a chance of getting decent light in there."

I thought a moment. "Then what we need is to find the real killer."

Cade nodded. "The sooner the better. I'd call the

sheriff's office and ask how the investigation is going, but I doubt they'd tell me anything."

"No," I said, "I meant *we* need to find the real killer."

He sat up, half straight. "Minnie, that's a job for the police, not a job for . . . for . . ."

"A girl?" I sat up, too, only I was all the way straight.

"For an amateur," he said gently. "The last thing I want is for you to get tangled up with a killer. This person murdered once. What makes you think he won't do it again?"

"I have no intention of getting killed," I said. "All I'm saying is that I poke around a little. Ask a few questions of a few people. We can make up a plausible story that I can go with. And I'm a librarian. I do great research. I might be able to dig up stuff the police would never be able to find."

He rubbed his chin and studied me. "Just questions. No sneaking around in the dark of night, no tiptoeing into dank and dark basements?"

I crossed my heart. "And no climbing rickety stairs with only a single candle to light my way."

"If you can do this, Minnie Hamilton, I will offer you anything you'd like."

"If I actually do it, I'll be happy with a thank-you letter."

He held out his hand for me to shake, and I took it.

"Deal," he said.

Chapter 7

I went straight from Lakeview to the library.

"Hey, Minnie." Donna, one of our part-time clerks, smiled, then frowned. "What are you doing here? I thought it was your day off."

I smiled but kept walking, barely even slowing as I passed the front desk. "Silly me, I left something in my office. Don't tell anyone I'm here, okay?"

She laughed. "Mum's the word."

I shut my office door behind me and fired up the computer. Leaving the overhead lights off would mask my presence to most passersby, but if any curious eyes happened to look in through the door's window, I was toast. Someone would see me, stop to talk, and then I'd get sucked into library tasks that needed doing.

So I got up to do something I'd never done before—pull down the window shade. I reached up as high as I could, but the shade's edge was just out of my reach. I jumped. Missed. For the second jump I crouched a bit, tried a little harder, and was rewarded for my efforts with the sound of the roller shade descending.

"Gotcha," I murmured. Snug in my office cave with

a much faster Internet connection than I could get at the marina, I started researching the life of Carissa Radle.

First off, of course, was to take a look at the most accurate information at hand, that of the Chilson District Library. I typed in her name, typed in every possible spelling of her last name that I could come up with, and still came up with nothing.

"No library card," I said, sighing and shaking my head. It never failed to amaze me how many people didn't have a library card. They were free and they gave you access to thousands of books. Maybe someday I'd understand people who weren't interested in reading, but probably not.

Next, I used the library's access code to log in to the archives of the *Chilson Gazette*, the local newspaper. Carissa's name came up fast, but there was only one entry. Her obituary.

I closed my eyes for a moment, wanting to reject the sight. She shouldn't have died so young. She shouldn't have died that way. I opened my eyes and found that my hands were balled up into fists.

I stretched out my fingers, releasing the tension, and looked at Carissa's obituary picture. She had been blond and pretty with a happy, wide smile, one of those smiles that made you want to smile in return.

Sighing, I started reading. Carissa Marie Radle, age thirty-nine, had died unexpectedly at her home in Chilson. She'd graduated from Wayne State University and Dearborn High School and had been employed by Talcott Motors. She was survived by her parents and two sisters. A memorial service was being planned for Labor Day weekend.

Hang on. Had that really said . . . ? I looked back. Why, yes, indeedy, it had said Dearborn High School. The very same high school that had given me a diploma. Me and my brother, Matt, who was only two years older than Carissa. What were the odds that out of the eighteen hundred or so students who attended Dearborn High, my brother had known her?

Probably low, but it didn't hurt to ask.

I unzipped my backpack, dug around for my cell, and scrolled down to my brother's number. Matt, his wife, Jennifer, and their three children lived in Florida and I didn't see nearly enough of them. Hardly a week passed all winter that I didn't get a call or an e-mail or a text from one of the five telling me how nice the weather was down in the greater Orlando area, so why didn't I abandon the snow and cold and come down for a visit?

Then again, hardly a week passed all summer that I didn't call or send an e-mail or a text down to Florida telling them how nice the weather was up here and why didn't they abandon the heat and humidity and come up for a visit?

Matt's phone rang once, twice. "Can't come this month," he said. "Ben has soccer camp."

"It's too hot," I said.

"They practice inside."

"Oh." I'm sure it made sense for the Florida heat, but playing an outdoor sport inside in the summer seemed weird to me. "That wasn't why I called."

"Yeah?"

From the way he spoke, I knew he wasn't paying attention to me, which served me right for calling in the middle of the day. My brother was a work-hard, play-hard kind of guy and on weekends he was always busy doing something. If not soccer, then softball, and if not softball, then swimming.

During the week, Matt worked as an Imagineer at Disney World, designing all sorts of things he could never talk about until they became reality. It was an extremely cool job, and if I hadn't been a bookmobile librarian, I might have been the teensiest bit jealous. "Can you talk for a second?"

"Mom and Dad okay?"

"They're fine. So is Aunt Frances and every other relative, as far as I know."

"So what's up? No, let me guess. You're finally getting married. Who's the poor sucker? Let me call and warn him about what you're really like."

I made a rude gesture in the direction of Florida. "I have a question about your dim, dark past. Did you know a Carissa Radle in high school? She was two years younger than you."

"Carissa Radle, Carissa Radle . . ." He made some humming noises that almost, but not quite, turned into an instrumental version of "Stairway to Heaven." "Carissa. You mean Chrissy?"

"I guess."

"Yeah, Chrissy Radle. One of my friends dated her for a while. Or was it a friend of a friend?" His voice drifted backward twenty-odd years. "Chrissy. Yeah, I remember. Blond, legs up to here, but not a lot of fun. One of those kids who took everything seriously. She had opinions on everything from pesticides to the World Trade Organization."

I tipped back in my chair. That didn't sound at all like the Carissa described by Barb and Cade and Kristen. Then again, people did change. Not that I could think of anyone who had done so right this second, but I was sure I could, given time.

"Chrissy Radle," Matt was saying. "Huh. I hadn't thought about her since high school. Why are you asking?"

"Ah. Well." I cleared my throat. Somehow I hadn't thought this conversation through to its inevitable conclusion. "Turns out she'd been living up here."

He caught the past tense. "She's moved?"

"Not moved, exactly," I said. "Matt, I'm afraid she's dead. Someone killed her." He was silent, so I kept going. "The police don't know who, but I'm sure they'll find out soon."

"Murdered?" Matt sounded far away again. "People I know don't get murdered. Are you sure?"

I read him the obituary. "So you haven't seen her since high school?"

"No," he said. "And my friend Bruce—they broke up even before we graduated. He went to MIT, then to Silicon Valley right afterward. He's hardly been back to Dearborn since."

I remembered Bruce. Far too good-looking to be an engineer, if anyone asked me, but no one ever had. "Sorry to be giving you bad news, but when I saw she was from Dearborn, I had to call."

"Chrissy Radle," he mused. "It's weird to know someone who's been murdered. It's not . . . right."

We were quiet for a moment. Since I agreed with him completely, there wasn't much else to say.

"Hey," my big brother said. "There's not a serial killer running around Chilson, is there? You're not in any danger, right? You'd be the perfect target, out on that bookmobile half the week. You even publish your route online. It'd be easy to . . ." He cleared his throat. "I don't suppose you'd consider carrying a handgun."

"Firearms are against every library rule ever," I said. "And do you know how unlikely serial killer deaths are? Statistically, you're more likely to be struck by lightning twice than be killed by a nutso wack job like that."

"Did you make up that statistic?" he asked.

"Absolutely."

"That's my girl," he said.

After we hung up, I poked around the computer for a while longer. Since I didn't find anything else about Carissa, I popped my head outside the office door to check for a clear exit and tiptoed out.

Monday was rainy and cool and windy, which made it an excellent library day. From opening to close, we were busy providing all the things that libraries do, from finding the perfect book for an eleven-year-old boy to tracking down a copy of a decade-old magazine to recommending materials on how to start your own worm farm.

Tuesday was a bookmobile day. "Which makes it a good day," I told Eddie as I gave him a cuddle before putting him into the cat carrier. "And since we're headed southwest instead of southeast, Thessie is meeting us at the library this morning. What do you think of that?"

If he thought anything of it, he didn't say. He was too busy rearranging the towel on the bottom of the carrier to his satisfaction.

Thessie arrived just as I was backing the bookmobile

out of the detached garage. I stopped and opened the door for her. "Good morning, sunshine."

"Morning!" She bounded up the stairs and into her seat. "Hey there, Eddie."

"Speaking of Eddie," I said, "we need to make a quick stop on the way out of town. Aunt Frances called this morning. One of her boarders has knitted a blanket for him."

"You hear that, Mr. Ed?" Thessie looked down. "You're going to get an upgrade from that ratty old towel."

It hadn't been ratty a few weeks ago. Back in my pre-Eddie days it had been my second-best bath towel. Now it had threads pulled out of it, and the corners were chewed to shreds. Eddie was almost as hard on towels as he was on paper products. What he was going to do to Paulette's handmade blanket I didn't want to think.

We drove through the back streets of Chilson and stopped at the curb in front of the boardinghouse. My aunt was waiting on the porch. "I'll be right back," I said.

Aunt Frances met me on the sidewalk. "Here it is. Sorry about the color, but Paulette wanted that particular type of yarn for Eddie's blanket and the yarn store didn't have enough of anything else."

I took the small, cat-sized blanket from her. It was soft and cuddly and warm . . . and so pink that every other color in the world would look washed out next to it. "Aren't cats color-blind?" I asked. "Tell Paulette thanks very much. Is she here? I have a couple of minutes. I can tell her myself."

Aunt Frances sighed. "Gone up to Mackinac Island

with Leo." She rubbed at her eyes, and that's when I noticed how red they were.

"You're not getting sick, are you?" I asked. Which was unthinkable, because my aunt never got sick.

"Not sleeping for beans," she said. "It's all . . . that." She tipped her head at the boardinghouse. "I need help."

I heard Thessie come down the steps. "Aunt Frances, have you met Thessie Dyer? Thessie, this is Frances Pixley, my aunt."

They exchanged nice-to-meet-yous; then Thessie asked, "What do you need help with? We're great at helping people find what they need on the bookmobile."

Aunt Frances smiled. "You're a sweet girl, but I'm afraid the solution to my problem isn't on the bookmobile. Unless . . ." She looked at me. "Unless, my dearest niece, my smart niece, my perceptive niece can find an answer."

My aunt was one of the most capable people I knew. She changed her own oil, was comfortable with power tools, and dealt with noisy neighbors herself instead of calling the police. To see her doubting herself was like the ground falling away from underneath my feet. "With Deena and Quincy?"

She nodded. "And Paulette and Leo." Her voice strung out the words tight. "This is all wrong and I don't know what to do about it."

"Who's Deena?" Thessie asked. "And those other people?"

Aunt Frances and I looked at her, then at each other. The matchmaking efforts were all done undercover; no one except the two of us had ever known about them. I lowered my voice. "She can keep a secret."

"So young?" Aunt Frances murmured.

"I'm not that young," Thessie protested. "I'm seventeen. I'll be a senior in high school."

Aunt Frances nodded. "And I'm going to guess that not only are you smart, but you have all sorts of ideas about how to fix the world."

"Well . . ." Thessie scuffed her toe on the sidewalk.

"She does," I told Aunt Frances. "Maybe she can help." Which would be a good thing, because I didn't have any advice regarding other people's love lives. Managing my own was often more than I could handle.

So Aunt Frances told Thessie about the summer boarders, about the secret matchmaking, about her years of success, and about this year's impending doom. Thessie started to grin a little when she heard the ages of some of the players, but when Aunt Frances said, "We all need love, no matter how old we are," the girl stopped smiling and started nodding.

"I just don't know what to do." Aunt Frances gripped and ungripped her hands. "It's a ghastly mess and I'm afraid it's going to end badly for everyone."

Thessie looked concerned. "So Deena should have been with Harris, but instead she's with Quincy. And Quincy's match was Paulette, but instead she's with Leo. This leaves Zofia, who was Leo's match, with Harris, who is young enough to be her grandson."

"In a nutshell," Aunt Frances said sadly. "Nothing I've tried has worked. Do you have any ideas? Anything at all?"

"Hmmm."

Thessie was going into think mode. I could tell from the small vertical crease between her eyebrows that the problem was getting the full force of her concentration.

"I'll let you know," I said, "if she gets any ideas. Sorry, Aunt Frances, but we have to leave right now if we're going to keep to the schedule."

I gave her a quick hug, tugged on Thessie's elbow, and escorted her back to the bookmobile. Through the window I gave my pensive-looking aunt Frances a cheery wave and we were off.

Thessie was silent for a few miles. Then she smiled and said, "I know. What she needs to do is have a party. We'll invite all the boarders and anyone who has met them. Then we'll get people to say how good Deena and Harris look together, how Paulette and Quincy look like they'd make the perfect couple, and how Zofia and Leo already seem as if they're married. If we can get those ideas into their heads, maybe that will help." She rattled on with idea after idea, each one more bizarre than the last.

I sighed. It had been accidental and with the best of intentions, but I'd created a monster.

The next day was a library day. I spent the morning working on a new policy for the display of artwork, a policy I'd thought about writing only after I'd helped put together a display of local artwork earlier that summer. I'd suffered pointed comments from two library board members about the inappropriateness of displaying seminude sketches in a public library and it was time to formalize things. My lunch hour was spent speed-reading reviews for books to add to the purchasing list, and then it was back to drafting the artwork policy.

By early afternoon, my eyes felt as if they were permanently focused at computer-screen distance. I pushed myself back from the desk and stood up, stretching, then winced at the tightness in my muscles. Maybe all those articles about getting up to move every half hour were right. I made a mental note to start doing that. Starting tomorrow. Next week at the latest.

The break room was empty, but considering that it was only an hour past lunchtime, that was only fitting. I poured myself a cup of coffee and stood there for a moment, feeling somewhat bereft. Not that I had to have someone around to talk to every minute of the day, but a certain amount of companionship was expected in a library. So, where were my companions?

I moseyed down the hall. At the front desk, Donna was helping a young mother and her two children check out teetering stacks of picture books. In the main library, Holly was showing a middle schooler the secrets of the Dewey decimal system. In the back room, Josh was elbow-deep in cables and electronics parts, muttering words that sounded suspiciously like curses.

Well.

I was walking idly down the hall when I noticed an extremely tall and baseball-capped figure leaning against the wall outside the doorway to the reading room. "Mitchell, what on earth are you doing?" I asked.

Mitchell Koyne looked down at me and put his finger to his lips. "I'm helping," he whispered.

I eyed the leaning Mitchell, who had recently begun sporting a scraggly beard. Whether the facial hair was intentional, was a result of sheer forgetfulness, or was due to the lack of a razor, we hadn't yet decided. "Thanks," I said, "but I'm pretty sure that the wall is going to keep on standing, even without your help."

The building itself had kept its upright position for

almost a hundred years in its various incarnations as K-12 school, elementary school, vacant building, and, starting just a few years ago, the Chilson District Library. I would have laid down money, and lots of it, that Mitchell's efforts weren't going to make any difference.

"Well, duh." He peered over his shoulder into the reading room. It was a large space filled with current newspapers and magazines, upholstered furniture, a fireplace, and a long window seat. "Ah, there's no one in there. Dang."

"Are you looking for someone?"

Mitchell nodded, the bill of his tattered baseball hat moving a fraction of a beat behind. "Yeah, I'm trying to help the cops catch whoever killed that woman the other night."

Right. "Do the police know that you're helping them?"

"Nah. Not yet, I mean. What I'm going to do is watch." He gestured at his eyes with the first two fingers of his hand. "Watch and learn, just like you did last month with who killed Stan Larabee."

My friend Stan. My mouth crumpled a little, but I straightened it out fast. "What makes you think the killer spends time in the reading room?"

He shrugged. "It's a good place to read the paper. Lots of people come here, you know? It just makes sense that whoever killed that lady will, too."

Maybe in Mitchell's world it made sense, but I wasn't sure it would to anyone else. The amount of time he spent in the reading room was directly related to the amount in fines he'd managed to accumulate for overdue books. Since Mitchell had no apparent intention of paying off the near-four-figure number, Stephen had cut him off from borrowing privileges. Any other patron would have found the money. Not Mitchell; he just spent more time in the library, reading in-house the books and magazines he would have borrowed otherwise to Stephen's displeasure—which I had been conveniently ignoring.

"Say," Mitchell said. "How about you and me team up together to find this killer? With your brains and my local know-how, I bet we'd figure it out in no time."

The thought of conducting an investigation with Mitchell curdled everything in my stomach, from the morning's cold cereal to the peanut butter and jelly sandwich I'd had for lunch to the coffee I was currently sipping. "That's nice of you to offer, Mitchell, but I'm pretty busy."

"You sure? Because I have these ideas all sketched out and—"

I patted him on the arm. "Thanks, anyway."

He took off his hat and scratched his head. "Well, if you're sure."

"Absolutely. But thanks again."

I headed back to my office and tried not to think about the conversation. Because though I was absolutely sure that I'd done my best to persuade Mitchell to leave off investigating, I was equally sure that he wouldn't pay attention to a word that I'd said.

"Minnie."

I stopped dead at the sound of Stephen's voice, then turned around to face him.

"It would appear," he said, "that you haven't made any progress regarding the situation I presented to you."

I sipped my coffee and tried to think of something to say. "I've . . . been busy this week."

"It's been more than two weeks since I tasked you with this issue. At the least I expected an outline of possibilities. A progress report would have been even better. Visible results better yet. What I've received from you, however, is nothing."

His face was getting a little red. "Nothing," he said, "and it's getting worse. Every afternoon, Koyne lurks there"—Stephen nodded down the length of the hall—"distracting the staff and annoying other patrons. As assistant director of this library, you need to learn to get to the heart of the matter. Do something about this, Minnie. And do it fast." He spun on his heel and marched up the stairs.

I sighed and took a sip of my coffee. Cold.

"Wow," Holly said, opening the door to the supply closet and stepping out, her arms laden with reams of paper. "Was Stephen saying what I think he was saying?"

I looked at her. "Did you jump in there when you saw him coming?"

"Anybody with the sense of a stick would have." She grinned. "Plus, we need more paper in the copy machine." She looked in the direction of Stephen's departure. "Was he really saying to kick Mitchell out of the library?"

"More like lure him away."

She snorted. "With what? This place is like his second home."

I had no idea and said so.

"Hmm." Holly twisted her mouth into a sideways shape and hummed a few bars of "The Wheels on the Bus." "Got it," she said, brightening. "Watch this. Come on."

We headed down the hall. She plopped the paper at the front desk and kept steaming ahead toward the reading room.

"Hey, Mitchell," she said. "Do you know what my husband told me?"

Mitchell twisted his baseball hat around. "Isn't he out west somewhere?"

She nodded. "He's in Wyoming, working at that big mine. He just got a promotion. He's making good money, really good, and he says there are jobs out there for pretty much everyone."

"Huh," Mitchell said. "He got a promotion? That's cool."

Holly's lips firmed, but she smoothed them out into a smile. "So, what I was wondering was, have you ever thought of going out there yourself? All those blue skies and open spaces, a big guy like you would get hired right away. I'm sure of it."

It was a good sell, so good that I almost wanted to go out there myself, but Mitchell was shaking his head.

"Leave Michigan?" he asked. "Leave God's country? Leave all of you? Not a chance." He reached out with both of his long arms and enveloped Holly and me in a big hug. My face was mushed up against the top of Holly's shoulder, and her chin was digging into the side of my head.

"It wouldn't be the same without you," I said, and escaped down the hall with as much grace as I could muster. Holly came along with me, whispering in my ear, "I'll see if I can get Josh to help. Sometimes he has really good ideas."

And sometimes his ideas were horrible, but right now I was willing to listen to anything.

*   *   *

"What I really need," I said to Eddie that evening, "is a magic wand. Wave it, say some really long words, and we'll find out who really killed Carissa. Wave it again and the boarders at Aunt Frances would get straightened around. One more wave and Mitchell would find something productive to do with his life. What do you think?"

Eddie didn't say anything.

"Yeah." I patted the top of his head. He squinched his eyes at every pat, but he didn't move. "I kind of figured that's what you'd say."

We were sitting on the roof of the houseboat, watching the sunset. At least I was watching the sunset; Eddie was still looking for the sparrow that had lured him onto the roof in the first place. Fifteen minutes ago, we'd been sitting on the chaise longues, me reading, him gently purring. Then the bird had zipped past.

Eddie exploded into action. He tore after the low-flying bird, jumped up onto the railing in hot pursuit, then launched himself onto the roof.

I'd put my book down and watched the activity with bemusement. When the bird flew into the wild blue yonder, Eddie had looked down at me.

"Mrrwr."

"You got yourself up there," I'd told him. "You can get yourself back down."

"Mrrwwrr!"

I could have left him there to figure out his own way, but I didn't want the entire marina and half of Chilson to suffer the yowls of an unhappy Eddie. Muttering about the uselessness of cats, I'd borrowed a ladder from the marina office and climbed up onto the roof.

"You know what?" I asked Eddie now. "If I don't figure out a solution to the Mitchell problem, Stephen might fire me. We'll be out on the street with no job in sight. Aunt Frances doesn't have room for us in the summer, and Kristen's living above the restaurant, so I'm pretty sure she wouldn't want a cat in there. We'd be homeless. What do you think of that?"

"Mrr." He butted his head against my cell phone. I'd brought it up onto the roof with me, just in case.

"And 'mrr' back at you." I ran my hand along his long tail. "For a cat who might be out on the street soon, you don't seem . . . Hey!"

He was still butting his head against the phone, and the furry action had turned on the calendar function.

"Cut it out." I dragged the phone out from underneath him. He gave it a swipe with his paw as I pulled it away, and the calendar rolled to last week. "Stop that, will you?" His white paw snaked out again, but I held the phone out of his reach.

"Leave it alone." I turned the phone off. "This is way too expensive for a cat toy."

He gave me a *but, Minnie, those are the best kinds of cat toys* look.

"Not this time."

"Mrr."

"Or ever."

"Mrr."

I gave up. It's hard to get the last word when you're having a conversation with a cat.

Chapter 8

"Who's going for lunch today?" Donna asked late the next morning.

"I went last week," Kelsey said.

"Pretty sure I went the week before." Josh kept his hands in his pockets, dodging the list that Donna was trying to pass to him.

Over the last couple of months, the library staff had fallen into the habit of ordering Wednesday lunch from the Round Table. Whoever happened to be at the main desk took orders, and the fetching task rotated among everyone else.

I was pretty sure that Josh had no idea about the last time he'd walked down for the orders, but I was very sure that the topic wasn't worth pursuing. "I'll go. It's a beautiful day."

Donna grinned and handed me the paper. "It's all yours, toots."

Toots? I looked down at the lengthy list. "All right, who's ordering onion rings? You know how Stephen hates the smell of onions in the library." I kept reading the list. "Four orders of onion rings? Are you kidding me?" I looked up, but they had already scattered.

"Weenies," I called. "You're all a bunch of weenies." Laughter came back to me and I shook my head, smiling. They *were* weenies, but I didn't know what I'd do without them.

I headed out into the warmth of a July day. In the not so far distance, Janay Lake was dotted by sailboats and powerboats with long tails of white-edged wake. Here in town, cars lined every street within three blocks of downtown. Ah, summer.

As I walked, I played the license plate game. Mostly Michigan plates, of course, but once I got to the main drag I hit the mother lode. An Ohio plate. New York. Missouri. California. Wisconsin. Colorado. And two Illinois for a total of eight out-of-state plates in a five-minute walk. A new record for Minnie!

I walked into the Round Table. Since it was summer and it was lunchtime, the place was packed with people I didn't recognize. Instead of the familiar faces I saw September through May, I saw sun-kissed cheeks and windblown hair and felt the infectious high spirits that people get when they're on vacation and having a good time.

"You're here for the library's order, right?" the young woman at the cash register asked. "It'll be up in just a couple minutes. You want to pay now?"

I handed over the bills that Donna had given me along with the list and smirked a little on the inside. "Keep the change." It would serve them right for the onion rings.

"Hello, Ms. Hamilton."

Behind me were Detectives Devereaux and Inwood,

the two police officers I'd dealt with a few weeks ago. Though we'd started off on the wrong foot, and then found that the other foot was also wrong, we'd ended up . . . well, perhaps not actually liking each other, but with grounds for mutual respect.

I nodded at the men. Both were in their late fifties; both had graying hair and tired looks. Then the similarities ended. I'd had trouble remembering which detective was which until a smart young deputy had told me about the letters. Detective Inwood was tall and thin, like the letter *I*. Detective Devereaux was shorter and rounder, exactly like a D, making him the embodiment of a *D* word.

"Detectives." *D* words, everywhere you looked. "How are you this fine day?"

Inwood grunted noncommittally. "So, how long have you known Russell McCade?"

"I know Barb a lot better." Which was true and didn't exactly answer his question, but I was okay with that.

"So you've known the McCades for some time?"

I put my chin up in the air, the better to stare him straight in the eye with. "Is this an official questioning?" I asked. "Because as I recall, Mr. McCade was released the other night. Seems to me that Daniel Markakis wouldn't take kindly to this line of questioning, not after what the medical examiner's report showed."

Detective Devereaux chuckled. Inwood sighed. "Ms. Hamilton, we're doing our job. All avenues have to be explored."

"Seems to me this one's a dead end," I said. It came out a little snappy, but these two had a gift for bringing out the snark in me. "There must be other streets to go down." I smiled, trying to be jovial. "Lanes, even. Alleys. Courts. Roads."

"Or drives," said a male voice. "Don't forget drives."

The three of us turned. Deputy Ash Wolverson stood a few feet away, looking from the detectives to me and back. Too late, he'd sensed the mild tension fizzing in the air. "Uh, Detectives. Ms. Hamilton, right? With the bookmobile."

I nodded. "Deputy." He was at least two decades younger than the detectives, making him maybe a few years older than me. He was also what many women would have called hot, with his muscular build, square jaw, and short brown hair. Right now, however, I would have called him uncomfortable. Which amused me on many levels.

"The library's order is up." The girl at the register hefted two large white plastic bags. Deputy Wolverson made a move to pick them up, but Detective Inwood blocked him and did the honors.

"Ms. Hamilton," he said, handing me the bags. "We're doing all we can to find Ms. Radle's killer. It's unfortunate if this offends your friends, but that's what police work can be like."

I sighed. "Yeah, I know. I don't suppose you can tell me if any of those other avenues are looking productive?"

"Inquiries are proceeding," Detective Devereaux said.

So, no, they couldn't tell me. I nodded and headed out but had to wait for a large family group to come in before I could get outside. While I waited, I craned my neck around to see the back corner. Bill D'Arcy, a new Chilson resident, was sitting in his normal spot, reading away on his computer, as per usual.

Sabrina, the diner's forever waitress, filled his coffee mug and leaned over to kiss the top of his head. As she did, the sparkle of her new engagement ring caught the light and flashed back to me, bright and shiny.

I grinned. Every once in a while, things really did work out.

Halfway back to the library, I stopped, put the bags of food on a bench, and dug my phone out of my purse. Seeing Sabrina and Bill's happiness made me want to talk to Tucker. And though Tucker had, in fact, called me as he'd promised, I'd been at the library with my phone turned off. Since then, we'd carried on a serious game of phone tag and it was getting a little silly.

I stared at my phone. Maybe a call wasn't the best idea. Maybe a text would be better. I squinted my brains into gear and thumbed out a message. *Miss you. When can we get together?*

The phone was in my purse and the bags were in my hands when I heard the *ping* of an incoming text message.

Down went the bags. I got out the phone and peered at the screen.

Me not Rafe?

I sat. What on earth was he talking about? So I typed that out. *What are you talking about?*

After a short but endless wait, he texted back. *Batteries in bedroom?*

"Oh . . ." Suddenly all was clear. When Tucker had stopped by the boat, Rafe had needed a new battery for his volt-doohickey. The only reason Rafe knew where things lived in my bedroom was that every spring he helped me open up my houseboat and get it in the water in exchange for my helping him with his spring yard work. But Tucker didn't know that. Tucker must have thought . . . I wanted to gag. Rafe was a good friend, but if we ever spent more than a single uninterrupted hour together, one on one, I'd have to muzzle him.

My thumbs got busy. I sent Tucker a long message about the spring chores. Before I hit the SEND button, I added the part about the muzzle.

Less than a minute later came a new message from Tucker.

Okay. Sorry I freaked out.

Right after that came a longer message that included his work schedule for the next couple of weeks, ending with *How about you?*

My schedule, naturally, was almost the complete opposite of his, but I did have a Saturday off in the not too distant future that matched up. I pointed that out, and he sent back a text. *We'll do something fun.*

A happy feeling filled me, lifting me, and making me grin like a kid on Christmas morning. I texted him back. *Count on it.*

At noon the next day, I headed off to do something I'd never thought I'd do—I drove onto the premises of Talcott Motors, the place Carissa's obituary had said she worked.

Sleek, shiny cars were placed just so on the grassy area between the road and the parking lot, cars that even car-challenged me knew were outrageously expensive. Cars from Germany, Italy, France, Scandinavia—and those were the ones I could identify.

I parked my sedan, which looked like something a

teenager of the hired help would drive, and walked into the showroom.

Car doors were invitingly open, hoods were propped up, and that new car scent was everywhere. Even though I knew I was being manipulated, I couldn't help walking up close to a sports car that looked fast even when it was standing still. "Wonder if Eddie would like this," I murmured.

"Eddie's your husband?" A middle-aged man, as smooth as the car against which he was leaning, smiled at me. "It's a beauty, isn't it?" He stepped toward me, one hand held forward for shaking, the other holding out a business card. "Bob Slocum, assistant manager of sales, at your service."

I shook his hand and took his card. "Hi, Minnie Hamilton, assistant director of the Chilson District Library."

His eyes, which had lit up upon hearing my title, dulled down at the mention of the library. The man clearly had a good idea of my salary. "Looking for a summer car?" he asked. "This is a top seller for us. Clients tell us that driving it is more fun than anyone should be allowed to have." He waved me toward the driver's door. "Take a seat, see what it feels like."

I put my hands behind my back and edged away. "Actually I'm looking for someone." Who exactly, I didn't know, but surely the line I'd prepared would work. "A friend of Carissa Radle's."

His gaze flicked briefly toward the row of offices lining the showroom's far wall. "Minnie, I'd love to help, but I hear my phone ringing. If you'll excuse me." He strode off, entered an office, and shut the door. Through the glass that made up the row's outside wall, I watched him lean back in his chair and pick up a magazine.

I mentally shrugged at the casual rejection—he was so good at it his coworkers probably called him Brush-off Bob—and walked toward the small office at which he'd glanced. It was occupied by a woman in her late thirties. Her sandy brown hair was cut short and stuck out into cute multiple spikes. I approached her open door, read her nameplate—Jari Mayes—and knocked on the doorjamb.

She looked up from the papers piled high on her desk. "Hi. If you're looking for a salesguy, they're down that way." She jerked her head. "If you have a bookkeeping question, though, you've come to the right place." Her smile was friendly, but her attention was clearly on the papers.

I introduced myself and said, "Could I talk to you a minute?"

"Uh, sure. What can I do for you?"

"It's about Carissa Radle," I said.

"About . . ." She swallowed and put her hand to her mouth, showing fingernails that were ragged from chewing. ". . . Carissa?" She blinked, once, twice; then the tears spilled over and down her cheeks.

After the tears that had overwhelmed Jari abated, I suggested that we head for lunch at the Three Seasons, my treat. Jari had sniffled, blown her nose, and agreed.

Once we were settled into a quiet corner, I'd spun Jari a story about being a friend of a friend who'd known the dead woman, that said friend was so troubled by Carissa's death that sleep was becoming impossible, and that I'd promised I'd try to find someone who could answer some questions about Carissa, that maybe this would help the friend sleep at night.

None of which made much sense if you thought about it for any length of time, but I was finding out that if you spoke well and sincerely, people tended to believe what you told them.

"So you and Carissa had known each other for a while?" I asked.

Jari sipped her water. "She started doing sales at Talcott, oh, around three years ago, I guess. I've been there since I graduated high school." She took another, deeper sip. "Probably be there until I die," she muttered.

Our server approached, carrying a platter laden with Kristen-directed food offerings. "Here you are, ladies," he said. "We're starting you off with Waldorf salads and rolls fresh from the oven."

I pushed the bowl of rolls over to Jari's side. "Have you had these before? Melt-in-your-mouth good."

She reached for her knife. "Oh, I shouldn't," she said, taking a roll and buttering it. As she took her first bite, her eyes closed and she gave a slight moan. "Oh, wow, this is so good."

Exactly. "You and Carissa were good friends?"

Jari dabbed at the corner of her buttery mouth with a white cloth napkin. "We ended up as friends the first week she started at the dealership." She looked at the roll in her hand as if she had no idea how it had gotten there. "Carissa was so much fun. One of those happy people, you know? It's just so wrong that she's dead." Her lower lip started to crumple.

I waited a short moment, then said, "Don't let your food get cold. I know for a fact the owner hates it when that happens." This was true. In the privacy of her office, Kristen had been known to stomp and rave at the top of her lungs about good food gone to waste. My hope, however, was that the eating and drinking process would keep Jari talking. My library friend Holly always talked when she held a beverage of any kind. I wondered briefly if her young children were aware of that quirk, and decided it was up to them to figure it out on their own.

"You know the owner?" Jari took another bite, then swallowed. "That's pretty cool."

It was, but I wanted to talk about her friend, not mine. "What did Carissa like to do? Did she have a boyfriend? Did she ski or have a boat or anything like that?"

"Ski?" Jari smiled. "The only place Carissa would have been at a ski resort was in the bar. You know, I bet she would have made a great bartender." Her pensive look was back.

I took a roll and pushed the bowl back in her direction. "No boyfriend?"

Jari's hand crept forward, hesitated, then snatched another roll. "She'd had a bad breakup just before she started at Talcott. She said she'd sworn off men her own age, that she was going to try dating older men and see if she had better luck."

Could this be . . . a clue? "So, was she? Dating an older man, I mean?"

Jari shook her head. "I'm not sure. When I was on vacation back in June, some guy came into the dealership. She said they went out a couple of times, but I'm not sure it was anything serious."

"What was his name?"

Jari kept buttering her roll. "She never said."

My eyebrows went up, and Jari sighed. "Yeah, I

know. I thought it was weird, too. I mean, you always tell your girlfriends the name of the guy you're dating. Always, unless . . ."

She stopped talking, so I filled in the blank. "You think he was married?"

"I don't know." Unhappiness crowded onto her face. "I can't think that Carissa would date a married man. That just wasn't like her."

I hoped not. "What did she say about him?"

"Not much. Only that he was kind of loaded, moneywise, and that he didn't look anything like the last guys she'd dated." Jari gave a vague smile. "She said it was time to break out of the lean build and sandy brown hair rut she'd fallen into."

So I had a wealthy older man as a suspect, one who was potentially married. Plus the bad-breakup guy. "Who was the guy she broke up with?"

"You mean the Weasel?"

I laughed. "Please tell me that isn't really his name."

"That's what she always called him." Jari gave a wan smile. "I never knew what his name was."

Our waiter scooped away the empty dishes and promised that our stuffed whitefish sandwiches would be out soon. I waited until he'd gone to ask the Big Question. "Do you have any idea who could have killed her?"

Jari clutched her water glass. "I wish I did. If I knew who did that to her, I'd go to the police so fast my head would spin around in circles."

"Do you know if anyone hated her? Or"—a brilliant idea came to me—"was really jealous of her?"

"She wasn't like that. I mean, she was pretty, so I suppose some wacko could have been jealous, but she was just fun. I can't imagine anyone wanting to . . . wanting to . . ." She sighed and took another roll.

I couldn't imagine it, either, and I hadn't even known the woman. Sorrow leached into and through me, another death diminishing me. What we needed was something for undiminishing purposes. A brand-new baby might work, although preferably not right here in the restaurant.

"There is one thing, though." Jari pleated her napkin. "She was big on Facebook. Always posting on there, real personal stuff. I kept telling her that she was opening herself up to trouble. I told her over and over that her house was going to be robbed, what with her posting where she was all the time and what she was doing and who she was doing it with. But she just told me not to be such a worrywart and laughed it off."

Jari's voice shook. "She said she was careful about her privacy controls and who she friended. She was all fun and games and she hardly ever took anything seriously. I wish . . . I wish I could be more like her."

I reached across the table and squeezed her hand. "That's a lovely thing to say and I'm sure that somewhere, somehow, Carissa is smiling down at you."

Jari swallowed a sob. "Do you think so?"

I did. But I also wondered if Carissa's Facebook page was still online.

That night the dinner menu was takeout Thai (me) and cat food (Eddie). A stiff breeze had whipped up out of the northwest and eating outside would have meant chasing napkins and keeping hair out of my mouth, so we were eating inside for the first time in days. Eddie had settled onto the top of the opposite dining bench and was studiously not paying attention to me.

"I'm sorry it's not nice enough to eat outside," I told him, "but you don't like the wind. You know you don't."

His mouth opened and closed in a soundless "Mrr."

I ignored him and turned the page of the book I was trying to read. It was the latest release from James Lee Burke, something I'd been looking forward to reading for weeks, but even Mr. Burke's lyrical prose wasn't capturing my attention.

I closed the cover. I probably shouldn't be reading a library book while eating something as slurpy as pad Thai, anyway. If I sprayed even the slightest spot of sauce on a page, I'd feel obligated to buy the book and my monthly book budget had taken a serious hit during the library's Fourth of July book sale. Two dollars a hardcover and a dollar a paperback are sweet prices to a bibliophile, but spend a couple of hours wandering the tables and you can still fork out a serious amount of money, no problem.

With no book at hand, I had two options. Read the newspaper or talk to Eddie. Since getting the newspaper meant I'd have to stand up, walk all the way across the room, bend down to get it out of my backpack, stand up, and walk all the way back again, I opted for Eddie.

"Not that you're second choice," I told him.

He turned his head and stared at me without blinking. I couldn't tell if he was thinking about how best to punish me for being a liar or if he was wondering how my food would taste if I keeled over dead.

"You wouldn't like tofu," I said. "Shrimp, sure, but I didn't order that today."

He went back to looking out into the windy world and I went back to talking to a cat that couldn't understand a word I said. Well, ninety-eight out of a hundred words. I was pretty sure he knew his name and what "No!" meant even if he didn't change whatever behavior was causing the command.

"So I need to find out more about Carissa Radle." I wound rice noodles around my fork, saw that it was far too big a bite, and shoveled it in anyway. Living alone allows you to do things like that. The trick is to remember to stop doing them when people are watching.

I chewed and swallowed. I might take big bites in the privacy of my own houseboat, but at least I didn't talk with my mouth full. A girl has to have standards.

Eddie stood and leaned backward to stretch his front legs.

"Stay out of my pad Thai," I warned him, but he didn't even glance at my food. Instead he jumped onto the floor and soft-footed it over to his water dish, where he crouched on the far side of the bowl and leaned all the way across it to drink.

I lived with the weirdest cat on the planet. Life was good. "So, Weird One, what should I do next about Carissa? How do I find out more about her?"

Eddie glanced up at me, a large drop of water hanging off his chin.

"Nice look." I spiraled up another mouthful of noodles. "Most times I'd ask Rafe or Kristen." Local knowledge had leached into their bones at birth. As a newcomer to Chilson, I was operating at a decided disadvantage. "But Carissa wasn't from here, so that network isn't going to be very useful."

Okay, so what would be useful? Talking to relatives. Friends. Neighbors. The only thing was, Carissa hadn't been up north long, and—

"Mrr."

I turned around. In the thirty seconds I'd had my back to Mr. Ed, he'd flopped on my backpack, wormed his back end inside, and burrowed around to make himself comfortable. In doing so he skidded my cell phone onto the floor.

"You are a cat of many talents." I crossed the kitchen to pick up the phone. "You even managed to turn it on to the calendar screen. How'd you do that?"

Once again, he didn't answer, but this time it was because he was sound asleep, deep into my backpack, the only part of him visible a pinkish nose.

Weirdest cat ever. No doubt about it.

Chapter 9

The first bookmobile visitors the next day were a boy of about seven and his mother. They'd been on the bookmobile once before, but the boy, whose name was Sheridan, had been too shy to say a word to any of us, and that included Eddie.

This time it was different.

Sheridan marched straight up to me. "Miss Minnie," he said in a strong voice, "I have a question."

I glanced at his mother, Tonya. She nodded, smiling. "Go right ahead," I told him.

"Your candy contest," he said. "You told me that if I'm closest to guessing the number of candies, I get the candies and the bookmobile will come to my house."

"Absolutely right," I said, crossing my fingers that the winner's driveway would be wide with a huge area in which to turn around.

He looked up at me with serious blue eyes. "If I win, does it have to come to my house?"

"You want it to go somewhere else?" This was a possibility I'd never considered.

"I want it to go to my grandma's. I want her to see

the bookmobile. It's my favorite place in the world. And I want her to meet Eddie."

We all looked toward the front of the bookmobile. The Eddie in question had perched himself on the passenger seat headrest. He was staring straight at us, the tip of his tail drumming to a beat only he could hear.

"Eddie is my favoritest cat in the world," Sheridan said. "We can't have cats at home because we live on a busy road. My grandma likes cats, too, and I want my grandma to pet Eddie."

"If you win," his mother prompted. "You might not, Sheridan."

"If you do," I told him, "we'll work something out."

Sheridan nodded. "Okay. Thank you." Business transacted, he headed off to the candy jar. Soon he was holding his pencil against the jar and muttering measurements and what sounded like volumetric calculations.

Tonya smiled. "He's only shy at first. Now you won't be able to shut him up."

"A kid who says the bookmobile is his favorite place in the world?" I smiled wide. "I forgive any transgression he's ever made and any he ever will make."

She laughed and started browsing through the books on CD. When another set of footsteps came up the stairs, Tonya turned and said, "Hi, Faye. How are you this morning?"

It was Faye of the Cookbooks. And the second she saw me, she spun in a half circle and fled back down the stairs.

Tonya and Thessie and I looked at one another. "I have no idea what that was all about," I said.

"She's my neighbor," Tonya murmured, "but I've never seen her do anything like that."

Before we could formulate a good theory, Faye came running back up the steps. "I had them in the car," she said breathlessly, and held out the stack of overdue cookbooks. "Here you go, Minnie, and I'm horribly sorry about them being so late."

Laughing, I took the books from her. "If I had a gold star, you'd get one for the most sincere apology I've ever had."

She rummaged around in the bottom of her purse for the change to pay the overdue fine. "But I have to tell you, the heavenly deviled eggs were a huge hit at the reunion."

Faye had borrowed the cookbooks to prepare for a family get-together. I checked in the books and tried to remember what weekend her reunion had been. "You had good weather, too, didn't you?"

"Chamber of commerce stuff," she said. "We had cousins show up that I'd never met."

Tonya looked over from her perusings. "Faye, don't you have a cousin who knew that woman who was killed?"

The back of my scalp prickled.

Faye's face crumpled a little with what looked like worry. "That was a few years ago," she said. "But you know what? I saw that Carissa a couple of weeks ago in Petoskey, all cozy with some guy who looked old enough to be her father."

I was twitching with questions. "Who was he? Do you know his name? What did he look like?"

She was shaking her head. "He looked familiar, but even that day I couldn't come up with his name. Maybe he was just that type. You know, mid-fifties, lots of money, and just good-looking enough that he figured every woman was half in love with him. Those guys all kind of look the same, don't they?"

We laughed, but she had a point.

The slippery sound of books starting a downward slide made me whirl around. "Eddie!" Before I could move, the books hit the floor. My furry friend looked up, his front paw still extended. He'd jumped, stealth-like, to the computer desk and had pushed at the pile of books Tonya had returned.

"You are a rotten cat," I told him, and crouched down.

"Here, let me help." Faye helped pick up the books, waving Tonya away. "No, we're all done." She put the stack back on the desk and patted Eddie on the head. "I'm sure he didn't do it on purpose."

I was sure he had, but I just smiled.

Faye selected two books—new releases by Nora Roberts and Tess Gerritsen—and promised to bring them back in short order.

"Before they're overdue is all I ask," I said, smiling. "And if you remember the name of that man Carissa was with, the police should know. The more information they have, the faster they'll find out who killed her."

She looked startled. "I never thought of it that way. You're right. I'll try harder to think of his name." She made her good-byes and left.

I was in the process of beeping the return books into the computer when Faye pounded back up the book-mobile's steps. "I remembered!" She reached for the books I was working on. "Here. This is what made me remember," she said, sorting through the stack and extracting a book that had a boat on its cover.

"The Boys in the Boat," I read. "Nine Americans and Their Epic Quest for Gold at the 1936 Berlin Olympics."

"It was wonderful," Tonya said.

Faye tapped the picture of the rowing shell on the book's cover. "The guy I saw with Carissa, it was Hugo Edel. Boats, that's what made me remember. He's that boat guy."

He certainly was. Edel, along with his wife, Annelise, were the founders of Crown Yachts, a local manufacturer of high-end boats. My cranky neighbor's boat, as nice as it was, probably cost a fraction of what a Crown would run.

So the question was, what had Carissa, who sold cars, been doing with a man like Hugo Edel? Certainly not buying a boat from him.

"That's great," I told Faye. "Call the sheriff's department and talk to either Detective Devereaux or Detective Inwood. They'll want to know."

At least I hoped they would.

The next day, Saturday, I'd scheduled the bookmobile to appear at the opposite end of the county, including a stop at the marina Chris had asked me to visit, so instead of sitting down to breakfast at the boardinghouse, I was driving east with Thessie at my side and Eddie in the carrier at her feet. He'd snuggled himself into Paulette's pink blanket so deep that only the tips of his ears were visible.

"Hey, did I tell you?" Thessie asked.

"Can you be a teensy bit more specific?" I checked the side mirrors, flicked on the right turn signal, and aimed the bookmobile at a shady spot created by a clump of white birches.

Uncle Chip's Marina East looked a lot like the Chilson version, which looked a lot like most fifty-year-old marinas I'd seen. Worn a little at the edges, but worn in a way that was comfortable rather than unsightly. Weathered docks, but no splintered wood. An elderly marina office built with small-diameter vertical logs. Boats of all shapes, sizes, and costs bobbed in the slips, and I could already see people out on their boat decks, pointing at the bookmobile and smiling.

"My mom and dad are going to take me downstate the week after next to look at colleges." Thessie bounced a little in her seat. "I can't wait. The University of Michigan and Wayne State have graduate programs in library and information science, but I've heard you shouldn't go to grad school where you got your undergraduate degree. So I was thinking about staying local for the first couple of years, but maybe I should start where I'm going to finish and if I go downstate maybe there will be chances to do an internship somewhere. Hey, wouldn't it be, like, the coolest thing ever if I got an internship at the Library of Congress?"

She suddenly noticed my lack of response. "Um, are you okay? I thought you'd be excited about this."

"Oh, I am," I said. And I was. But if Thessie was going to be away the week after next, I was going to have to quick-a-minute find a bookmobile volunteer. Both Stephen and the library board had been adamant that the bookmobile had to have two people aboard at every stop. I might skirt a rule here and there, especially ones that could involve cats, but the two-at-a-time proclamation was one I dared not flout.

We went through the regular motions for the beginning of a bookmobile stop. Opened the vent in the roof, released the bungee-corded chair at the back desk, fired up the computers, opened the door, and made sure everything was shipshape.

"Mrr."

I snapped my fingers. "Sorry about that, pal." Between Thessie's excited chatter about college and my own concerns about finding a volunteer on short notice, I'd completely forgotten about releasing Eddie.

"Yes, I am a horrible kitty mommy," I said, hurrying toward the front of the bookmobile, "and you have every right to scold me. I hope you don't, of course, but I'm sure those hopes will be dashed to bits as soon as I open this door."

Thessie laughed. "Do you always talk to him as if he can really understand you?"

"Mrr," Eddie said.

She stopped laughing. "He, uh, sounded kind of annoyed, didn't he?"

"You're not annoyed, are you, Eddie?" I scooped him up into my arms and snuggled him. "Not with Thess. She's your second favorite human and . . . hey, cut that out."

He was doing that wriggle and squirm thing, the one that turned him into a slippery liquid mass that was impossible to hold.

"Come on, Eddie, chill a little." I tried to pet him calm. "She was just joking and . . ."

And he was out of my arms, on the floor, and zooming down the carpeted aisle of the bookmobile.

"Eddie!" I called. "Don't you dare go—"

Down the stairs and out the door he went, running flat-out fast, a black-and-white streak of cat-titude.

Thessie shrieked. "He's out! Minnie, he's out! He never wants out! We have to—"

"He'll be fine," I said with as much calm as I could muster. "But I need to go get him. If you could take care of things for a minute, I'd appreciate it." Because there were people clattering up the stairs and into the bookmobile. Thessie was many wonderful things, but she did have a slight issue with claustrophobia. Too many people on the bookmobile gave her the absolute willies.

She bit her lower lip, eyed the newcomers, and nodded. "I'll be fine," she said. "You have to get Eddie. Just . . . don't be long, okay?"

I patted her on the shoulder. "Be back in a jiffy with the kitty." It didn't exactly rhyme, but it was enough to get a smile out of her. I headed off, welcoming new patrons as I went, aiming a few at appropriate areas of the bookmobile, and smiling all the while.

My smile dropped off as my feet hit the asphalt. "Rotten cat," I muttered. "If he does this one more time, I swear I'm never going to bring him on the bookmobile ever again."

It was a hollow threat and Eddie wouldn't have taken it seriously if he'd heard it. "Eddie? Here, kitty, kitty, kitty." I turned in a small circle, scanning the area. "Where are you, pal? Eddie!"

A distant "mrr" caught my ear. I called his name again and listened carefully. A second "mrr" had come from the opposite side of the marina, close to the office. Instead of taking the sidewalk, I trotted across the lawn, keeping an eagle eye out for the fuzzy escapee.

I kept trotting, dodging picnic tables and pieces of playground equipment. "Eddie? Here, kitty, kitty. Here, Eddie kit—"

And there he was, occupying the top of an already occupied picnic table. At the table were two men sitting on opposite sides, one of whom was fussing with what looked like a very expensive camera. Both men looked vaguely familiar.

Brett, that was it. And the baseball guy. What was his name . . . ? I snapped my fingers. "Greg," I said out loud, and he looked up at me.

"Hey," he said easily. "Minnie, right? From the marina. Thought this cat looked familiar." He scratched Eddie behind the ears, which was just the way he liked it. "He pounded across the lawn like a bat out of you-know-what a minute ago."

"Faster than a speeding bullet," Brett said, laughing.

I moved closer to Eddie, but he slid backward, out of my reach. "He has a habit of doing that. But you don't look as if you're having a stroke, so you should be okay."

"A stroke?" Greg frowned. "That golf ball got me pretty good the other day, but other than that I feel fine."

Me and my big mouth. I gave a quick explanation that didn't make much sense. Then, needing to change the subject, I said the first thing that popped into my head. "Too bad about that woman who was killed. Did you know her? Carissa Radle?"

Greg, who had been tickling Eddie's toes, glanced over at Brett. "Carissa," he said. "I knew of her, I guess. But I didn't know her know her if you know what I mean."

Sort of. "Where did you meet her?" I asked.

"Don't really remember. Ready to head out, Brett?" Greg stood, and so did his friend. "We need to get going," Greg said. "Chris Ballou sent me over here to look at a boat, and these pictures aren't quite what I wanted, so I need to get some more. See you later, okay?" He sketched a quick wave and walked briskly toward the parking lot.

"Well, that was weird." I scooped an unresisting Eddie into my arms and we headed back. "If he's going to take more pictures of that boat, he's headed in the wrong direction."

"Mrr."

Then we were at the bookmobile. I had to introduce Eddie to a new circle of admirers, and I put the odd conversation to the back of my mind.

After an early dinner, Eddie and I hung out on the front of the houseboat, watching the boats cruise past and enjoying the gentle breeze and sunshine that was just starting its evening slant.

I picked up the newspaper and watched as the sports section slid out down to the deck. Convenient for me, since I never read the sports section. "Say," I asked Eddie, "did you see the look on Thessie's face when I told her I'd been talking to Greg Plassey? I think the girl was a wee bit starstruck."

One of Eddie's ears twitched, but other than that, he didn't seem to care about retired Major League Baseball players.

"That conversation with Greg was a little weird, wasn't it?" I asked. "Kind of makes you wonder. It was almost as if—oof!"

Eddie's leap from his chaise longue to mine ended in a wild sprawl halfway across my lower abdomen and all over the newspaper. The now-crumpled newspaper.

"Jeez, cat," I said, pulling the newsprint out from underneath him. "You could have given me some warning. I know that kind of thing isn't part of your genetic makeup, but maybe you could evolve a little? Just for me?"

He rotated one and a half times, settled onto my legs, and started purring. Which I'm pretty sure was cat for *Not a chance, but it's cute of you to ask.*

I muttered about rotten cats, gave him a few pets, then tried to uncrumple my paper. I wasn't one of those people like my father, whose day could be ruined by a newspaper that wasn't pristine, but even I preferred my printed news to be on sheets that didn't have peaks and valleys in every paragraph.

"You know," I told Eddie as I smoothed the pages, "you could have jumped on the end of the chaise and walked up. That way you wouldn't have crinkled anything. Okay, I know, I know. The way you did it was much more fun for you, and that's what really counts."

Outstanding. Not only was I talking to my cat; I was also answering for him. The habit was getting a little out of hand and—

"Huh," I said. "Would you look at that?"

Given his body language, Eddie wasn't going to look at anything except the insides of his eyelids, but I kept going anyway.

"There was a boat explosion a couple of weeks ago, remember?" I was sure I'd read the short article to him. "That big one that blew up out on Lake Michigan? Well," I said, scanning to the end of the article, "it turns out that the guy on the boat was Hugo Edel, can you believe it?"

Eddie apparently did, because he sighed and settled down deeper into my lap. I kept reading.

"This says Edel was out on the big lake alone. He was thrown from the boat in the explosion. Then another boat zoomed over to the site and picked him up." Except for Edel's name, that much had been in the newspaper before. Eddie started moving around, but I kept sharing my stream-of-consciousness thoughts.

"Anyway, the investigation is over and they're saying it's an accident. I wonder how close that boat explosion was to Carissa's murder, timingwise. Which kind of makes you wonder if the two things are related somehow. And I wonder if Faye has called the sheriff's office about Edel. Do you think I should—"

"Mrr-rrrooww."

I lowered the paper and looked at my cat, who was now lying along the length of my shins with his chin propped over the tip of my right flip-flop. "Was that a yawn," I asked, "or is your dinner disagreeing with you?"

"Mrr."

"Back at you, pal." I dropped the newspaper and pulled him onto my lap for a good snuggle. "Back at you."

Chapter 10

Sunday passed as my Sundays often did, with morning chores, a few hours at the library, and dessert with Kristen. Monday I didn't have to work at all, so of course it started out cloudy with a spattering of rain. Then, just as I was gathering my dirty clothes to haul to the marina's coin laundry, the sun broke through the clouds. What had been a gray day of mild summer gloom instantly transformed into an outstanding morning.

Eddie, who had been following me, twining around my ankles and criticizing my cleaning efforts as only a cat can, spotted his favorite square of sunshine and settled down in the middle of the kitchen floor with a purring sigh.

I looked at the piles of laundry, looked out at the enticing blue sky, looked at my cat. "What do you think, Eddie? Should I be a responsible adult and do the chores that need doing, or should I skip out into the sunshine and play the rest of the day?"

He opened one eyelid, gave me a brief look, then went back to sleep.

Play. He'd clearly said play. No doubt about it.

I ate a quick lunch of peanut butter and jelly, scrawled my vague plans on the kitchen whiteboard as I promised my mother I would always do, and headed out.

"So much for playing," I said. Or that's what I would have said if I'd had the breath to talk. The hill up which I was riding my bike was far steeper than any hill had a right to be. And I had a feeling that the hill wouldn't seem nearly as precipitous when going the other way. How a hill could be twice as steep riding up as riding down, I didn't know, but it was one of those harsh realities of life.

After leaving the snoring Eddie, I'd decided a bike ride was a good idea and hauled my bicycle out of my marina storage unit. Then I'd decided it would be an excellent idea to take a look at Carissa's house. I used my cell to call Jari for the address, then set off. Then up. As in serious amounts of up.

At long last, I topped the hill and turned onto a tree-lined street. The houses on the right were set back from the road, perched on the edge of the hill with a fine view of Janay Lake. These were old homes, built in the early nineteen hundreds by upper-middle-class people come north from Chicago or the Detroit area for the summer. Lots of clapboard, lots of gingerbread trim, lots of porches and swings and irrigated lawns.

The houses on the left were a little different. Most were ranch houses set close to the road, and looked as if they'd been built in the last thirty years. Nice enough, but none had anywhere near the class of their across-the-street neighbors.

I had slowed to the point of wobbliness while reading the house numbers. Carissa's address was half of a duplex. The left side of the house had curtains drawn across every window, so I swung down my bike's kickstand and walked to the front door on the right, where the windows had half-open blinds. On a Monday morning in July, the people who lived here were probably at work.

Knocking on the door, I imagined a young family renting this place while trying to save money for a down payment on a house. I had started visualizing their dog as a golden retriever when the front door was flung open.

"What do you want?" The man barking at me was tall and wide and hadn't shaved in at least two days.

I smiled at him, which wasn't an easy thing to do in the face of his glower. "Hi, I'm Minnie Hamilton. A friend of mine knew your neighbor, Carissa, and he's so upset about her death that I thought I'd stop by and ask—"

His frown went so deep it was probably etching grooves in his skin. "You got a warrant?"

"A what? No, of course not. I'm not a police officer. I'm a friend of—"

His bloodshot eyes glared at me. "I'm not talking to nobody about nothing unless they bring a warrant."

"Sure, I understand, but—"

The door slammed so hard that the wind of its passing rocked me back a step. I retreated to my bicycle, toed up the kickstand, climbed aboard, and pedaled off.

The road felt much rougher than it had a few minutes ago. I glanced at the asphalt. Didn't see any noticeable cracks, bumps, or potholes. Why, then, were my bicycle handlebars quivering so much that I was afraid of being tossed onto my head?

I slowed to a stop. Put my feet on the ground, released the rubbery grips, and stared at my hands.

They were shaking.

I took a deep breath. Another. Looked at my hands again. Still shaking, so I swung my leg over the bike's crossbar and looked around for somewhere to sit. Providence was with me, because there was a nice Minnie-sized rock at the end of the driveway across from the duplex. Perfect. I walked my bike over, leaned it against the rock, and sat down.

The stone was in the sun, and its warmth spread into my skin, soothing and relaxing me. Soon my breaths came easier and my hands stopped shaking.

Yep, I'd been silly to let that man get to me. I was used to dealing with recalcitrant types—it was part of being a librarian—so why had this particular brand of crankiness bothered me so much? Was it because part of me had been afraid that he'd killed Carissa and that I might be next?

"Hello."

I jumped high enough that, when I landed, I came down half on the rock and half off, then slid in a very ungainly way to the ground.

"Oh, dear." The woman frowned in concern. "Sorry about that. I didn't mean to startle you. I just saw you sitting on my rock, looking like you lost your best friend, and I wondered if you needed some help."

I clambered to my feet, my brain still stuck firmly in awkward mode. "No, I'm fine, thanks. I just . . . had an odd encounter and I needed to sit for a little. Sorry about using your rock."

The woman peered at me, her short salt-and-pepper hair framing a square face that topped a body trending to, but not quite achieving, plumpness. "You look familiar. Do I know you?"

"Minnie Hamilton. I'm the assistant librarian here in Chilson. That's where most people have seen me. Or on the bookmobile. I drive that two or three days a week."

She was shaking her head, then switched to nodding sharply. "Three Seasons. You're Kristen Jurek's friend, aren't you?" She grinned wide, exposing teeth with wide gaps. "You look like you could use something to drink. Come on up to the house."

Ten minutes later, we were sitting in white wicker chairs, the kind that lived on almost every front porch in Chilson, only we were sitting on a back porch of the home's second story with an amazing view of Janay Lake, the channel, and beyond.

"That's a great view of Lake Michigan," I said, taking in the watery vista.

"Only from the second floor, though," Abby said, "because of all the trees. That's why my great-grandfather designed the house backward, or so the family story goes."

My hostess was Abby Sterly, who was the head honcho loan officer at the bank where Kristen had applied for the money to fund her restaurant's renovations. Abby had given me the nickel tour of the rambling cottage she'd inherited. "No one else wanted to take care of the old place," she told me, "let alone pay the taxes. But it would have broken my heart to have the property go out of the family, so I found a way to make it work."

She'd made it happen thirty years ago by building the

duplex where Carissa Radle had lived. "Those rents have paid the property taxes nicely, but now I'm thinking about selling it. Don't suppose you would be interested, would you?" She eyed me over her glass of soda. "No, never mind answering. I can tell already what you'd say."

I laughed. "I'm not a property-owning kind of person. My houseboat is about all I can deal with right now."

She made a "hmm" sort of noise and I suspected my name was being entered into a mental list titled "Contact at a Later Date."

"Besides," I said, "the guy who lives there gave me the creeps."

"Rob Pew?" Abby blotted her glass on a coaster. "He's not a bad guy."

My mother had taught me, if I couldn't say anything nice, not to say it at all. And maybe someday her lessons would sink in. "He scared the snot out of me," I said honestly.

Abby half smiled. "He works the night shift at Northern Fabrications. He hates being woken up before his alarm goes off. I'm surprised he even answered the door."

So there it was: a simple explanation for the extreme surliness of a large man named Rob. Not justification, of course, because there was none for rudeness, but a little explanation could go a long way.

"What did you want from Rob, anyway?" Abby asked.

She'd been so nice to me that I almost told her the whole truth and the entire truth right then and there, but something in her sharp gaze stopped me. There was no reason for her to know about Cade, and you never knew who might say what to whom and then the whole town would know that the famous artist guy had been tossed into the slammer—however briefly—for murder. And they'd also know that the bookmobile librarian was trying to help him clear his name, and that was a complication I could do without. Certainly the library could do without it. So I sort of made something up.

"Carissa Radle and I came from the same town," I said. "It's just a little weird, if you know what I mean."

"You grew up in Dearborn, too?" Abby toasted me. "Dearborn High or Edsel Ford?"

"Dearborn High."

"Hail, fellow graduate well met!" She held her hand high and leaned forward so we could slap palms. "Was Mrs. Koch still teaching Latin when you were there? I loved that woman. Did you know she spoke five languages?"

"She'd retired by the time I got there," I said.

"Too bad. And how about the Beefeater?" She switched easily from education to food. "My grandparents took us there every Sunday after church. Short dresses and tights and those shiny black shoes with the strap across the instep that was always either too tight or too loose." She laughed, but it ended fast. "So long ago."

"Lives on in your memories, though," I said.

Her face brightened a little. "Yes, it does, doesn't it?" Then she sighed. "Just like Carissa will for her parents."

After a pause, I said, "Kristen said she would have liked to hire Carissa, but she needed people with experience."

"Makes sense, but I'm sure Carissa would have learned fast." Abby put her feet up on a low table. "From what I heard, she was already getting a return clientele at Talcott. Still . . ." She stopped talking to kick off her sandals.

When she didn't start up again, I asked, "What's that?"

"Well, it's just a little odd. When Carissa was moving in, I stopped by the duplex to see if she needed anything. We got to talking, so I helped her unpack a few boxes. In one of them was a framed diploma from Wayne State University, and textbooks with all sorts of medical titles. So . . . it's a little odd." She shrugged. "But then lots of people can't find jobs in their fields these days, so I didn't ask about it."

"What degree was the diploma for?"

But she shook her head. "I didn't get that close a look at it."

After a pause, I asked, "What was Carissa like? Her personality, I mean."

Abby pointed to Janay Lake. "Like that. All shiny and sparkly. She was one of those happy people, the kind that make you smile when they walk into a room. I can't think of anyone who didn't like her."

"Even her neighbor, Rob?"

She smiled. "Even Rob. He's been all broken up since she died. Not that there was anything going between them. He and his girlfriend have been dating forever. Carissa was like a little sister to Rob."

Enough like siblings that murderous anger could have been spurred up during a spat of teasing? I gave the idea some thought, then gave it a pass. If the killer had been so obvious as to be the next-door neighbor, the police would already have latched onto him.

"Did you know Carissa very well?" I asked.

There was a moment of quiet. "I'd like to say yes," she said, "but since I got the news, I've realized that I hardly knew her." Abby watched the lake far below us. "I didn't know her hopes and dreams and I didn't know what she lay awake at night worrying about. I didn't even know why she moved up here."

Her sadness tugged at me, but I knew what she meant. There were people who let us into their lives, and people who didn't.

"I worry about losing my eyesight," I offered.

Abby pulled in a shaky breath and smiled. "I worry about knee replacement surgery."

"I moved up here because this is my favorite place in the whole world, even in March."

She lifted her glass to me. "Here's to Chilson."

"To Chilson." We tinked glasses. My hand, I was happy to notice, didn't shake at all.

After riding back to the marina, switching my bike for my car, and taking a short drive, I walked through the main entrance of Crown Yachts and into a cavernous showroom featuring extremely large, very shiny, and amazingly expensive boats. A chair at the desk near the front of the room was occupied by a twentysomething guy whose attention was completely focused on his smartphone.

At my question, he made an over-there gesture with his head. "Hugo? I think he's in his office."

The guy's thumbs were moving rapidly, but from

this angle I couldn't tell if he was texting or playing Angry Birds. "Should you call ahead, let him know I'm coming?"

"Nah. Hugo's okay."

His being okay wasn't what I was worried about; it was whether or not he'd be annoyed at my unannounced arrival. I wanted him friendly, not irritated. But I shrugged and made my dwarfish way around the massive boats, being exceedingly careful not to touch anything. My mother had instilled the "if you break it you buy it out of your allowance" creed in me at a young age.

The first office door off the showroom floor was large and spacious and sported a brass label that read HUGO EDEL, PRESIDENT. The man inside, who was fit with short hair and tanned skin, was standing in front of a paper-covered desk, staring at a set of boat plans, talking on a cell phone, and tapping a particular spot on the plans over and over.

"Phil, I know you want that storage compartment next to the head, but—" A torrent of words came through the phone's receiver. Edel listened, then said, "Right. I'll get the designer to work on it." He clicked off the phone and looked up at me. "Good morning," he said, then frowned. "No, wait. It's afternoon, isn't it?"

The phone in his hand buzzed. He looked at the readout. "Sorry. I have to take this. Sit down, if you can find a spot."

I tried not to listen in on his conversation, but it was a little hard to pretend I couldn't hear him when we were less than ten feet apart. I picked up a pile of Crown Yachts brochures, sat down in the chair where they'd been, and did my best to show an interest in boats I would never be able to consider purchasing.

As soon as that phone call was over, another one began. He held up his index finger, indicating that he'd be with me in a minute, and I contented myself with choosing what color fabric to upholster my yacht's master suite in.

"No more." He turned his phone off and tossed it, skittering, across the boat plans. "Hugo Edel. What can I do for you?" He came around the desk to shake my hand.

I introduced myself, adding that I was the bookmobile librarian.

He smiled, and ten years dropped off his face. "I've seen you driving around. That looks like a great job. I'm a little jealous."

"It's not all fun and games." I said, then grinned. "But to tell you the truth, a lot of it is."

He laughed and leaned against the edge of his desk. "So, what does the bookmobile librarian want with Crown Yachts?"

I made my smile as warm as I could. "As the library's assistant director, I get stuck with doing everything that the director doesn't have time to do. In this case, it's fund-raising. I'm contacting the area's most successful businesses and asking them to consider a donation." It was a brilliant idea, and I was glad I'd thought of it that morning.

Edel was losing interest fast. "I'm afraid our donation budget is tapped out for the year."

I nodded. "Sure, I understand. That's why I'm talking to you now, so you can keep a donation in mind for next year." I handed him my card. "Do you have any questions? Lots of people want to know about the bookmobile."

Sadly, he didn't have a single one. This meant I was forced to take a more direct approach to the Carissa question than I would have liked.

"Say," I said, "I know where I've seen you before. Didn't I see you having dinner with Carissa Radle a couple of weeks ago? You know, that poor woman who was killed?"

"Rotten thing to have happen," he said. "But sure, I had dinner with her. There's lots of wining and dining in this business. She was asking about boats for some car client of hers from downstate." He tipped his head back, considering me. "You're not thinking that I had anything to do with her death, are you?"

I opened my eyes innocently wide. "What? Oh, gosh no. I just remembered seeing you, that's all." Well, technically Faye had seen him, but that was close enough.

"Okay, then," Edel said. "Because if you thought she seemed interested in me, you're wrong. Once we got done talking about boats, she mostly talked about how much fun it was to hang out on the set for that TV cooking show they film around here."

"*Trock's Troubles*?" I asked.

"That's the one."

And I suddenly had another lead to follow.

The twentysomething guy waved at me as I left. "Have a nice day!"

I walked into the small vestibule area, and, with my hand reaching for the doorknob, came to a sudden halt.

A trim, fiftyish woman was using the door's glass as a mirror. She pushed a stray strand of hair into place, patted a little color into her cheeks, checked for lipstick on her teeth, gave herself a bright smile, then opened the door.

"Oh!" She stopped abruptly. "I didn't know anyone was there."

I'd stepped backward, but there was no getting around the embarrassing fact that I'd caught her primping. There were two options here, either politely ignore the incident or make the most of it. I smiled and said, "You look great."

A faint red stained her cheeks. "Thank you," she murmured. "I hope you have a nice day." She gave me a nod and walked into the showroom.

"Hey, Mrs. Edel," I heard the twentysomething say. "How you doing?"

So the woman who was so concerned about how she looked was Annelise Edel, Hugo's wife. *Hmm,* I thought, as I left the building.

Definitely *hmmm*.

Chapter 11

I'd been wanting to check on Aunt Frances, so I headed over to the boardinghouse after work on Wednesday.

As I was trotting up the porch's wide steps, I spotted young Harris and the approaching-elderly Zofia sitting side by side on the porch swing, Zofia with her legs tucked up underneath her, Harris using his long legs to push them gently to and fro.

"Hey, you two," I said. "Do anything fun today?"

Zofia patted the strong shoulder next to her, the colored glass of her costume jewelry rings flashing bright in the sunshine. "This gentleman spent the day updating the statistics for his fantasy baseball team. A nice task for a summer day, don't you think?"

All I knew about fantasy sports leagues was that they could occupy an inordinate amount of time, even more so at the beginning of your sport's season. I knew this because the upcoming professional football season was all that Josh wanted to talk about, in spite of the facts that it was barely August and that no one else on the library staff cared about football.

Once, Holly had told Josh to talk about football to someone who cared, like maybe Mitchell Koyne. Poor Josh had looked so hurt that I'd felt obliged to ask a couple of questions about his picks. Two years later, I was still paying the price. So instead of asking Harris about his fantasy baseball team, I gave him a smiling nod and headed into the house.

Inside, young Deena was practically sitting on the lap of the balding Quincy. They were paging through an old scrapbook of vintage postcards, their heads almost touching. While their gazes were ostensibly on the book, it was clear from the lingering touches and sidelong glances that they were only interested in each other.

My genial wave in their direction went unnoticed. I passed through to the empty kitchen, poured two glasses of lemonade, checked the cookie jar, put four oatmeal cookies on a plate, got out an old Coca-Cola tray, and carried the lot onto the screened-in porch that overlooked the forested backyard.

Aunt Frances smiled up at me from the rocking love seat. "Just what I needed. How did you know?"

"Years of experience." I put the tray on a low table and sat next to her. "It's what you always brought me whenever I was upset."

As soon as I was old enough to be put on a Greyhound bus, I'd begged to be sent north to stay with Aunt Frances for the summer. She'd nursed me after I'd fallen out of a tree and broken my arm, hugged me when the boy I'd liked had called me a Mini-Munchkin, and wiped away my tears when I'd been rejected by my top college choice. Every occasion had been eased with lemonade and cookies.

She reached forward, broke a cookie in half, and handed me the larger share. "And it's what my grandmother always brought me."

It was a cozy thought. We rocked back and forth, eating cookies and sipping lemonade, enjoying each other's company in companionable silence.

Finally she said, "I'm worried, Minnie. Nothing is working out like it's supposed to."

Never before had I seen my aunt look so anxious. It didn't suit her at all. "Things will work out," I said.

"Do you really think so, Minnie?" Her light blue eyes gazed at mine with intensity. "Do you really?"

I had no clue if it would or not, but at that moment I would have done almost anything to wipe that look of desperation from her face. "Absolutely." I hesitated, then said, "And I'll do everything I can to make it happen."

"Oh, Minnie!" She reached out and hugged the stuffing out of me. "You're the best niece ever!"

"And you're the best aunt," I said into her shoulder. I gave her a squeeze. "Thessie had an idea. What do you think about hosting a party?"

My aunt looked dubious. "What good would that do?"

"Invite dozens of people, including the boarders. Then we'll prime people to say how nice Deena and Harris look together, how Paulette and Quincy seem like the perfect couple, and how Zofia and Leo already seem as if they're married. If we can get those thoughts into their heads . . ."

But Aunt Frances was shaking her head. "It's not a bad idea, but either one or another of them has day-trip plans the next three weekends. After that it'll be too late."

"Okay. Let me think a minute," I said, deciding not to mention any of Thessie's more outlandish theories, especially the one about love potions. I was almost sure she'd been joking, but not completely.

My thoughts brushed up against the ideas of love and companionship and friendship, and how it can be found in the most unexpected places. Look at me; who would have thought I'd find a boyfriend while taking Rafe to the emergency room? And then there were people who looked too hard for a companion.

Was that what Carissa had been doing with Hugo Edel? He said no, but Faye had said they looked cozy, and that was a hard thing to mistake.

Edel had to be at least fifteen years older than Carissa, but age didn't matter. I glanced over at Aunt Frances. I knew her well enough to be sure that she wasn't concerned about the age differences between her mismatched boarders; it was just that they weren't setting up to be the matches she'd so carefully constructed.

"Maybe it's time for a more direct approach," I said, getting to my feet.

In the living room, Deena and Quincy were still pseudostudying the scrapbook. I plopped down on the couch across from them. "Hi," I said. "Where's Paulette?"

They looked up at me. "Uh . . ." Quincy blinked. "Paulette?"

"You know," I said. "Nice lady, early fifties, likes to wear flip-flops, could make a fortune selling her needlework projects online. Her."

Deena laughed. "She reminds me of this neighbor of my parents, only Paulette doesn't have eight cats."

"How do you know?" Quincy asked. "Have you ever asked Paulette if she has cats?"

For some reason, the two found this hilarious.

They were still laughing when Harris came in through the front door. I called to him. "Come on over," I said. "Have you seen this scrapbook?"

"Sorry," he said. "I'm going kayaking and I need to get changed." He waved and headed up the stairs.

"Kayaking," I said brightly. "Doesn't that sound like fun, Deena?"

She squinched a face. "Sounds wet and probably cold. I hate being cold." She gave a fake shiver.

"We can't have our Deena cold," Quincy said. He put his arms around her. "Is that better?"

The stars in her eyes told me the answer to that question, and more. I murmured a good-bye that they didn't hear and went to report my failure to Aunt Frances.

On Tuesday, I'd sent Rafe a first draft of his after-school reading program, so that night he was finishing up the electrical work on my boat. Or what I hoped was the finishing up of the work. School was starting in less than a month and soon he'd be too busy doing middle school principal–type tasks to think about much else for weeks. Not that you could tell. Maybe someday, somewhere, Rafe would look harried and frantically busy, but right now he looked as if he had all the time in the world.

"You know," I said, "this would get done a lot faster if you didn't stop to look at every good-looking female who walks past."

"Not every one." He glanced up from the spaghetti-like tangle of wires that surrounded him. "I skip right over any female who looks younger than twenty."

Which was probably true. Rafe was many things, but he would never dream of being age-inappropriate. On the low end, anyway. "Do you have an upper age limit?" I asked.

"Nope." He pulled out a long wire and eyed it critically. "I mean, someday I'm going to be old. Wouldn't make sense if I couldn't appreciate the female form in its later years. Plus, have you taken a close look at your neighbor?" He tipped his head in the direction of Louisa and Ted's boat. "I don't care how old she is, she's downright hot."

"I'm sure her husband would appreciate the sentiment," I said.

Rafe was impervious to the sarcasm. "Yeah, he probably would. I mean, who wouldn't like to have a hot wife?"

He went on about the happiness of hotness, but I'd gone backward a little, to thinking about neighbors. "Hey, Rafe?"

"What's that?"

One nice thing about Rafe was that he didn't mind switching topics in the blink of an eye. Did that come of working with middle school kids? Or was it his innate ability to do so that made him good with the kids? I pushed the questions away. "Do you know a Rob Pew? He lives in a duplex up the hill, in the unit next door to where that woman was killed a few weeks back."

"Pewey Lewey?" Rafe grinned, his teeth showing white against his skin, which, since it was late summer, was a deep burnished red. "Sure. He's one of my hunting buddies, come November."

Ha. I knew what "hunting" meant for any group of guys that included Rafe. It meant a week of staying up late, playing cards, imbibing copious amounts of adult canned beverages, sleeping late, then waking up and doing it all over again. "When was the last time you actually got a deer?"

Rafe's grin went even wider. "Need-to-know basis, Miss Minnie. Anyway, what about Pewey?"

I started to frame my question, but Rafe was still talking. "Wonder if Pewey's going to make it up to deer camp this year. He works nights for what's their names, that company making interior panels for cars. They got a big new contract and Lewey's been signed up for double shifts, afternoon and midnights for over a month now." Rafe squinted at a green wire. "Nuts, if you ask me, but he's trying to save money for a log cabin up near Newberry. Why do you want to know?"

So there was no way Rob Pew could have killed Carissa. And so much for that gut feeling of imminent danger that I'd had when he answered the door in such a surly fashion. All I'd been reacting to was the man's response to extreme sleep-deprivation, just as Abby had said. Still, I was glad I'd corroborated with a second knowledgeable source. "Does anyone call him Rob?"

Whistling, Rafe picked up his wire cutters and stripped off the end of a yellow-coated wire. "Not even his mother."

At noon the next day, I pushed back from my desk and looked at what I'd accomplished so far.

I'd moved Stephen's notes on employee handbook revisions from one side of my desk to the other. I'd tidied up the books sent to the library for donation purposes and for which thank-you letters should be sent. I'd scrawled out a short list of possible Thessie Replacements, made a few phone calls, and subsequently had to draw a line through each of the names.

So, how much had I accomplished that morning? Basically nothing. Clearly, what I needed was a hefty dose of caffeine.

My empty Association of Bookmobile and Outreach Services mug and I made our way to the break room, which was also empty. Odd, for noon, but I reminded myself that I wasn't there to socialize. No, indeedy, I was there for fluid replenishment and to stretch my legs.

Still, I took my time, sipping at my coffee until it was half-gone, then filling the mug again slowly. I watched the dark liquid stream down, watching its smooth texture, thinking about the long history of coffee, wondering how far these particular beans had traveled, guessing that they'd come much farther than I'd ever gone and—

"Hey."

My arm jerked, coffee spilled, and a small brown puddle spread itself across the counter. "Hey, Josh." I put the carafe back on the burner and yanked a paper towel out of the holder. "How was your weekend?"

I heard a male grunt followed by the whir of a dollar bill being sucked into the soda machine followed by the *thunk* of a can dropping out of the machine. I tossed the sodden paper towel into the garbage and got out a fresh one.

"That good, huh?" I asked Josh. "I thought it was the big second date with Megan. Weren't you going up to the Side Door?" The Side Door Saloon in Petoskey, with its multiple televisions, was a hot spot for the sports-minded. It had excellent food, too, but I wasn't sure Josh cared much about that.

Megan was a neighbor of Holly's, and ever since Megan had stopped by to talk to Holly about babysitting Holly's children, Josh was smitten. He'd been casting goo-goo eyes at her for months, and we'd all cheered when he finally found the gumption to ask her out.

Josh shoved the can of diet soda into an outside pocket of his baggy pants and whirred another dollar into the machine.

I finished cleaning the counter and turned to face Josh. "Are you okay?"

The second soda can dropped down. He picked it up, popped the seal, and slugged down half the contents. He wiped his mouth with the back of his hand. "We got talking about baseball."

Josh was a big football fan, but he was a *huge* baseball fan. Huge with a capital H, U, G, and E. He cared about things like spring training and openly pitied anyone who didn't understand the infield fly rule. He could recite baseball statistics from before he was born and was too much of a purist to consider putting together a baseball fantasy league.

"You know," I said, "it's okay if she doesn't like baseball. Some really smart, funny, and good-looking people don't know much about the sport." I tossed my hair back, but he wasn't catching on. "Maybe you could teach her. Maybe—"

"She likes baseball just fine." Josh upended the soda can, tapped its rim against his lower teeth, then tossed the empty can into the box of returnables.

"Well, that's good, isn't it?" I tried to imagine a scenario in which having a baseball-fan girlfriend would upset Josh. Remembered one of his rants and dredged up a comment. "She's not a fan of the designated hitter rule, is she?"

"She's a White Sox fan," he snapped.

I almost choked on the coffee I'd been swallowing. Josh was a true-blue die-hard Detroit Tigers fan. Listening to him talk about his team often brought to mind the reality that the term "fan" was short for "fanatic."

"Her parents are from Chicago." He shoved his hand into his pants pocket and extracted another dollar bill. "She said going to the old Comiskey Park is one of her earliest memories."

I watched him jab the dollar into the machine and made a mental note to call the vending guy for an early refill. "Well," I said lamely, "at least she's a baseball fan."

He pounded the machine's plastic button with his fist. "The White Sox," he muttered. "I can't believe it."

I couldn't believe he was so upset over what was essentially just a game, but I also knew better than to say so. Of course, I'd once broken up with a boyfriend after a heated debate about the usefulness of a public library system in the age of the Internet, but that was much different.

Since Josh was obviously determined to wallow in his bad mood, and I wasn't quite ready to go back to work, I wandered out of the break room with the intention of chatting with Donna, this morning's front desk clerk.

I was barely halfway there when Stephen barked out my name. "Minnie!"

Through a combination of sheer luck and exquisite hand-eye coordination that no one except me would ever appreciate, I did not spill the contents of my coffee mug. I pasted on a polite smile and turned to face my boss. "Good morning, Stephen. How's the report progressing?"

One of Stephen's pet projects was a multipage saga presented to the library board on a quarterly basis. He would have loved to present one at every monthly board meeting, but they'd kindly told him that his time was valuable and could be better spent directing the library, and that a quarterly report was fine. Annual might be even better.

"The report is exactly why I'm down here." Stephen adjusted his tie, today a knit version. "I've come to the section regarding any difficulties in the library and I need to know that you have the situation in hand."

I looked at the mug I was holding. No, that couldn't be what he was talking about. Or was it? Though he hadn't laid down a forbidding law, Stephen did frown on liquids anywhere except in the break room. The transportation of a spillable item from coffeepot to an individual office was tolerated, but only because no tragedy had yet occurred. If anyone, especially anyone whose name started with the letters Minnie, ever had an accidental spill on library-owned material, a new policy would be instituted at eighty words per minute and posted on walls everywhere. "Um . . ."

"Minnie," he said sharply. "Please tell me that you remember our conversation regarding a particular library patron."

"Of course I do." I just wasn't sure what to do about it. My thoughts must have leaked onto my face, because Stephen held up his index finger. "Two weeks, Minnie." The words came out almost as a growl. "I want to see progress within two weeks. If there is none, the library board will be apprised of the situation."

I watched him stride down the hallway, his pant legs swooshing lightly against each other. Only when he started up the stairs and left my field of vision did I let out the sigh that had been building inside me.

Bleah. Where on earth was I going to find the time to solve the Mitchell Koyne Conundrum? "Almost sounds like a Nancy Drew title," I murmured, which amused me immensely. All I needed was a roadster, a housekeeper, an attorney father, and a couple of good friends and I'd be all set.

What color was that roadster? I frowned, trying to remember. Blue? No, it was red. Or was it—

There was a thump on my shoulder. "Ah!" My shriek filled the echoing hallway and my backward leap flung coffee all over the tile floor.

"Good jump," Mitchell said, nodding approvingly. "Your vertical must have been six inches."

I made an ineffectual attempt to brush coffee drips off my jacket sleeve. "You could have said something instead of scaring me like that." How such a big man could have moved so silently was another mystery for Ms. Drew.

"I did," he said in a hurt voice. "Honest, I did, Minnie."

Which was undoubtedly the truth as he knew it, because Mitchell had a complete inability to see the world from anyone else's point of view. Of course, in many ways this made his life far simpler than mine, which didn't sound bad right now. "Sorry," I said. "What can I do for you, Mitchell?"

He twisted around to look over one of his shoulders, then the other. "I heard what your boss said. You got two weeks to fix something or he's going to fire you."

Only the library board could terminate me, but Stephen could definitely make my life uncomfortable. And if he truly wanted me gone, he could turn the situation into a case of insubordination, tell the board I was impossible to work with, and convince them to give me the boot.

The muscles at the back of my neck tightened into taut cords. No matter how much I disagreed with Stephen's point of view regarding Mitchell, Stephen wanted it dealt with and I was his assistant. I should be doing what he asked me to do. Only . . . how?

Mitchell shuffled close enough that I could see how badly his beard needed trimming. "I can help," he whispered loudly enough for anyone within fifty feet to hear.

"You can?"

"Sure," he said. "I know Stephen can be a pain to work with. Just tell me what the problem is and I'll be glad to help. What are friends for, right? And hey, I'm pretty good at figuring things out. Like that Carissa Radle? I'm real sure she was killed by her boss. You ever met him? Anyway, he's a real jerk and it's got to be him. I've told the sheriff's office, so I'm sure an arrest is coming soon."

Though it was almost out-loud laughable that Mitchell was volunteering to help me get rid of Mitchell, I was touched that he wanted to help me. However, the last thing I wanted was Mitchell's help for almost anything. "Um . . . ," I said.

"Hey, sports fans," Josh said, walking up to us. He

turned his head and gave me a wink. "Well, not you, Minnie. I'm talking to Mitchell here."

"What's up?" Mitchell asked. "Did you see the game last night?"

Two Tigers fans and me standing in a group. There was no way I was going to get in a word edgewise. I started to slip away, but Josh winked at me again.

"Great game," he said. "But I wanted to tell you about this really great Web site. They have tickets to minor league ball games for next to nothing. If you can get a little bit of cash together, you could spend the rest of the summer driving around the country, going from ballpark to ballpark. Sounds pretty cool, don't you think?"

Mitchell rubbed his chin. "Sounds okay. But it might be good to have someone to share the driving, you know? What are you doing the rest of the summer?"

Josh's mouth flopped open, but nothing came out.

I walked away, quietly snorting with laughter.

After work, I walked to the marina office to pay Chris Ballou my monthly slip rental. Typical for this time of day, Chris was comfortably seated. "Just leave your check on the counter," he said. The other three men in the office, Skeeter and Rafe and Greg Plassey, looked just as comfortable and just as unwilling to move.

I looked at Rafe. "Aren't you supposed to be doing that last work on my boat?"

"The day's young," he said lazily, tipping back in an ancient director's chair, wood and canvas creaking underneath him. "Say, how you coming along with the next draft of the after-school reading program?"

"I'd be coming along a lot faster if I knew my boat was going to get fixed before school started."

"And that, gentlemen," Skeeter said, "is why any permanent relationship between a woman and a man is doomed."

The four men clinked their beer cans. I rolled my eyes.

"So, what's the story with your doctor boyfriend?" Chris asked.

"Yeah," Skeeter said. "Hardly ever see him around. You sure you two are dating?"

"Now, boys." Rafe smirked up a smile. "I saw him just the other day. Course, he didn't stay long, and come to think of it, he left in kind of a hurry."

While that hadn't been Rafe's fault, I didn't see any harm in saying so. "It was you he was trying to get away from," I said.

The other three hooted and tinked beer cans. The tightness that had snaked up my back when they mentioned the Tuckerlessness of my life eased a little. It was our schedules that was the problem: both of us working some evenings and some weekends and the twain was hardly ever meeting. Except for the day after tomorrow. We had plans and they were etched in stone this time.

And these men weren't trying to hurt my feelings; they were just being guys, and in spite of their extreme guyness, I liked them very much.

"Speaking of not around," I asked Greg, "where's your friend Brett? I thought he was a part of this motley crew."

"Downstate," Greg said.

"Sucker." Chris grinned. "What could be better than this?"

I squinted at him. "You could be outside in the fresh

air and sunshine instead of sitting in this dingy, poorly lit office that hasn't been cleaned properly in decades."

"Hey, now," Rafe said. "I saw Chris here wiping down the countertop just last month."

Skeeter smirked. "Only because he spilled his coffee all over it."

"Chris drinks coffee?" I asked. "When does he do that?"

"After the Fourth of July," Chris said, wincing. "Man, I'm getting too old to stay up all night."

I left the Four Stooges to their stories of all-night parties and headed to my houseboat for a quick dinner of nacho chips and cheese. With salsa, which would count as a vegetable with anyone except my mother.

While I ate, I pondered the looming cloud on the horizon that was Thessie's upcoming college trip. All the people I'd already called had pleaded houseguests or other commitments and I had no idea what I was going to do.

After dishes and a see-you-later hug for Eddie, I set out to visit Cade at Lakeview to let the volunteer problem bounce around in my head. There were a couple of people interested in taking over from Thessie once school started, but in summer it was difficult to get people to donate their time.

I yearned for the day that Stephen was going to recognize how much the bookmobile was doing for the library. Outreach, image, and presence were all improving in an anecdotal evidence sort of way, and circulation was up compared to this time last year.

"October board meeting," I said out loud as I walked into Cade's room.

"Why wait?" he asked. "Do it in September."

"But you don't want to rush things, either," Barb said. "Maybe November would be better."

I looked from one McCade to the other and laughed. There was no possible way they could have known what I'd been mumbling about, yet they'd joined into my narrative without a pause. "Can't do September," I said, "because I won't have time to get the August circulation numbers into report form before the meeting. And by November everyone is concentrating on the holidays."

"Sounds as if you have whatever it is well in hand."

"Don't I wish." I sat down. "But my most immediate problem is that I'm losing my bookmobile volunteer for a week and the library board insists on having two on board."

Sadly, it had to be two humans. There had been one time that I'd danced closely with prevarication and led Stephen to believe that there were two people on board when it had actually been just Eddie and me, but I didn't want to push my luck.

"Does this volunteer actually drive the bookmobile?" Barb asked.

I grinned. Thessie kept trying to convince me that letting her drive made sense—"for backup, just in case you break both feet, or something"—but it wasn't going to happen. "Library policy is employees only," I said, "and any driver has to take a commercial driver's license class." Truck-driving school would have been better, but it was a long and expensive course. "The bookmobile volunteer checks materials in and out, helps patrons find books. Normal library stuff, only it's on a bookmobile."

Barb grabbed her purse and excused herself.

"Hey, watch this." Cade lifted his weak arm, made a fist, then released it. "Not bad, eh?"

I clapped loudly. "That's fantastic! You'll be painting again in no time."

He started to make another fist, but this one fell apart halfway through. "Time being a relative term," he said, but there was humor at the back of his voice. "So, tell me." He glanced up at the open door. "Have you made any progress with . . . with . . ."

"With you-know-what?" I supplied.

His face, still uneven from the stroke, twisted into a smile. "Exactly."

"Sort of," I said.

"As I recall," Cade said, "our deal was that you ask a few questions of a few people. You're sticking to that agreement, yes?"

I filled him in on what I'd found out so far, ending with the fact that Hugo Edel had mentioned Carissa hanging out on Trock's set. He did some nodding and some frowning, then said, "Trock Farrand. I've met the man. A little flighty, I'd say. Be careful, Minnie. Someone killed Carissa, and I don't want anything happening to you."

"Careful as I'd be in a crystal shop."

"One more thing," Cade said. "Please don't say anything about your efforts to Barb."

I blinked. And here I'd thought they shared everything. "If that's what you want, sure. But why?"

"For her own peace of mind. Please. The police have been silent for days and if she hears you're looking into this, she'll be worried and get upset all over again and I don't want that for her."

I swallowed. True love. That's what these two had. I couldn't speak, so I gave a weak nod instead.

It must not have been very convincing, because Cade leaned forward. "I'm sure you think it's silly, but—"

"That man thinks everything is silly," Barb said as she breezed in. "Don't take it personally, Minnie. The only thing he's ever taken seriously in his life is his painting, and I'm not always sure about that."

She smiled at her husband fondly. "Now, what was it you two were arguing about?"

"Whether or not 'de rigueur' is a real *D* word," I said. "What do you think?"

She considered the question, then made her pronouncement. "Doubtful."

"Darn," I said, sighing dramatically, and left them to their evening.

Chapter 12

Two things accompanied me to bed that night, a brand-spanking-new copy of Bernard Cornwell's latest historical novel and an Eddie. Both were heavy, but both gave me comfort, and after a relaxing hour of reading about the early days of England, I turned off the light and slept the night through.

The next morning, I was halfway through my pre-work preparations when I realized I wasn't scheduled to work that day. And since I was the one who made up the schedule, there was no excuse for my early rising.

"Here I am," I said. "All dressed up and almost ready to go. Now what?"

I asked the question of Eddie, who had squeezed himself onto the houseboat's small dashboard. Since I docked the boat nose-out, the dash not only allowed a view of Janay Lake and the passing boats, but also showcased seagulls, mourning doves, swallows, the occasional evening bat, and every so often a bald eagle.

He hunched down and made a cackling noise at the feathered creatures that were wheeling about.

"You do realize those birds are on the other side of the

window, don't you?" I spooned up the last bite of cereal. The bottom of the bowl held a cat-sized pool of milk. "Ready, Eddie?"

The second he heard the light *thump* of the bowl hitting the floor, Eddie leapt down and trotted over for his morning treat.

I listened to the noise of his laps. "You know, my mother always said to eat with my mouth closed." Eddie ignored me. When he finished with the milk, he sat down and began cleaning his back leg, which had mysteriously gotten dirty when he was drinking.

That wasn't something I had much interest in watching, so I started sliding out of the booth.

My movement startled Eddie. He jumped, squirreled sideways, and fell over, all four legs scrambling for purchase on the smooth flooring. After an eternity of effort, he managed to right himself. One long jump later, he was back on the dashboard, staring at the birds as if nothing had happened.

But one thing had. Eddie's bumbling antics had given me an idea for the day's activities.

A little bit of Internet searching and one phone call later, I tracked down the location of the day's filming of *Trock's Troubles*, the cooking show that had made Trock Farrand a national celebrity.

Or at least a national celebrity in certain circles. For someone like me, who wasn't overly interested in food except as fuel, the man's name had scarcely been heard except from my aunt and my down-to-earth best friend who started talking in giggles when asked if there was any chance her restaurant was ever going to be featured on the show.

However, since said best friend was also the person who had confirmed that Farrand's show was being taped at his house today, I forgave her future giggles and even made an internal vow not to make fun of her for turning into a bedazzled thirteen-year-old at the mention of the man's name. After all, if I ever met Nancy Pearl, the famous librarian, I might get a little giggly, too.

I parked my car on the side of the road and walked up Farrand's driveway. At this point, however, it looked more like a parking lot than anything else. Vans, SUVs, pickup trucks, and even a few sedans crowded the asphalt from garage door to right-of-way.

People milled about, some looking bored, some looking worried, some looking tense. But since none of them were paying any attention to me, I waltzed on past as if I belonged, nodding vaguely to everyone I passed.

"Morning," I said calmly, and every one of them nodded back. Though I'd thought there'd be some sort of security in place, I didn't see even a single guard keeping an eagle eye out.

It seemed weird, because *Trock's Troubles* was a long-running television show and they were bound to get gawkers who could make a nuisance of themselves. But what did I know about taping a television show? I didn't even know for sure if they called it taping or filming, and I certainly didn't know who got to eat the food that was made during the show. Kristen said I was a Philistine to even think about something like that, but I thought it required careful consideration.

"Oh, man," a male voice at my right shoulder muttered. "Not again. I can't freaking believe it."

I glanced at the guy. A few years older than me, with sharply defined arm muscles and white-blond hair, he was shaking his head and tucking a cell phone into his pocket. "What's the matter?" I asked.

He looked at me. "You must be new," he said, smiling in a sour way that still managed to be friendly. "Our friend Trock has a habit of changing the meal plan just as we're starting to shoot. Throws everything off schedule something fierce. Trock says that's part of the show's charm, but I say he's nuts." He stared in the direction of the most activity. "The troubles that get on the air aren't half of the troubles we have to suffer."

I smiled and stuck out my hand. "Minnie Hamilton." Whoever this guy was, and in spite of his harsh-sounding words, it was clear that he had a deep respect for Trock Farrand.

"Scruffy Gronkowski."

I eyed the sharp crease in his khaki pants and the perfectly rolled collar of his polo shirt and raised my eyebrows.

He laughed. "Nickname from when I was a kid. It's better than the name on my birth certificate, so what do I care? And since I'm the producer on this wretched show, I should probably know what you're doing here."

So there was security. It just came in a different form than expected. "I was hoping to talk to Mr. Farrand. I'm a friend of Kristen Jurek's. She owns a local restaurant, the Three Seasons—it's on your short list for being featured on the show—and I was hoping to put in a good word for her. I'm sure you hear this all the time, but her restaurant is something special. The only thing is, she thinks the Three Seasons is good enough to speak for itself. She's too proud to come out there and promote herself."

"And you're not?" Scruffy asked, raising his own eyebrows.

"Not when it comes to asking for help for my friends," I said seriously. "And it's an outstanding restaurant—it really is."

Scruffy picked a piece of invisible lint off his shirt. "Outstanding restaurants are a dime a dozen."

"Sure, but how many of them are only open three seasons a year so they can offer only fresh and local ingredients?"

"That cuts it down quite a bit." He squinted down at me. "You got anything else?"

"She grew up in Chilson, went away to multiple colleges, got a Ph.D. in biochemistry, hated every second she worked for a large pharmaceutical company, and came back home to open a restaurant."

A slow grin spread across his face. "Now, that's a good story."

I beamed at him. "Isn't it? But she doesn't like talking about it. She's annoyed that she wasted all that time and money."

"Education is never wasted," he said. "After all, you never know when you'll need to know Avogadro's number."

"Six-point-zero-two-two times ten to the twenty-third, the number of atoms in a mole, but I have no idea why anyone would need to know that, or even what it means, exactly."

He laughed. "If you want to talk to Trock a minute, he's over there." Scruffy nodded at a large, very round man who was mopping his forehead with a towel.

"And you'll have my undying gratitude if you can point him back to grilling pork tenderloin. Tell him we can do the whitefish some other episode. Just not today."

I squared my shoulders and saluted. "Yes, sir. I'll do my best, sir."

He gave me a sharp return salute. "Good luck to you."

Smiling, I made my way through the snaky maze of cables and wires, staying behind cameras and trying very hard to stay out of everyone's way. At long last I reached the table where Trock Farrand had seated himself. He'd crossed his oversized arms and slid down in his chair far enough that a strong breeze would have pushed him onto the bricked floor of the massive patio.

"Mr. Farrand?" I asked. "Scruffy sent me over here. He—"

"Whitefish," he growled. "I will not listen to another lackey sent by Sir Scruffy. I suppose you have yet another point to make in favor of the porcine product?"

"Nope," I said. "But that's not what I wanted to talk about."

"Eh?" He lifted his head. "You don't have an opinion on pork tenderloin versus whitefish?"

"Not really, sir."

He sat up and lost his sulky expression. "Ye gods, a woman of pluck, discernment, and wisdom. Give me your hand, young lady. I would press your flesh but lightly."

I blinked and held out my hand for shaking purposes.

"Milady." He took my hand gently in his and kissed the back of it. "I am your devoted servant, yet I don't even know your name. Sit, please."

Suddenly I understood the attraction to his show. It wasn't the food; it was him. Sitting and laughing, I said, "Minnie Hamilton. I'm a librarian. I drive the bookmobile and—"

"Ah, a bookmobile!" His pudgy face lit up. "What a glorious conveyance. I have seen your bookmobile whilst out and about, and now I've met its beautiful young driver. What luck!"

"I'm glad you think so, sir."

"Trock," he said, patting my hand. "No sirs on this set. Makes me feel as if I'm about to get paddled by my sixth-grade teacher. Now tell me why the bookmobile librarian is on my set."

I told him about the Three Seasons and about Kristen and about how good she'd look on his show.

"Attractive, is she?" He smoothed his eyebrows.

"If you think a slender, blond, and almost six-foot-tall woman could be attractive, then yes."

"Hmm." He kept smoothing his eyebrows. "I will send young Scruffy to investigate. Meanwhile, since you are not making any movements regarding leaving, methinks you have more to say."

Bumbling he might be, but Trock Farrand was also perceptive. I used the looking-for-bookmobile-donations spiel again and got about as far as I had with Hugo Edel. And that was my link to divert the conversation.

"I asked Hugo Edel for a donation," I said, sighing, "and got about the same level of excitement."

Trock smiled. "Dear Minnie, you need to find an

emotional connection. Intellectual appeals are all well and good, but you need to tug on the heartstrings."

An excellent tip. "I think Mr. Edel's heartstrings were a little damaged," I said, mostly, but not completely, lying. "He knew that woman who was killed a couple of weeks ago."

"Carissa," Trock said, and the name came out almost as a curse. "I wish I knew nothing of her. She was nothing but a pain in the behind. It's situations like hers that might drive me to have a closed set." His voice grew loud. "This show has enough troubles with timing and schedules and I'm the one who has to—" He stopped. Breathed in and out. Sighed. "But I'm sorry she's dead, of course I am. Especially since she seemed to have found a new love interest. A new man who, I hoped, would make her very happy indeed."

I'd been sitting up fairly straight, but my spine suddenly went even straighter. "Do you know his name?"

"Dear heart." Trock gave me a pitying smile. "I barely remember my own."

"Trock!" A wild-haired woman in shorts, canvas sneakers, and a tie-dyed shirt appeared in front of us. "We need a decision and we need it now."

He sighed heavily and turned to me. "Which do you think, Lady Minnie? The exquisite whitefish creation I so long to bring to platter, or the staid pork tenderloin that will do nothing for the history of culinary arts."

Out of Trock's view, the woman clasped her hands and got down on her knees, mouthing a single word over and over: *Pork!*

I gave her a tiny nod. "What do you think about doing your whitefish some other day?" I asked Trock.

"With a little time to plan, you could make a show around it, maybe go out on the boat and help catch the fish."

Trock's eyes opened wide. "Minnie, that's an outstanding idea, simply outstanding."

I wasn't sure it was a good idea at all, but maybe I was wrong.

"But . . ." He hesitated. "The pork. So bland. So basic. So blasé."

"Not after you get done with it, I'm sure."

His sudden smile was wide and deep and he looked sincere as Santa Claus three days before Christmas. The man had charm out the wazoo. Maybe I'd ask Kristen to record some of his shows. It was possible I'd even learn something about cooking.

On my way out, Scruffy pulled me aside. "I heard you talking to Trock," he said. "That Carissa? She was a big fan. We all liked her."

I eyed him. Was he trying to establish that no one from the TV show had anything to do with the murder? "Okay," I said, "but Trock seemed to have some issues with her."

Scruffy shrugged. "Trock has issues with everyone. And that new guy she was seeing?" He glanced away as Trock started shouting orders to fetch the pork. "Hallelujah," he muttered. "Anyway, I don't know his name, either, but I know he used to play some sport. A professional sport."

"Football?" I asked as casually as I could. "Basketball? Baseball? Hockey? Tennis?"

But he was shaking his head. "No idea. I'm not into that kind of thing. Sorry."

*   *   *

Eddie and I had a late lunch out in the sunshine of the houseboat's front deck. Or rather, I ate a nice lunch of grilled cheese and a salad while Eddie batted around the three cat treats I gave him.

"You know," I said, "those are to eat, not to play with."

Since Eddie was intent on his new game, the rules of which seemed to change at any given moment, he ignored me completely.

"So, you know what I've done today?" I asked him. "I talked to Trock Farrand. And you know what I found out? That Carissa was seeing a professional athlete."

Eddie licked at one of the treats, got it wet with cat spit, rolled it around a little to spread the spit around, walked away from it with the obvious intention of never returning, then came straight over and whacked my shin with the top of his head.

"Yeah, I know," I said. "It's probably Greg, isn't it?" Maybe not, but probably. There were other sports guys around; I'd heard of a few retired NFL players who had places nearby, and a number of hockey players, but given Greg's reaction when I'd talked about Carissa, he definitely had some connection to her.

The knowledge was depressing. Though I barely knew Greg, I liked the guy. Thinking that he was hiding something made me feel icky inside.

"And if that's not a medical term," I told Eddie, "it should be."

He jumped up next to me on the chaise longue and rubbed the side of his face against my arm.

"Of course," I said, pulling him onto my lap, "there are variations of ick. Take the way you just rubbed Eddie spit on me. That's also icky. I mean, you don't catch me doing that to you."

He bumped his head against my leg, which almost always meant *Pay attention to me. Now!*

I started to pet the thick black-and-white fur. Full, purring rumbles began half a second later. "Greg lied," I said quietly. "But I don't think he's the only one."

Eddie's mouth opened in a silent *Mrr.*

"I agree. I think Hugo Edel and Trock lied, too." Or at least hadn't told me everything. Now all I had to do was figure out why.

Saturday morning was unseasonably cool and threatened rain. I pulled on long pants and a fleece pullover and drove up to the library to back the bookmobile out of the garage. It was odd not to have Eddie with me, but the morning's schedule wasn't a suitable one for a cat.

Though it wasn't anywhere near as big as the famous art fairs in Charlevoix or Petoskey, the Chilson version was enjoying a steady growth that boded well for the local arts world. I'd talked the director into believing that having the bookmobile parked at the fair would be an asset and hoped that it would be true.

From eight until eleven, I opened the bookmobile to one and all, answering questions, checking out books, and even giving out a few new library cards. Though the morning was chilly, I was warmed by the many smiles, especially the smile that walked up the steps at eleven sharp.

Tucker looked around. "So this is the bookmobile. Nice. It's a lot like one of those bloodmobiles they have downstate."

I nodded. "The company that fabricated this also

does medical vehicles." I gave Tucker the tour, then said, "All I have to do is drive it back to the garage at the end of the day."

"Sounds good," he said. "Lunch first or fair first?"

We discussed the question as we descended the steps, kept discussing it as we browsed through a dozen booths of varying displays of art, and only ended the discussion when we walked up to a trailer selling corn dogs. We kept discussing if that was enough food for lunch until we found a booth offering hamburgers. The dessert discussion ended at the booth selling elephant ears. Tummies contentedly full, we wandered through the booths, admiring most of the work and being puzzled by some, but enjoying the crowd and each other's company.

And the crowd was large—poor boating weather often made for well-attended summer events. I saw half the regular library patrons and my marina neighbors. I also saw Hugo and Annelise Edel, Greg Plassey and his friend Brett, and though I didn't see him I could have sworn I heard Trock Farrand's voice.

Tucker and I had walked through about half the booths when one particular display caught my eye.

"Hello." A woman sitting on a tall stool smiled at me. "How are you?"

"Excellent," I said. "How about you? Busy?"

"The little ones are selling." She waved at the show-cases. One case was full of Petoskey stones cut into the shapes of bears, turtles, and wolverines. Another case contained Petoskey stones formed into drawer pulls, switch plates, clocks, and doorknobs. Yet another case was full of raw stones. "You're familiar with them?" she asked.

I nodded, knowing that the stones were fossilized coral. I also knew it was great fun to find them on the lakeshore. I'd picked up a couple myself. "How expensive are the big ones?" I nodded at the softball-sized behemoths.

When she named the price, my eyes bugged out. She laughed. "Petoskeys that large are hard to find. You typically don't find them any bigger than small paperweight size."

Tucker admired the shined-up surface. "I didn't know you were interested in Petoskey stones, Minnie."

I gave the price tag one last disbelieving glance, then edged out of the booth. "I'm not, not really. It's just . . ."

Tucker put his hand in mine as we walked. "It's just what?"

Could there be anything nicer than walking hand in hand with your boyfriend? I sighed happily. "Well," I said, "it's just that a Petoskey stone was what killed that woman a while back. Remember when that happened?" Tucker nodded and I went on. "The police think that a friend of mine killed her. But there's no way he did it, none at all."

Tucker didn't say anything for a moment. "How long have you known this guy?" he finally asked.

I glanced up at him. "Long enough to know that he's not a killer." My voice had a little edge to it. "You don't have to know someone very long to know that."

He stopped, and since my hand was still in his, I stopped, too. The park was full of people, but they walked around us like the water in a stream breaking around a rock. "Minnie," he said, "I know you're a smart person, but I also know you like to think the best of people. If the police think your friend killed someone, have you considered the possibility that they may be right?"

"No," I said shortly. The afternoon was taking a sudden turn for the worse.

Tucker sighed and shook his head. "Minnie—"

"Hey, Kleinow, you slumming it today?" A tall, broad man was walking toward us.

Tucker squeezed my hand, then let go. "Minnie, this is Dr. Miller Alvord. He's an orthopedic surgeon. Miller, this is my friend Minnie."

Friend? Not girlfriend? My stomach clenched and I was pretty sure it wasn't because of the corn dogs.

"Charmed, I'm sure." Miller gave my hand a perfunctory shake and turned his attention to Tucker. "Say, I've been wanting to talk to you. What do you think about helping me convince the higher-ups to buy a new X-ray machine?"

I stood first on one foot, then the other, waiting for Tucker to finish his conversation. When they segued smoothly into a discussion of treatments for dislocated hips, I told Tucker I was heading back to the bookmobile.

"What's that?" He looked over at me with a distracted look. "Right. Okay. See you later."

My thoughts were black as I wandered through the fair. If he wasn't calling me his girlfriend, what was I doing calling him my boyfriend? And if he wasn't my boyfriend, why did I already know his birthday, birthplace, and shoe size?

I was so mired in my own miserable thoughts that I was halfway up the bookmobile steps when I realized that I hadn't unlocked the door.

The bookmobile had been unlocked. Unlocked and unattended for hours.

I pounded up the rest of the steps, freaking out a little, scared that there'd been vandalism or theft or . . .

Or nothing. I looked around and saw absolutely nothing out of the ordinary. Books, magazines, and CDs all tidy. Computers in place. All was well.

Except for me. I sat down hard into the driver's seat and tried not to think dreary thoughts. I sighed. What I wanted was Eddie and the comfort of his purrs. Maybe even some of his cat hair.

I looked down and picked an Eddie hair off my sleeve and sat there, just holding it.

The art fair was over, the bookmobile was tucked away, and with the heavy cloud cover, darkness was coming on fast. I typically loved this time of night, just before it got truly dark, when the lights in people's houses were glowing cozily through their windows and children were being called inside by moms and dads. Evening walks were my second-favorite kind, right after early morning walks, but that which I usually found calm and soothing was lost to me tonight, thanks to the things whirring around in my brain.

I was wandering along, my hands in my pockets, thinking about Carissa and my aunt's boarders and how Tucker had ditched me to have dinner with Miller and one of the hospital's biggest benefactors. I was thinking hard and not completely present in the world when a movement caught my attention.

A man was walking out of the shadows and into the light from the downtown streetlights that were shaped like old gas lamps. A man, shortish and rounded on his belly side but with a straight back, a man shaped like the letter *D*. Detective Devereaux.

Now what should I do? The detective and his partner and I were being mutually agreeable to each other
at this point, but if Detective Devereaux and I started
talking, he was bound to know something was up. He
was a detective, after all. They were trained to sense
these kinds of things, and I wasn't ready to share what
I knew about Hugo or Trock or Greg without proof. A
feeling of ickiness probably wouldn't count for much
to them.

Besides, I didn't want the detective to tell me to stay
out of police business, and what they didn't know
couldn't hurt me.

I slid sideways into the dark cast by the bank building, then eased even deeper into the darkness by edg-
ing toward the narrow walkway that led to a rear
parking lot. Silently, holding my breath, I moved behind a tall container plant and waited until Devereaux
walked past.

When he was gone, I waited. Waited a little longer.
Then, just after I started to feel like an idiot for hiding
behind a plant for no good reason, I slipped out of the
alley and walked away.

Chapter 13

After dinner at a local sandwich shop, I wandered on home, trying hard not to think about Tucker. It was a pleasant walk punctuated by short stops to chat with numerous library patrons from the cane-carrying Mr. Goodwin to the cookie-baking Reva Shomin to the thriller-reading Jim Kittle.

"Must be the cool weather," I told Eddie, tossing my backpack onto the dining table's bench, sliding in next to it, and putting my feet up on the opposite bench. "It's fooling people into thinking that it's after Labor Day and the summer people are gone."

Eddie was again on the houseboat's small dashboard. In spite of the precariousness of his perch, it was now his favorite place for seagull spying.

At this particular moment, however, the only wildlife Eddie could possibly see was himself, since it was dark outside.

"I can't believe you're paying more attention to your reflection than to me." I slid into a comfortable slouch. "Why is it people have cats, anyway? I feed you, water you, clean up your messes, wear your hair everywhere I go, and what do I get out of it?"

Eddie turned to look at me. Blinked, as if my appearance were a sudden surprise. Then he oozed off the dashboard, hit the floor, sauntered over to me, jumped up on my lap, and immediately started purring.

"Okay." I patted his head. "You win. Purrs trump all that other stuff, hands down." I gently picked up one of his front legs and we exchanged a paw-to-palm high five.

He purred a little louder.

There couldn't be many cats who would let you handle them like that. Eddie didn't care, however. I could stuff one of his back paws into his ear and he wouldn't twitch.

I was starting to do just that when my cell phone came to life with a plain old electronic beeping noise, which meant it was a number to which I hadn't assigned a ring tone. I dug through my backpack and turned it on. "Hello?"

"Minnie, Barb McCade here, and I have the answer to all your problems."

"You've discovered a way to keep all of Eddie's hairs attached to him? Outstanding."

"Let me rephrase that. I have the answer to one particular problem."

"Better than nothing. What do you have?"

"My mother has decided she's coming north to spend the rest of the summer with us. Mom has more energy than I know what to do with, so I always have a project for her. She is practically giddy with excitement over the possibility of riding along with you on the bookmobile."

Though I'd never asked, I assumed Barb was in her early fifties, making her mother seventy, at the absolute minimum, and probably older. "Well," I said slowly, "that's a wonderful offer . . ."

"Then we're settled." Barb's voice held a tone that indicated a dusting off of hands after a job well done. "I'll have Mom drop by the library to get an orientation. Would eleven work?"

I gave up. If Barb's mother was completely unsuitable, I'd leave her behind at the library and abscond with one of the clerks. As plans go, I'd had worse.

"Of course," I said to Eddie as I thumbed off the phone, "maybe there's a good reason Barb is so eager to get rid of her mother." Frightening images of harridans and shrews pinged into my brain.

Eddie tipped his head up and around so that he was looking at me almost upside down.

"Mrr," he said.

The next morning I got up bright and early. That is, if eight thirty on a Sunday morning can be considered early, which I did, in spite of the admonitions of my mother all through my youth. It was a known fact that you weren't a slug on a Sunday morning until the hour hit the double-digit range.

"Comparatively," I told Eddie, "half past eight is practically dawn."

The Eddie-sized lump that was under the comforter didn't say anything. I leaned close to make sure he was still breathing, then slid out. The poor boy needed his sleep, after all. Yesterday he'd barely had eighteen hours.

I was halfway through a bowl of cereal when my cell

rang the *Scrubs* theme song. Tucker. I would have asked Eddie if I should answer it, but I was in the kitchen and he was still on the bed. I would have flipped a coin, but I didn't have one handy.

I wasn't sure I wanted to talk to him, but if he was going to break up with me, I might as well get it over with now. That way I could metaphorically dissect him that night with Kristen.

"Hey," I said into the phone.

"Hey yourself," he said. "First off, I want to apologize for yesterday. I was being an inconsiderate jerk and I'm sorry. I shouldn't have ignored you like that when Miller and I were talking and I shouldn't have left you to have dinner with him and that donor."

Relief sang through my bones, but I pushed it down. I wanted answers. "If you know you shouldn't have, then why did you?"

I heard him swallow. "Because I'm stupid."

Don't laugh, I told myself. *Don't laugh.* "Probably," I said. "But I'd like a little more detail."

His sigh gusted into the phone. "Because I'm still new at the hospital. I've worked so hard for so long to get this kind of job and I'm worried that if I don't think 'hospital' twenty-four-seven that I won't be taken seriously." He stopped. "Minnie, are you still there? What are you doing?"

Smiling, actually. "I had no idea that men had self-esteem issues."

"Of course we do," he said. "We just don't talk about them. I'm breaking the Man Code by even hinting that I wasn't born with a massive ego."

This time I did laugh.

*   *   *

"So you forgave him?" Kristen asked.

We were sitting in her office, spooning up crème brûlée. "When he brought over that big bunch of flowers, it wasn't that hard."

"Carnations? Daisies?"

I shook my head. "Roses."

She whistled. "Not bad. This guy might be a keeper."

"Still too early to tell," I said. "Say, have I ever told you how good your desserts are?"

"Only every time you eat one."

"Come on, I tell you more often than that." I debated telling her about what Scruffy and Trock had said about stopping by the Three Seasons, but decided not to. No point in getting her all excited over something a TV person said. Maybe it was unfair of me to assume they were unreliable, but professions get stereotyped for a reason.

"So, what have you learned about Carissa?" she asked. Only after she swore on a stack of *Bon Appétit* magazines to keep her lips zipped had I told her about Cade's short stay at the county jail and my later vow to help him stay out of jail.

Cade had said I could tell her, that anyone I trusted was guarantee enough for him, but the magazine thing was a requirement for me. Plus, it was fun listening to her make the vow.

"Not enough." I told her everything I'd learned. Unfortunately it didn't take long.

"All you have is guesses," she said. "What you need is some proof."

I looked at her.

"Yeah, yeah." She grinned. "Like, duh, right?" She spooned up the last of her custard. "How's it going with trying to kick Mitchell out of the library?"

I toyed with the sprig of mint that had formerly garnished my dessert. "About as well as you'd expect. Stephen's really out to get me fired this time."

She leaned back in her chair. "You know, did I ever tell you about the time I had to kick a state senator out of here?"

"You did not."

"Did, too. Ask Harvey."

"That's not proof. Your sous-chef is so infatuated with you that he'd say anything you wanted."

She waved off that particular truth. "I must have told you about the time a softball team came in to celebrate some championship game. All women old enough to be my mother."

Now, that story she had told me, and every time she told it I was sure my curly hair was going to go straight. I settled back, smiling. "Make sure you tell the dancing-on-the-tables part. That's my favorite."

We spent the rest of the evening sharing stories and laughing. It didn't get me any closer to a solution to any of my problems, but I did go to sleep with a smile on my face.

The next morning, I woke up refreshed and perky. Eddie, not so much. The cool weather was still in full force and he seemed much more inclined to nap on the bed than get up and watch me eat a bowl of cereal.

"I'll let you lick the bottom of the bowl," I said.

He opened one eye briefly, then shut it again.

"You do realize that tomorrow you're going to have to be out of bed at this time if you're coming on the bookmobile."

He started purring. I wasn't sure if that meant *Of*

course I'll be ready to go at this time tomorrow or *That's twenty-four hours away; why are you bothering me with it now?*

I kissed the top of his furry head and left him to sleep the day away.

Monday mornings at the library could be one of two things, frantically busy or quietly slow, and you never knew which one it was going to be until it started happening.

This particular Monday started out quiet, but half an hour after I unlocked the front door, e-mails started piling up, the phones started ringing, and people started pouring inside. It was All Hands on Deck time, to the extent that Stephen descended from his second-floor office to help out.

I was taking a stint at the reference desk, so when I saw Donna talking to a trim, gray-haired woman and point her in my direction, I readied myself for a reference question.

The older woman strode over to the desk and held out her hand. "Good morning, Minnie." Her smile was wide and calm. "I'm Ivy Bly."

"Hi, Ivy," I said pleasantly. "What can I do for you?"

There was a short beat of silence, and then she said, "My daughter wound me up and pointed me in your direction, so here I am."

"And I hope I can answer whatever question you have." I smiled. "Animal, vegetable, or mineral?"

A tiny line appeared in the middle of her forehead. Not quite a frown, but not nearly the smile of a moment ago. "Didn't Barb tell you I'd be here this morning?"

Light dawned in a great blinding flash. I blinked from its intensity. "You're Barb McCade's mother?" This woman didn't look anywhere near old enough to be the mother of someone in her fifties. Maybe she was a stepmother. Sure, that was it.

She laughed. "Had Barb when I was twenty-five. Give you a piece of advice, Minnie. Slop on that sunscreen and stay active."

I looked her up and down, admiration plain on my face. "I'll take that into serious consideration."

"The best day of my life was when I turned seventy," she said. "Around here, they practically give you ski passes for free at that age. Do you ski?"

"A little."

"Keep it up. Do squats every day," she recommended. "Even if you don't have time to do anything else, everybody can find a minute to do twenty squats."

And this was the woman I'd been afraid would be too frail to help out on the bookmobile. Then again, there were other things to consider. "How are you with computers?" All the books got checked out and in through a laptop. If Ivy wasn't computer-savvy, we had a problem.

"Spent the last twenty years of my career teaching computer programming to inattentive college students," she said. "As long as you don't want me to work in Java, I'm okay."

I was pretty sure she wasn't talking about coffee, so I moved on to the next question. "Do you get along with kids?"

"Love 'em."

I looked left and right, then leaned forward. "How about cats?" I whispered.

"Have three of my own," she whispered back. "They love it at Barb and Cade's place."

Which settled the deal. I told her to meet me by the bookmobile garage early the next morning and advised her to pack a lunch. She nodded, sketched a wave, and headed off to whatever her next appointed task might be.

I watched her go, thinking that I suddenly had a new role model for what to be like in retirement.

My thoughts were interrupted by the sight of Stephen standing in front of the desk, his hands on his hips.

"I would like a progress report regarding The Situation," he said.

Meaning Mitchell. But since I'd made no progress, there wasn't much of a report to give him. I hesitated, then asked, "In a case like this, what would you do?"

"I," Stephen said in a voice loud enough for everyone to hear, "would give the problem to the person who was hired to take care of such things."

"Oh," I said. Then I remembered I wasn't afraid of Stephen and bucked up. "To tell you the truth, I don't see it as a real problem."

"What you don't see," Stephen snapped, "is the bad side of anyone or anything. Take care of this, Minnie."

I watched him go, wondering why being optimistic was such a horrible thing. Then the phone rang, I was asked about the origin of the ampersand, and the Moratorium on Mitchell went to the back of my brain.

"What're you doing, Minnie?"

I looked away from the computer screen to see Mitchell's hands flat on the front of the reference desk.

Classic Mitchell: on the edge of rude, but not so far over the edge that you had to say something.

"Research," I said, pushing back from the computer. And I'd been at it way too long. Not only was it more than an hour past my scheduled work time, but it was past my stomach's preferred suppertime. I started to stand.

"What are you researching?" he asked, leaning around to look at the screen.

"Grants," I said. "I'm looking for operational funds for the bookmobile." I'd also been trying to find anything that might help prove Cade's innocence, but that wasn't something you could put into a search engine.

Mitchell didn't appear to be interested in the bookmobile problems. "Say," he said, "know what I found out?"

"No idea." This time I stood all the way up.

"Let me show you." He came around and sat in the chair I'd just left.

I sighed. "Mitchell, you can't use the reference desk computer."

"Hang on, this will just take a second." He tapped rapidly at the keyboard. "Remember I said the police were going to arrest Carissa's boss? Well, looks like the real killer was someone else."

Surprise, surprise. "Mitchell, you really can't—" I stopped. The Web site materializing on the screen was Cade's Facebook page.

"See this guy?" Mitchell pointed. "What I hear is that he's the one they're tagging to be the killer."

"How did you hear that?" I asked, so fiercely that the patrons sitting at nearby tables turned to look. I smiled. When they turned away, I turned back to Mitchell. "How do you know?"

He shrugged. "I hear things."

I'd just bet he did. Sometimes I wondered if he and Rafe were related. Closely. "Sorry to break this to you," I said, "but Cade has an alibi."

"He does?"

"A solid one." At least I hoped so.

"Well, shoot." Mitchell squinted at the screen. "Here I thought I was going to help the police by seeing something in this Cade guy's Facebook posts."

"His wife is the one who puts up the pictures and writes the posts."

"How do you know?" Mitchell asked.

"I hear things," I said, grinning, but Mitchell just nodded.

"Sure, you probably hear lots of stuff, being a librarian and everything." He was scrolling down through Cade's page. "And out on the bookmobile, you . . ." He stopped at a photo. "Say, that's Carissa, isn't it? With that guy? Huh. He's a lot older than I would have figured." Mitchell clicked the button to read all of the comments that had been posted regarding the picture. "Uh, Minnie? Did you see this?"

We both read the comment. "One down, one to go," it stated.

For a second I couldn't breathe.

"Um . . ." Mitchell's voice cracked. "Is that the killer?"

"Maybe," I said, and I was happy that my own voice was steady. Mostly, anyway.

"Hey," Mitchell said. "If the killer's posting on Facebook, that'll help the police find him, right?"

I looked at Cade's number of Facebook fans. Eight hundred forty-five thousand, nine hundred and fifteen. No wonder his agent had pushed for a social media presence. "Look at the name. 'John Doe.' That's probably not on the guy's birth certificate."

"Oh." Mitchell deflated. "Still, the police are probably figuring something out from the guy's Facebook identity."

I thumped him on the shoulder. "You know something? You could be right."

And I sincerely hoped he was.

The next morning, as the sun was heaving itself up over the Chilson skyline, I gave Ivy a lesson on the inner workings of the bookmobile. She was a fast learner, and we had time for a stop at the back door of Cookie Tom's before we hit the road. Earlier in the summer, that wonderful man had promised me a discount rate and speedy service anytime the bookmobile wanted to stop for provisions on the way out of town. Sometimes there were even cookies left over for the patrons.

Ivy peered into the bag. "Lovely. Nothing like coconut chocolate chip."

"I'm glad you're okay with cookies," I said. "My other volunteer has become so health-conscious that I feel guilty eating anything as horrible as oatmeal raisin."

"Practically health food." Ivy leaned down and reached her fingers through the wires of Eddie's cage. "Hey, Mr. Ed. You doing okay in there?"

I glanced over. Eddie was rubbing up against her and I could hear his purring even over the bookmobile's engine. "If he's not, it's his own fault."

"Oh?" Ivy sat back and rearranged her shoulders, making herself comfortable. "I hear a story coming. Tell all."

So we drove across the county, west to east, me relat-

ing the main story of Eddie the Stowaway and How He
Managed to Become a Fixture on the Bookmobile and
then the almost as important substory of Why the Library Director Must Never Know.

Ivy was an excellent audience, laughing, gasping,
and sniffling in all the right places. When I came to the
end, she reached down and gave Eddie another scratch
as we drove into the outskirts of the village where our
first stop was scheduled. "You've created quite a di-
lemma for Miss Minnie, Mr. Eddie."

"Mrr," he said.

Ivy laughed delightedly. "It really does feel as if he
knows what you're saying."

"He excels at sarcasm," I said. "Especially when—"

"What's the matter?" Ivy asked.

There was concern in her voice, but I didn't look at
her. Couldn't, really, because my gaze was stuck on the
sight of two of my aunt's boarders walking along the
sidewalk, hand in hand.

I squinted. Maybe I was seeing things. It was early,
after all. Maybe my eyes weren't all the way awake yet.

"Minnie?"

But no. The sight was undeniable. There was Paulette, whom Aunt Frances had matched with Quincy, side
by side with Leo, whom Aunt Frances had matched
with Zofia. They were gazing happily into each other's
eyes, goopy smiles on their faces. "Oh, jeez."

"You're sure you're all right?"

This time I spared a glance away from the road and
looked at Ivy. "Sorry. I'm fine, it's just . . ." The idea of
explaining the inner workings of the boardinghouse
was daunting. How could I possibly start this story?

"It's just what?" Ivy asked. "Tell me, Minnie. You

look troubled and who better to confide in than someone you barely know?"

I thought about it. In lots of ways, she was right.
"Okay. I have this aunt . . ."

By the time I flicked the turn signal in preparation
for the wide right turn into the parking lot of an elementary school, I'd already described the typical
boardinghouse summer. I braked the bookmobile to a
complete stop, and by the time we opened the doors,
I'd pretty much covered everything.

"So you see the problem?" I asked.

"The only problem I see is getting your aunt to stay
out of other people's business."

She'd spoken with a smile, but it was clear that she
thought Aunt Frances's efforts were misguided. Up until that moment I'd thought Ivy and my aunt could be
great friends. Now I realized that it would be best if
they never met.

"Any more problems I can help with?" Ivy asked,
laughing.

"How about employee relations issues? Any experience there?" Not that Mitchell was an employee, but I
didn't want to tell anyone I had a problem with a library patron.

"Not an ounce. One of the beauties about working
for yourself and then teaching college is not having employee issues." We greeted a young woman and three
children coming up the steps; then Ivy turned back to
me. "Minnie, I know you're looking for answers, but
sometimes there aren't any. Sometimes you have to go
with your instincts and hope for the best."

I sighed. "I'm not sure my instincts are up to the
job."

Ivy clapped me on the shoulder. "Now, don't go all whiny on me. You're smart and you'll figure things out."

"Oh, honey," the young woman said. "You should have asked first."

I whipped around. Her little honey had stuffed his mouth full of Kristen's maple-flavored candies. Candies that had come out of the jar for the guessing contest.

My knee-jerk reaction, which was to shriek at the top of my lungs, warred with my training to take everything in stride. There was a short battle, but my training slid into the lead.

I took the jar out of the child's hands. "Sorry," I said politely but firmly, "this candy is for a contest." I handed out the slips of paper. "Here's a form for guessing the number of candies. If your guess is closest to the correct total, you win the candy and the bookmobile will come to your house."

"But Charlie ate some of the candies," one of his siblings said. "You don't know the number anymore."

"Yeah," said the remaining sibling. "And maybe other people have taken candies, too. How are you going to pick a winner if you don't have the right number?"

My smile grew more fixed. "We know the number of candies we started with. We'll count them again and use the average for the winning number." And after the recount, I'd tape the lid down with half a roll of duct tape.

The kids protested that it wasn't fair. I nodded, agreeing that it probably wasn't, introduced them to Eddie, and they immediately went into cat rapture.

I watched, shaking my head. Eddie had saved the day. Wonders truly never did cease.

"I can't believe you talked me into this, Minnie-Ha-Ha."

I looked over at Chris Ballou. We were about to walk through the front door of Crown Yachts, and Chris was still whining. "What I can't believe," I said, "is that you're complaining about talking to some guys about boats."

At lunchtime, I'd been thinking about what I knew and didn't know about Greg Plassey and Trock Farrand and Hugo Edel. In pursuit of more information, I'd called Crown to ask Hugo if Carissa had said anything about a professional athlete. And if, during our conversation, he let something slip about the depth of his involvement with Carissa, well, that would be just a little bonus, wouldn't it?

When I'd been told he was out for the day, I'd had the brilliant idea of getting Chris to come with me to Crown after work. It was my experience that every employee is more forthcoming when the boss isn't around. Chris could legitimately talk to a salesguy about a boat for Greg, and while he was talking I could show the picture of Carissa around and see what I could see.

At the end of the bookmobile day, I'd dropped Eddie off at home and gone to the marina office to coerce Chris into helping. It had taken the promise of a six-pack of The Magician from Short's Brewing Company in nearby Bellaire, but he'd eventually agreed.

"It's not that," Chris said now. "It's that you didn't give me time to get ready."

"For what?"

"Asking about Crown boats. I got a reputation to keep up. Don't want these guys thinking I don't know what I'm talking about."

I raised my eyebrows and opened the door for him. "A smart guy like you?" I asked. "I'm sure you'll manage."

"Yeah, well." He grinned. "Whatever you got cooking, I can play along. You ever going to tell me what this is all about?"

I smiled but didn't say a word. If you told Chris anything, it was best to assume the entire town of Chilson, half the county, and a hefty percentage of the region would have the same information within a day. Or faster.

"Good evening." A middle-aged man came toward us, his hand outstretched. He wore a navy blue jacket, a white polo shirt, khaki pants and . . . I looked down . . . yes, deck shoes without socks. "How can I help you?" he asked.

In seconds, he and Chris were deep in a conversation about boats suitable for a former Major League Baseball pitching star, complete with pantomime of a curve ball delivery. At least that's what Chris said to the guy, claiming he was taught the windup by Greg Plassey himself.

I glanced around the end of a monstrously sized boat and spotted a wall clock. Twenty to six. Thanks to my speedy parking of the bookmobile and a complete neglect of the usual vacuuming of Eddie hair, I had twenty minutes before the place shut down for the night. I eased away from Chris and the salesguy—neither one of them so much as flicked a look in my direction—and went off in search of a talkative employee.

"Hey there." Another middle-aged guy approached, dressed in a navy blue jacket, red polo shirt, off-white pants, and penny loafers. Not quite twin clothing to the other guy, but close. "Is Rob helping you and your husband?" he asked.

I tried not to make a horrified face. The notion of being married to Chris Ballou made my head want to turn inside out. Nice enough guy, but not husband material. At least not for me. I pulled the obituary picture of Carissa out of my purse and held it out. "Do you remember seeing her in here?"

The guy looked at me. "What are you, some kind of cop?"

I babbled on about Carissa's death, about being a friend of a friend, and about trying to help her family. When I saw him nodding agreement, I nodded back. "So, you can see what I'm doing here. Just trying to help, right?" I held the picture a little closer. "Have you seen her in here?"

He looked, frowned, then nodded. "Too bad about her being killed and all. I heard a girl died, but I didn't know it was her."

"So you knew Carissa?"

"Not by name," he said, "but she's a hard one to forget. One of those sparkly people. Shame that she was murdered."

I slid the picture back into my purse with care. "Yes," I said. "It's a great shame." I waited a moment, then asked, "Was she in here to buy a boat?"

"Now, that I don't know." He tipped his head in the

direction of Hugo's office. "She came in and talked to the boss. Not sure what that was all about," he said, half grinning, "but Annelise didn't like it at all."

Annelise. Mrs. Edel. The co-owner of Crown Yachts. The woman who'd felt the need to primp before coming into her husband's workplace. So Annelise didn't like another woman talking to her husband. Yet the husband had said it was strictly business.

Hmm.

"So," I said, "Annelise didn't like Carissa?"

He was still grinning. "Annelise doesn't like any female younger than eighty getting close to Hugo. The jealousy thing happens to women, sometimes," he said seriously. "That change-of-life stuff."

"Really?"

My sarcasm was clear, but the guy didn't seem to notice. "Yeah. I can tell you stories." He laughed, then said, "Of course, that boyfriend of hers didn't like it, either."

I frowned. "Annelise has a boyfriend?"

"Nah, that Carissa. He came in here all mad about Hugo taking his girl out to dinner, but he came in on a Saturday, and Hugo's never here on the weekends."

"What did the boyfriend look like?"

"Ah, I don't know. Kind of scrawny, but not real scrawny. Had hair the color of a living room wall, if you know what I mean."

A soft electronic *ping* went off. The guy looked toward the front door. "Excuse me," he said, looking at an elderly couple who'd just walked in.

Timing is everything, and this was perfect. I said thank you and good-bye, yanked Chris out of a discussion of trout fishing, and headed home.

*   *   *

"Hey!" I called through the houseboat's screen door. "What do you think you're doing?"

Eddie looked at me. He was sitting exactly in the middle of yesterday's local paper, which meant he was also sitting in the middle of the dining table, a place where he wasn't allowed to set foot. At least when I was in the room. What he did when I wasn't within scolding distance was something over which I had absolutely no control.

More than once I'd walked down the marina's dock and, through the houseboat's windows, spotted Eddie sitting on the kitchen counter, napping or idly grooming himself. I'd pound up the dock and burst through the door, reprimands at the ready, only to find my cat sitting innocently on the floor. I had yet to decide whether that whole routine was a coincidence, or whether it was something he planned with the precision of a Swiss watchmaker.

Now I clapped my hands three times—the "Stop that right now!" signal—and watched Eddie slither off the table and onto the bench seat. "You are a horrible cat," I told him. "And stop looking at me like I'm the stupid one. If you didn't do the things I tell you not to, I wouldn't have to yell at you, see?"

Bonk!

"Eddie! Will you cut that out?" I reached for him and snuggled him to my chest, because the loud bonking noise had been his head thumping against the edge of the table. "That had to hurt, you silly thing." I kissed the back of his furry neck and sat down on the upholstered bench. "You'll give yourself a concussion if you keep that up."

His deep purrs indicated that there was nothing wrong, but what did I know about cat head injuries?

I snuggled him again. "You be careful or you'll end up like Greg Plassey, thinking that getting whacked in the noggin with a golf ball is a perfectly normal occurrence."

"Mrr."

"Well, exactly." Carefully, I gave his head a slow pet. "There's got to be something seriously wrong with him to shrug something like that off. Just because it's an accident doesn't mean he shouldn't take it seriously."

Eddie jumped off my lap and back up onto the newspaper. I started to swipe him off the table and back onto my lap, but he reached out with a paw for the newspaper and snagged it with his slightly extended claws.

Rip!

"Oh, good job." I detached him from the newsprint, slouched, and settled him on my chest. "Don't tell me that was an accident, buddy boy. I've known you long enough to know when something was intentional."

Eddie stared at me through unblinking yellow eyes.

"Huh," I said. "I wonder . . ." But no. The idea was far too far-fetched.

Or was it?

I looked at Eddie. "Am I nuts?" He didn't say anything, which was probably the safest possible answer. "If I sound nuts, just tell me, okay?"

He dug his front claws into my shirtfront just the slightest bit, then retracted them. I took the action as a reply of "Have I ever held back from telling you that you were being stupid?" To which the answer was, of course "No."

Since both of my hands were busy with Eddie, I used my elbow to tap the newspaper. "Greg Plassey had that accident with the golf ball. That didn't make the paper because he didn't tell anyone, but there were other accidents that we've read about in the last couple of weeks."

Eddie's eyes opened ever so slightly.

"There was Trock's bicycle accident, remember?" I ran my hand over Eddie's back, and his eyes closed again. "He was run off the road by an SUV. And then there was that boat accident, the one where Hugo Edel was almost blown up." It hadn't made sense then and it didn't make sense now, because how could a guy who made and sold high-end boats for a living blow up his boat? Okay, it could have been an operator error of some kind, but from what I knew about Edel, he was as safety-conscious as a first-time mother.

"So that's three accidents this summer," I told Eddie, who might—or might not—have been interested in what I was saying. From the sound of his snores, I was guessing he wasn't, but maybe it was a trick. "Three typical summer accidents, but they all happened within a couple weeks of each other and they all happened to guys about the same age."

"Mrr," Eddie said sleepily.

"Yeah," I murmured, "I know. The odds seem against it, don't they? And . . ." Another piece jiggled into place. "And I'm sure that Greg Plassey was holding something back about Carissa. What if he had been involved with her in some way? What if his accident had something to do with her death? What if all of them did?"

Maybe I was wrong, but maybe I was right, and that

meant someone would have to find out more about the relationships between these men and Carissa.

"That someone being me," I said, and for some reason that got Eddie purring and settling into my lap as if he had no intention of ever moving.

My thoughts went darker.

Suppose that Greg's, Trock's, and Hugo's accidents weren't truly accidents. Maybe, somehow, they had something to do with Carissa's death. Maybe someone was out to get all the men Carissa was linked to.

Not only did I have to make sure Cade didn't go to jail; I might have to save them all from being killed.

Eddie deepened his purr and curled up into a tight furry ball.

"Then again," I said, "I might be wrong about all this. Maybe one of these guys is actually the killer."

Eddie stopped purring and reached out with one paw to bat me on the back of my hand.

"Sorry." I started petting him. "How many strokes would you like, Sir Eddie? Two? Three?" I paused. "An infinite number?"

That's when he started purring again.

Chapter 14

The next morning I looked up the phone number for Faye, the cookbook lady, and called as soon as the first flurry of library activities was over.

"Good morning," I said. "This is Minnie from the bookmobile and—"

"Those books can't be overdue already, can they?" she asked. "I've only had them just over a week. Were they a short-term loan? I am so sorry!"

I laughed. "Faye, don't worry. It's more than a week until we come back to your stop. At the speed you go through books, you'll have plenty of time."

She sighed her relief into the phone. "You had me worried for a second."

"No need. Matter of fact," I said, "I was a little worried about you and that's why I called. You seemed a little upset about your cousin on the last bookmobile run, and I wanted to make sure you were okay."

"That's so sweet," she said.

I winced at myself a little, because I was calling under mostly false pretenses. Sure, I had been a little concerned about her, but I was mostly interested in her cousin, the one who'd known Carissa. If I could get her name, maybe I knew her, or maybe I could call her and find out a little more about Carissa.

"Thanks so much," Faye said, "but I'm fine now, pretty much."

"It was your cousin that you were concerned about, wasn't it?" I asked.

"What a good memory you have! Yes, I'd been a little worried about Randall. It must have been so frightening, to have the police come talk to him like that."

I stared out my office window but didn't see anything. "Your cousin's name is Randall?"

"Randall Moffit," Faye said. "First cousin on my mother's side."

Why had I assumed her cousin was female? I tried to remember exactly what she'd said that day, but it was long gone out of my head.

"Anyway," Faye was saying, "somehow the police knew that Randall had dated Carissa for a little while."

I sat up straight. "He had?" How had I not known this?

"It was a long time ago," Faye assured me. "Even still, I'm so glad he had a nice, solid alibi for the night she was killed. He was downstate to a Tigers game with some friends. They'd dressed up silly with blue paint and whatnot. They were shown on television and it's hard to get a better alibi than that."

"How nice," I said faintly.

"You are a sweetie, aren't you?" Faye laughed. "So Randall's safe, and I don't have to worry about him a bit."

I hung up and continued to stare at nothing. So the

detectives were indeed looking for other suspects. As they'd said that day at the Round Table, they were doing their job.

But if Faye wasn't worrying any longer, I still was. Because what suspect was ever going to look better than the man who'd been at the crime scene with the murder weapon in his hand?

That evening, I watched with concern as Tucker rubbed his nose. It was a beautiful Wednesday evening, and we were about to take our first official bike ride as a couple. The plan was for a shortish ride, then a return to his car for a picnic supper, then another ride. On the way home from work, I'd stopped by a downtown deli for sandwiches, pasta salad, and chips. It all fit nicely into the wooden-lidded picnic basket I'd originally used for an Eddie carrier—recycling at its finest—and I'd been adding bottled water when Tucker had arrived.

"Hey there." He'd knocked on the screen door and let himself in. "Is that dinner? Looks good."

I'd laughed and given him a hug. "The lid is closed. You can't possibly know what's inside, so how can you say it looks good?"

He'd picked it up. "A full picnic basket is a good picnic basket, so—" He'd gotten a funny expression on his face, dropped the basket back onto the counter, buried his face in his shoulder, and started sneezing.

Now, as we fiddled with unloading the bikes from the top of his car's rack, I eyed him. "You sure you're okay?"

"I'm fine," he said.

"That was a pretty nasty sneezing fit you had back

there. You're not coming down with something, are you?"

"Nope." He flipped my bike off the rack and thumped its tires on the ground, bouncing it a little.

I moved over to take it from him. "Don't they say that doctors make the worst patients?"

"They do, but that doesn't mean I can't diagnose myself." He reached up and started unlatching his bike. "The good news is that Dr. Kleinow says I'm fine."

"And the bad news?"

"Is that we have only two and a half hours before the sun sets." He turned and grinned over his shoulder.

When he did that, he was downright gorgeous. My skin tingled a little. This smart, gorgeous man was all mine for the evening and—

An electronic noise sounded from Tucker's belt. *Eee-ooo, eee-ooo*.

"Is that . . . ?" I nodded at his cell phone. The ring tone had sounded a lot like an ambulance siren.

"Yeah. It's the hospital. But I'm not on call, so . . ." He put the phone to his ear. "Dr. Kleinow." As he listened, he gave me a long glance. Then he reached up to refasten his bicycle. "Yes," he told whoever was on the other end. "I can be there in half an hour."

He thumbed off the phone, turned to me, and took my hand. "Minnie, I am so, so sorry, but I have to go."

"It's okay," I said. "You're a doctor. I understand."

He kissed the back of my hand, and my skin tingled again. "This shouldn't have happened," he said, "but there's been a multicar accident and they need all hands." He blew out a breath and looked at my bike. "I'll take you home, but then I have to—"

"No, you don't."

"What?" He blinked at me. "Of course I'll take you home."

But I was already rolling my bike out of the way of his car. "You get to the hospital. They need you and I can take care of myself. Been doing it for, oh, three or four days now without any problems."

He smiled briefly. "I don't know. It doesn't feel right to leave you."

"Don't be a mother hen." I threw one leg over my bike. "I ride by myself all the time. I'll be fine."

"You're sure?"

"Get going," I said. "And don't forget to eat your sandwich."

"Minnie . . ."

"Go!" I ordered, using my Librarian Voice. "Go forth and heal!"

He gave me a kiss, and left.

I took the road that ran along Lake Michigan. Well, along and above Lake Michigan, since the road ran along a steep bluff that dropped precipitously to the water. Hundreds of feet, if what I'd been told was true, and from the distant look of the whitecaps, I believed the stories.

On the horizon I could see the shapes of North and South Manitou Islands. The Native American legend surrounding the creation of the islands was one of the saddest stories I'd ever heard, so when I saw a small county park, of course I wheeled into it.

The park wasn't exactly abandoned, but it had an air of loneliness that only compounded the effect of the island's story. A weedy gravel parking lot, a single worn picnic table, no restrooms, and no fence to keep kids from falling into the brink. I propped my bike against a tree and walked to the edge of the bluff, trying to see back in time.

To a great forest fire in Wisconsin. To a mother bear and her two cubs trying to escape the heat and crackle of the fire. To the bear family swimming across the miles and miles of Lake Michigan, trying to reach safety. To the smallest baby bear dropping behind, then the other. To mama bear, making it to land, lying down, and waiting for her cubs to reach the shore. To the sand drifting over the drowned cubs, creating the Manitou Islands. To the sand drifting over mama bear, creating the Sleeping Bear National Lakeshore.

It was a story that always made me a little sniffly, and I felt tears tug at the corners of my eyes.

"Great view, isn't it?" said a voice at my elbow.

I jumped high, spun in the air, and landed facing the direction of my speaker. A man in his mid-fifties, shorts and a T-shirt, baseball hat, camera around his neck. I panted, my hand to my chest, and realized that he looked familiar. Not only did he look familiar, but I knew him. "Hey, Greg."

He smiled. "Sorry for scaring you. I thought you must have heard me." He tipped his head, indicating his black SUV in the parking lot. "I've been trying to get some pictures of the islands. And tonight the light's just right."

A black SUV. Hadn't Trock's bicycle accident been caused by a black SUV?

Possibilities tumbled through my brain at a speed that made me realize my thoughts usually operated at maybe thirty percent capacity. I edged away from Greg, ever so slowly.

What if one of the three men—Greg, Trock, or Hugo—had killed Carissa? What if whoever it was had only faked his accident so he could point suspicion in some other direction? What if the killer was Greg? What if he was coming after me now for poking around where I wasn't wanted and asking too many questions?

The conclusion was obvious: I'd been colossally stupid.

"You know," Greg said, moving closer to me, "the spot I've picked out is right where you're standing. I'll be able to get those trees in the frame. That'll give some foreground interest." He had his gaze on the horizon and took another step in my direction.

This, on top of what my brain had just concluded, freaked me out completely. "Gotta go," I said, stumbling backward. "I'm probably late for . . . an appointment. Yep, pretty sure I am. See you later." I turned and fled as fast as my legs could carry me.

"Hey!" Greg called. "Wait, okay? I want to talk to you!"

I sincerely doubted it. What he wanted was to toss me over the edge of the bluff, to send me tumbling head over heels those hundreds of steep feet, my bones breaking on the rock-studded slope, my head cracking open, my breaths ending by the time I rolled into the water like a rag doll.

"Not a chance," I muttered, and ran on.

Unfortunately there wasn't anywhere to run. The park was small and tall fences coursed down the length of both sides. And even if I reached my bike, he'd chase me down with that SUV in seconds. I couldn't take the chance that he'd left his keys in the ignition, so where was there for me to go? Nowhere but down.

His running footsteps were practically on my heels. I might have been twenty years younger, but he'd been a professional athlete for longer than that.

"Just wait, will you?" he called.

He was approaching fast. Maybe I could slide a little way down the edge of the bluff, crab sideways to a friendly neighbor, and call the police from a nice safe cottage with a loud security alarm. I glanced down.

Nothing but air. This part of the bluff was close to vertical.

I spun around in a half crouch. I was small and quick. When he made his move I'd dodge to the side, give him a push, and send him over the brink, just as he intended on doing to me.

"Look," Greg said. "I don't know why you're running, but I want to talk to you, okay? This has been bugging me. I hate lying to anyone, let alone someone like you."

Which meant what? That he hated lying to the people he was about to kill? How commendable. I stayed in my crouch, tense and ready.

"It's about that Carissa." He adjusted his hat. "I kind of lied about knowing her," he said, taking hold of his camera and fiddling with one of its many buttons. "But that doesn't mean I had anything to do with her death."

Not necessarily, but the evidence wasn't looking so good, buddy boy.

"And I didn't kill her," he was saying. "Why would I? So, I mean, yeah, I knew her, kind of, but lots of people did. You're not going to tell anyone, are you?" He wasn't moving, but the emotion in his voice was sharp and deep. "All I want is to be left alone," he said. "Is that so much to ask?"

Not in my book, because what I wanted most at that very moment was for him to leave me alone.

"Say something, will you?" He held his hand out.

I jerked back, afraid of his touch, afraid to die, afraid that what had happened to Carissa was going to happen to me.

"Minnie, will you just—"

I was still moving back when I heard a noisy trickle of sand. I looked down. In my retreat, I'd reached the edge of the bluff. The crumbling edge. The ground beneath my feet was vanishing fast, dropping down, down, down, tumbling at a speed that made me dizzy.

The only thing I felt was fear. I was caught between a killer and a crumbling cliff. Not good odds, either way, but maybe I could . . .

Suddenly there was no time for decision-making. Square yards of ground were heaving and sliding and falling. I had to move, had to do something, couldn't just stand there and die.

Faster than I'd ever done anything, I summoned all my strength and all my power and all my will to jump to solidity and safety.

But even as my feet left the ground, I knew there was no way I'd make it.

Chapter 15

All of my senses were on full alert. I heard the sound of sand cascading out from underneath my feet. Felt the sickening emptiness where ground should be. Smelled my own terrified sweat. Tasted the tartness of adrenaline. And I saw the wonderful sight of a hand reaching out to me.

"Grab my hand, Minnie!" Greg shouted. "Now!"

I reached, flailed, felt the whispering brush of his fingertips rushing past mine. Felt myself falling falling, falling. Saw my future end in a very short time. And then I saw him lunge forward and his strong pitcher's grip was circling my wrist.

"Hang on," he said from above me. "I've got you."

I looked up. Greg was laid flat out on the bluff's edge, hanging on to me with one arm. Under my feet was . . . nothing. My mouth opened, but no words came out. I felt nothing. I heard nothing except the sound of my heartbeats. And there was nothing I could do to save myself.

"Just stay still," Greg ordered. "I'm going to pull us back. Stay still."

I closed my eyes. If I looked down, I'd see my feet dangling in thin air, freak out, and do something stupid, like move. If I looked up, I'd see the man who, mere moments ago, I'd thought was going to kill me. Then I'd freak out and do something stupid, like move. So I did what Greg said. I stayed still.

From above I heard grunts and groans and scrapings of feet and then I felt myself pulled higher. A few grunts more and I could feel my face being shoved against the glorious dirty sand. More grunts and my shoulders were scraping against the edge of the bluff. A couple more and my hips were pivoting past the danger point. Then my knees came up and over and cleared, then my ankles, and finally, happily, thankfully, my toes.

He dragged me a few more feet for good measure, then released me and rolled onto his back. "Man," he breathed. "Good thing you're little, Minnie. If you'd been much heavier I never would have been able to haul you over that edge."

I flopped onto my side, then sat up. From head to toe I was covered in sand, dirt, and bits of leaves and grass. I brushed off my face and looked at Greg. He was just as dirty as I was, if not more so.

"Thanks," I said. "If it hadn't been for you, I would have fallen for sure." Then again, if it hadn't been for him I wouldn't have been skating the edge of the bluff in the first place, but I couldn't see how it would be a bad thing to offer up some gratitude.

"Hey, no problem," he said, his breaths already slowing to normal speed. "Glad to help." Then he gave me a look that seemed to be half question, half wondering if I was bat crazy.

If he was Carissa's killer, surely he would have let

me drop. But he'd risked his own safety to secure mine, so he probably deserved an explanation.

"Well," I said, "for a second there, I thought you might have killed Carissa. And that maybe I was going to be your next victim. Sorry about that."

"Huh." Smoothly, he sat up into a cross-legged position. "I guess my feelings should be hurt, that you'd think I could be a murderer, but you know what?" He grinned. "It's kind of cool that you'd think I could be a dangerous bad guy."

I blinked. Men were mysterious creatures. Not as mysterious as cats, but close.

"Thing is," he said, "I have a great alibi for the murder. I had to call the veterinarian and he was out here all night. Dr. Joe, do you know him?"

The vet? What on earth was he talking about? "Sure, but what does that have to do with anything?"

Greg rubbed his chin, considering me. "Tell you what. Pop your bike into my rig and I'll take you over to the house. You can get cleaned up and I'll tell you everything."

"Oh. Uh . . ." Was this the proverbial offer from a stranger? What was he going to do next, offer me candy?

"Come on." He jumped up easily and held out a hand to me. I took it and he lifted me to my feet as if I weighed nothing. "It's just down the road."

I dusted off my shirt. My shorts. My arms. Legs. Face. Dusted some more while thinking about how to turn down his offer without seeming ungrateful for saving my life.

"I haven't told hardly anyone any of this," he said, "but Chris Ballou says you're okay. He said that if any woman can keep a secret, you can."

"Chris said that?" I looked at the sky and all around. "Where's the lightning? It must be about to strike."

Greg laughed and bumped his fist lightly on my shoulder. It was a brotherly sort of gesture and it comforted me in an oddly deep way. If he was willing to trust me with his secret, whatever it might be, maybe I should be willing to trust him.

At least a little.

"Hang on." I trotted over to my bike, upzipped the handlebar pack, took out my cell phone, and pushed at the buttons. "Hey," I said loudly into Kristen's voice mail. "I'm headed to Greg Plassey's house. I'm on my bike, so if I'm not home by dark, come looking for me, okay?"

I thumbed off the phone and looked up at him. "Ready when you are."

The wide gates at the entrance to Greg's driveway swung open slowly. My jaw dropped at approximately the same speed. How on earth had he done that? There were no humans, or even elves, around to do the opening, and his hands had never left the steering wheel.

He glanced over at me and grinned. "Pretty cool, huh? I had a guy install a transmitter on the front bumper. Don't have to push a button or anything."

We drove through the gate of closely spaced metal bars, a pattern that repeated itself in the tall fence that appeared to march all around the property. So, in addition to Greg's being a gadget guy, he was also a man who took his privacy seriously.

Trepidation started to ooze into me. Why did he need security like this? Maybe he was famous to sports fans, but he hadn't played baseball in years. And no matter how much money he'd made as a pitcher, there were lots of summer people up here who had more and I couldn't think of anyone who had this kind of protection.

"Do you have a security guard?" I asked.

"Nah." Greg braked and we came to a stop in front of a new and large brick house. It looked strange to me. Houses around here were sided with wood, not brick. Which only made sense because a good share of the Midwest's early buildings had been built with lumber from Michigan's forests. Brick? I blinked away the oddity and listened to what Greg was saying.

"Well, I had a guard at first, but he got bored pretty fast, so I didn't replace him when he quit. All I really want is privacy, and people pretty much leave you alone up here."

We got out of the SUV and started up the front steps. They, too, were made of brick, and my legs, almost half as short as Greg's, found the spacing uncomfortable. I felt as if I were a little kid again, clambering up the stairs at my grandma's house.

"So, anyway," Greg was saying, "I knew I didn't want a place on the water. Too many people around, you know? This property was exactly what I wanted. Nothing and nobody as far as the eye can see."

He unlocked the front door, a massive wooden slab, and it swung open. "Come on in." Once we were inside the soaring entryway, he pointed to a door to the right. "Lots of towels, if you want to clean up."

I thanked him, but once in the plush bathroom of marble floors, gilt mirrors, and shiny fixtures without a single water spot, I made a quick decision. Tempting though the shower was with its multiple jets, it would have felt too weird to take off all my clothes in the house of a guy I barely knew. A washcloth and a little soap would have to do until I got home.

Marginally refreshed, I emerged from the bathroom into the vacant foyer. "Greg?" My voice echoed off the hard surfaces and I didn't want to think of the noise level if Greg ever hosted a party.

I moved into the main part of the house, calling Greg's name. If he'd thought I'd take a shower, maybe he was doing so himself. Maybe I should just wait in the living room.

"There, there, little one."

His voice was distant, yet clear enough thanks to the room's acoustics. I wound my way through the living room, dining room, and kitchen and found a partially open door. I pushed it wide . . . and stood stock-still in amazement.

"You're a handsome little guy, aren't you?" Greg was sitting in the middle of a long upholstered sofa. "Yes, you are," he crooned. "You're the handsomest one of all. Except for you, of course." He looked to his left and scooped a gorgeous long-haired rabbit onto his lap, crowding the rabbit that was already there.

"So," I said slowly, "I take it you like rabbits."

It was the understatement of the decade. Filling the room were short-haired rabbits and long-haired rabbits. Big rabbits and little ones. Floppy-eared rabbits and rabbits with their ears sticking straight up. White rabbits and black rabbits and multicolored rabbits. Rabbits in cages, rabbits on furniture, rabbits on the floor. I tried to count, but they moved around so much that I stopped when I reached twenty for fear of getting a headache.

A black-and-white guy hopped over and sniffed at my shoes. "Aw . . ." I sat in the middle of the floor. "Can I pet him?" I asked, my hand hovering over fur that looked deliciously soft and pettable.

"Sure," Greg said, "but he's a her. That's Rosie. She's an English spot."

I sank my fingers in and was delighted to learn that I'd been correct regarding the pettableness. "She's gorgeous." I gazed around. "They all are."

Greg grinned. "I thought you might like them."

"They're adorable." A small, floppy-eared fellow with thick fur hopped close. "And who are you, my little friend?" His fur didn't look as soft, but it looked thick.

"That's Baldy. He's a fuzzy lop."

Of course he was. How could he not be?

Greg went on to name each of his furry pals. Then came the breeds, their parentage and their weights. I quickly passed through the stage of full interest and moved happily to pet-the-cute-bunny status, hoping that Eddie wouldn't get all uptight about me petting other people's pets. Of a different species, no less.

I'd decided my favorite was a big-eared golden girl with a twitchy nose when Greg said, "So, you see, don't you?"

What I saw was a roomful of happiness, if you didn't count the litter boxes. "See what?"

"Well, this." He spread his hands. "Last thing I want is people calling me the rabbit guy. Or worse, the bunny guy. I'd never live it down. I have an image to keep up, and if people found out I have more than thirty rabbits, well, you can just hear the jokes, can't you?"

Thirty? I glanced around and almost started counting again. "Wouldn't taking a few jokes be a lot cheaper than all this secrecy?"

He looked up from the Angora-looking bunny he was petting, and the expression on his face wasn't one easy to read. Exasperation, a little condescension, a touch of humor, and a lot of . . . it couldn't be sadness, could it?

Whatever it was, he didn't reply to my question. "When Carissa was killed, my favorite female was giving birth, and she was having a hard time. Dr. Joe and I were by her side the entire night. No way would I have left her."

But I hadn't seen any baby bunnies.

"They're in another room," Greg said, correctly interpreting my not-very-covert glance. "I keep the mamas and babies out of the general population for a couple of months."

"They'd be what, almost three weeks old? Can I see them?"

"Sure, if you want." He carefully moved the rabbit from his lap to the floor and stood. "They're over here." He opened a door. "The gray ones, in the closest cage."

And they were adorable little balls of cuteness. I longed to take one, no, two, home with me, but they were far too young to be taken away from their mother. Plus, I wasn't sure how Eddie would feel about roommates.

"Yeah, Shadow there wasn't doing well," Greg said, draping his long arm across the length of the cage and looking in with a concerned eye. "This was her first litter, and those can be tough."

"Oh, sure." Like I'd know. The closest I'd ever come to the birthing process was seeing an extremely pregnant library patron turn an unusual shade of white and clutch at her belly. "Call my husband," she'd gasped, and I'd been more than happy to do so.

Greg smiled down at the little family. "I always worry about first litters. That's why I paid Dr. Joe a fortune to be here the whole time. Just in case, you know?"

"He's a nice guy." Dr. Joe was also Eddie's vet.

"Yeah, but did you ever wonder about his sense of humor? Seems a little off, if you know what I mean."

I'd never thought about Dr. Joe that way, but I didn't have thirty rabbits, either.

"My wife says I need to lighten up about him," Greg said. "She says most vets wouldn't make house calls for small animals and I should cut him some slack."

I could almost feel my ears twitching, rabbitlike. "Your wife? Is she here?"

Sighing, he worked his fingers through the wires of the cage to pet one of the babies. "Nah. She went back downstate right after Christmas. I got her a giant chinchilla buck, thought maybe that would get her interested in the rabbits. . . ." His voice trailed off.

I watched him for a while, then asked, "I take it the chinchilla didn't work?"

He shook his head. "She said it was them or her. I thought she'd be back. I thought she'd get to miss them, but it hasn't happened." He sighed. "So I have to get rid of them, I guess." His fingers sank deep into the gray fur, almost disappearing. "I keep hoping she'll change her mind. Do you think she will?"

Not only was I not a matchmaking assistant to Aunt Frances, I was also not a marriage counselor. "I'd ask her that question."

"'Them or me,'" he quoted mournfully. "It was after I got an e-mail from her saying 'Them or me' that I went out with Carissa after meeting her at that car dealership. It was just that once; she didn't know I was married. She was a lot of fun. But it wasn't right."

"Because you're still married?" I asked.

"I love my wife," he said. "I'm going to figure out a way to get her back. And anyway, I don't want anyone else to know about the rabbits, so I stay away from women in general."

"Sorry?"

"Ah, you know what woman are like. They want to get to know you." He rolled his eyes. "They want to talk about feelings. Guys are easier. They just talk about sports. You can know a guy for years and not know anything about him."

Which didn't make any sense, but I knew what he meant. And though I also knew his blanket statement was by no means true for all women and all men, I did know a lot of them who fit nicely into his pigeonholes.

"You're the only person I've told about the rabbits outside of my family. Well, you and Dr. Joe."

I used my index finger to make a cross over my heart. "Hope to die and stick a needle in my eye, I won't tell a soul."

"Thought so." He thumped me on the shoulder. "Like I said, Chris said you were okay and I trust Chris."

"Really?" My eyebrows went up. "I mean, that's nice. It's good to trust people." I winced at my inanity, but Greg didn't seem to think my statement was stupid.

"You got that right," he said. "That's why I felt okay telling the county cops about Carissa and why I couldn't have killed her."

"The detectives talked to you?"

"Yeah, short, fat guy and a tall, skinny one? They were out here a couple days after Carissa died. Guess she'd been on Facebook about the time we had dinner," he said. "Just what I need, my name all over social media. But, hey, at least she didn't know about the rabbits." He grinned.

"So, why did you lie to me earlier, about knowing her?"

He lifted his shoulders. Let them drop. "The whole thing is so hard to explain. If I'd told you I was separated from my wife and only went out with Carissa that once, would you have believed me?"

Maybe. Then again, maybe not.

The indecision must have shown in my face. "See?" he asked. "You're not sure. To have it all make sense I would have had to tell you everything, and I didn't want to. Sometimes it's easier to lie than to tell the truth, right?"

Sure. But that didn't make it right.

"All I want is to be left alone," he said. "That's why I'm looking for the right boat. Out on the water no one will bug me."

"Or the bunnies?"

He flashed me a wide smile. "Or the bunnies."

First thing the next morning I called Dr. Joe, the vet.

"Greg Plassey?" he repeated. "Sure, he's one of my clients. Him and his . . . uh . . ."

"His rabbits," I said.

Dr. Joe made a noise that didn't sound quite like a laugh. If I hadn't known Joe to be a large African-American man in his mid-forties with a wife, three children, and a thriving veterinarian practice, I would have said he giggled. But the idea of a six–foot-three, two-hundred-and-fifty-pound man giggling was so unlikely that I pushed it to the outside edge of probability.

"Oh, you know about the bunnies?" Dr. Joe asked. Then he giggled.

"I was introduced last night," I said. "Greg showed me his new litter and I was wondering how old they were. He couldn't quite remember," I lied, "but he said you were out there that night."

"Yeah, held his hand more than anything else. Weird way to spend a Friday night." There were a few keyboard clicks and he gave me the date of Carissa's murder.

For a brief second, I considered the possibility that Greg had bribed Dr. Joe to lie for him. Then I discarded the idea. I'd once overheard Dr. Joe berate his youngest son, who worked at the vet clinic after school, for not telling the complete truth about cleaning a dog cage. This was not a man who would lie for a client.

"The little bunnies," I said, "they're really cute."

"Cute, sure." Dr. Joe chuckled. "I keep trying to come up with the right phrase, only Plassey's name doesn't rhyme with any rabbit breed I know about. Greg, either, come to think of it."

"Phrase?" I asked.

"Like for a headline. Hey, you're the librarian. I bet you could come up with something good. No, wait, I got it. Baseballer's Bunnies! No, wait, here's a better one: Pitcher Plassey's Penchant for Plush Pets."

He laughed loud and long, and though I'd basically rolled my eyes at Greg's assertion that he'd never be able to live down the jokes, I was beginning to understand the isolated house and the tall fence. If Dr. Joe, a man who loved animals of all shapes and sizes, was laughing at Greg's much-loved pets, the response of an average Joe would be even worse.

Having a fortune might be nice, but I was suddenly very, very glad I wasn't famous.

That evening, as I was finishing up the dinner dishes of a plate, knife, and fork and tossing a foam container from the Round Table into the trash, my cell phone rang with the *Scrubs* theme song.

Eddie, in his new favorite sleeping spot of smashing himself against the window while perched on the top of the dining bench, twitched his tail at the noise.

Smiling, I picked up the phone and thumbed the phone on. "Hey."

"Hey yourself," Tucker said. "Are you doing anything? Thanks to coming in yesterday when I didn't have to, I have an unexpected night off."

Still smiling, I sat down and gave Eddie a few pets. Immediately cat hair shot straight up toward the ceiling, then drifted about while deciding what object it was going to grace with its final resting place. "Well, I had a busy night planned. I was going to finish reading a book, watch the sunset, then go to bed with a brand-new book." I watched as a majority of the Eddie hair wafted down onto my navy blue T-shirt.

"Hmm. You sound swamped. Is there any way you could be persuaded to modify your plans?"

I started to cite the quote of "I might, rabbit," but changed my mind. There were enough rabbits in my head without adding a cartoon version. "I'm certainly willing to listen to another offer."

"How about the same basic plan, but replacing the reading with some quiet conversation?"

It sounded wonderful. "I think that could be worked into my schedule."

"Excellent." His voice sounded odd. I heard a knock and looked up. Tucker was standing at the screen door, flowers in one hand, a bottle of wine in the other, and my picnic basket at his feet.

Grinning, I went to the door and swung it open wide. "What would you have done if I hadn't been home?" I took the flowers and gave Tucker a kiss.

"Donated the flowers to the hospital and saved the wine for another occasion."

"Clever man." The houseboat's storage capacity didn't provide room for extras like flower vases, so I trimmed the ends of the colorful blooms and popped them into a white mixing bowl while I told Tucker where to put the picnic basket. "There," I said, putting the flowers in the middle of the dining table. "They look happy there, don't they?"

"Eddie doesn't look so sure." Tucker nodded at Fuzz Face, who was reaching out with a paw to touch bright pink petals.

"Hey," I said, pulling away the bowl. "Not a cat toy."

Eddie gave me a look of pure disgust and flopped himself onto the seat.

Tucker laughed. "Did you see that look he gave you? I swear he understood what you were saying."

I turned and scrounged through the kitchen cabinet for the stemmed glasses Kristen had given me last summer so she didn't have to drink her wine out of plastic cups. "I'm just afraid of the day when he starts talking back."

Tucker looked at Eddie. Eddie looked at him. "Yeah," Tucker said. "I see what you mean. Knowing exactly what he's thinking might not be comfortable."

I handed Tucker the corkscrew and he popped the cork out of the bottle with an efficiency Kristen would have smiled to see. Wineglasses in hand, I pushed the door open with my elbow and headed out. Tucker paused. "Can Eddie . . . ? Oh, wait. Never mind."

Having scooted out between Tucker's feet, Eddie was already outside and choosing which chaise he'd lounge upon.

"It's fine," I said. "We're often out here." I took the Eddie chair. Tucker sat on the edge of the other and poured the wine.

"To summer nights," he said, holding up his glass.

"Long may they last," I said.

"Mrr," Eddie said.

Tucker blinked. "You're sure he can't . . . ?"

"Absolutely not," I said firmly. "He's a cat. He can't possibly understand human speech."

"I'm sure you're right." Tucker reached forward to give Eddie a cautious pat. "His fur is so soft. Do all cats have fur like this?"

My eyebrows went up. "Eddie is the first cat you've ever touched?"

"My parents were dog people. I must have had friends who had cats, but I don't remember petting one. Maybe I did." A breeze blew at Tucker's hair and he pushed at it with his free hand. Which, I noted, now had pieces of Eddie hair on it. "Doesn't seem possible that I could be thirty-five years old and never petted a cat."

"I'm thirty-three and I've never petted a llama."

"Well, there you go," he said. "We have a lot in common."

I smiled and he smiled back. This was a good thing, being able to be silly with each other. A very good thing. This was extremely good compared to every other relationship I'd ever had. Most times I'd had to repress my silliness for fear of being mocked, but maybe this time . . . just maybe . . .

"I hope I'm not getting sick." Tucker sniffed, then rubbed at his eyes. Scratched at his face. Rubbed the palm of his hand against the edge of the chaise. "My eyes are watering like crazy."

And, just like that, the pieces fit together, tight and snug. I pulled Eddie into my arms and stared at Tucker. "You're not sick," I whispered. And he hadn't been sick the other night, either. "You're allergic to cats."

Chapter 16

Tucker had denied reality until his skin had started to turn a splotchy red. Even then, he'd said he'd be fine. It was the steady stream of eye and nose drippage that sent him home.

Eddie had been nestled in my lap throughout Tucker's ordeal, saying nothing but blinking every so often, almost as if he were calculating.

I looked over at him. Over and down, to be exact, since he was in his cat carrier on the floor of the bookmobile. Ivy had pulled the carrier up against the bottom of the passenger's seat, and her legs were draped over the top of the carrier.

What had Mr. Eddie been thinking about last night? Though it was great fun to think that Eddie comprehended everything that was going on around him, it wouldn't do to anthropomorphize him too much. He was a cat, with a cat's brain and a cat's sensibilities. He wasn't a small furry human and he didn't think like one. It was far more likely that Eddie had been studying Tucker's every move to make sure the stranger wasn't a threat to him than that he'd been calculating how to get rid of a rival.

"Ivy?" I asked. "How smart do you think cats are?"

She turned and looked at me, a quizzical expression on her face. "You sure you want to ask a question like that so close to lunchtime?" I laughed, but she shook her head and tapped Eddie's carrier with the toes of one sandaled foot. "And do you really want to have that conversation where this one can hear? If you think there's any chance at all of—"

"Mrrrroowww!"

I winced and jumped at the same time. "Eddie? Are you okay?"

"MrrrRROOWW!"

Ivy was already bending down and examining the howling, yowling critter that Eddie had suddenly become. "He looks all right," she said, "but—"

"MRRRR-rrrr-OOWW!"

It was the three-syllable howl that got to me. It sounded as if Doom were heading straight for Eddie with no turns in sight.

We were halfway between bookmobile stops, pretty much out in the middle of nowhere. There was only one decent place to pull the bookmobile over, and it was just ahead.

"Hang on, pal," I told Eddie. "I'll get this buggy stopped in a minute."

My promise did nothing to soothe the savage-sounding beast, because he continued to howl and groan and moan the entire time I slowed, braked, and turned into the parking lot of a small restaurant where there was a nice large tree to shade the bookmobile.

At last we came to a complete stop. I unbuckled myself and leaned across to open Eddie's cage.

"I hope he's not sick," Ivy said.

I was fervently hoping the same thing, but as soon as the cage door was open, Eddie stopped howling and looked at me. Blinked. He flopped over onto his side, reached out for my fingers with one white-tipped paw and held my hand.

"He's purring," I said flatly.

"Maybe he was a little carsick," Ivy suggested. "And now that we're stopped, he feels fine?"

From the doubtful tone of her voice, I don't think she believed that scenario any more than I did. Eddie had ridden along on the bookmobile perfectly fine for weeks. Why would he suddenly start getting motion sickness?

"I'll get him some water," I said, pushing myself to my feet. "See if he can keep that down."

He could and he did. When he was done, he sat up, dried his whiskers with his paw, and leapt to the headrest behind the driver's seat.

I sighed. "He's purring again."

Ivy laughed. "You sound almost disappointed that he's not sick."

"Can you have a cat who cries wolf?"

"Cats can do pretty much anything they decide they want to do."

I looked at Eddie and was very glad that he didn't have opposable thumbs. "Well, since it's lunchtime and since we're in the parking lot of a restaurant, we might as well get something to eat."

"I thought you'd never ask," Ivy said, getting up

and opening a cabinet door to retrieve her purse. "I love this place. Fried everything. They even have fried Oreo cookies for dessert."

"Mrr," Eddie said.

"You," I told him, "do not get fried anything."

"Mrr."

"Yeah, well, if you're still hale and hearty when we're done with lunch, you'll get some cat food." I kissed the top of his furry head and locked the book-mobile's doors behind me. Even though it was the middle of August, it wasn't anywhere near hot outside, and since I'd parked the bookmobile in the shade, it would take hours before the bookmobile's interior warmed up to anything Eddie might pant at. He had water and a serious number of cozy places to sleep. What more could an Eddie want?

Inside the restaurant, Ivy was already sliding into a wooden booth. At least I hoped it was Ivy; the place was so dark that I was going by assumption. Dark wooden floor, dark wood-paneled walls, and a dark ceiling that might have been tin, but because it was so dark, I couldn't tell.

"What can I get you ladies to drink?" A beefy young man slid plastic-covered menus across the tabletop.

I opted for ice water. Ivy grinned. "I'm going to be bad," she said to me in a stage whisper. To the waiter, she said, "Give me a large soda. Lots of caffeine and none of that diet stuff. I want the fully leaded version."

"Gotcha."

He started to turn away and Ivy put out a hand. "And we'll want an appetizer while we make up our minds about lunch. Let's say an order of onion rings. And some ranch dressing to go with."

I pushed my menu over to her. "How about if you order for me? I'm not allergic to anything that I know of, and the only thing I don't like is mushrooms."

Her face lit up. "You are a treasure. Barb and Cade are so health-conscious. Every time I manage to drag them out here, they read over the menu a hundred times before ordering a side salad. And then they sigh when it shows up and it's nothing but iceberg lettuce with a little cheese on top."

I smiled, but I was thinking about allergies and cats and boyfriends and futures. Then I shook my head and cast my gaze about the darkness.

"Restrooms are over there." Ivy tipped her head sideways. "You'll want to shade your eyes going in. It's as bright in there as it is dark out here."

She was right. The glaring fluorescent fixtures that some heartless soul had installed on the ceiling were bright enough that I squinted from entry to hand washing. Then, just as my eyes started to adjust, it was time to leave.

When I pushed open the door with my elbow, light flooded out into the dining room, illuminating the scars in the worn booths and the scratches on the floor. It also brushed light across the face of the sole occupant of the booth in the dining area's farthest corner.

I stopped. Peered into the gloom. Couldn't make up my mind. I backed up and opened the restroom door again. This time, when the light came across the man's face, he turned away, pulled his hat down lower, and rearranged his sunglasses.

But it wouldn't have mattered if he'd painted his face purple with blue polka dots. It wasn't his face that I recognized so much as his large, rotund shape, his bulky shoulders, his massive arms, and his sausagelike fingers.

Hmm.

I walked closer. He hunched over his drink. I slid into the booth across from him. He bent his head lower and sipped through his straw, making a gurgling noise at the bottom of the glass.

"Didn't your mother tell you not to do that?" I asked.

Trock Farrand flicked me a glance. "Dear heart. What are the chances of you going away and pretending you never saw me?"

"Isn't your show all about organic food and healthy eating and sustainable living?"

"What television show doesn't have some small element of fiction?"

The waiter came over, his arms laden with plates. Platters, really. Fried fish. Fried chicken. French fries. And a plate of fried something or other that could have been anything from cauliflower to cheese.

I gestured at the array of unhealthy, but undeniably yummy, food items. "This is what you call a small element?"

Trock tossed aside his sunglasses and looked at me earnestly. "Minnie, my love, my paragon of a bookmobile librarian, my shining star, what can I do to earn your silence? If word gets out about this little incident, my credibility will be a thing of the past and, like the dodo bird and the passenger pigeon, it will never return."

I eyed the plates and said nothing. I was not going to out this man to anyone, but he didn't need to know that. Not yet, anyway.

"Minnie, Minnie, Minnie, please understand. I am a man with a deep need for fried food. There are only so many days I can go without. If I do not ingest items such as these lovelies on a weekly basis"—he cast a longing look at the cooling items—"there is a strong possibility that I will curl up and die."

He caught my sardonic glance. "Well, perhaps I won't die, but I will become irritable and annoying and even more difficult to work with than I already am." His quirk of a smile gave me the distinct feeling that his on-set antics were intentionally staged. "If I get more irritable, the show will suffer, and in all honesty, my sweet, it's in enough trouble as it is."

My first instinct was to suspect him of straightforward Minnie Manipulation. My second was to think he was telling the truth. He didn't even look at the food for seven straight seconds, but stared at his hands, a bleak expression on his face.

"Are those mushrooms?" I asked, pointing.

He brightened. "Nothing remotely that healthy. Cheese, my dear. Large chunks of sharp cheddar cheese." He pushed the plate over. I picked up one piece and dipped it into a white goo that I assumed was ranch dressing.

"Let's make a bargain," I said, holding the delectable morsel in front of me. "I'll keep quiet about your eating habits if you tell me everything you know about Carissa Radle and her boyfriend."

He looked at me with brown basset hound eyes. "Can't we make another type of bargain? Perhaps one of those Faustian varieties will do."

"Carissa." I popped the glorious hunk of cheese into my mouth.

"Even from our short acquaintance, I sense that you are a woman of your word. You swear upon your honor that you will not pass my current location to members of the press, any social media site, or worst of all, the suave and debonair Mr. Scruffy?"

I gave him a single nod, then firmly said, "Carissa."

He sighed, added malt vinegar to the fries, and started talking. "We have many spectators at the local shoots as a matter of course. Carissa had been showing up on a regular basis. It was fine at first, but then I realized her presence was slowing down the filming. Slow filming means more time on the set means higher costs."

"You sound like Scruffy," I said.

"For good reason." Trock waved a fry at me. "He's my son. Don't be fooled by the last name. You didn't think I was christened with this name, did you?"

I hadn't really thought about it, but now that he mentioned it, Trock Farrand did sound made up. "Carissa," I said.

He smiled, his white teeth appearing Cheshire cat–like in the dim light. "I predict you will go far. It is focused minds like yours that get results. Carissa. Yes. I finally had to ask her to stay away. It wasn't her, but the aftermath. Every time she watched a filming, that man would appear the next day, asking questions."

"What kind of questions?"

"Odd ones. Who had Carissa talked to, had she talked to anyone in particular, what had she said?" He studied his plate and chose what I thought was a small piece of chicken. "It made everyone on the set uncomfortable because Carissa had told everyone she was seeing an athlete, and this young man was clearly not the athletic type."

"Why didn't you just ban him from the set?" I asked.

"We don't have the budget for real security, and the network is already threatening to cancel the show. The contract is up for renewal in two months, and if I can't deliver these last episodes on time . . ." He buried the last of his sentence in a huge bite of fried chicken.

"So Carissa was more or less a threat to the renewal of your contract?"

He chewed and nodded.

"You know," I said, "that's not a bad motive for murder."

He swallowed, reached into his pocket, and pulled out a wad of receipts. "Perhaps. However, I have a lovely alibi. The night she died, I was down on Torch Lake, eating at the Dockside on the deck's farthest corner. Their fried shrimp are delectable." He sorted through the flimsy pieces of paper. "Here, love. There is no possible way I could have signed that credit card receipt and driven all the way up to Chilson to kill that poor woman."

I brought the smudgy receipt close to my nose. Read the handwritten note: *Thanks! Whitney* with a smiley face. Read the time and date stamp. He was right; there was no way the timing could have worked.

Then again, he was a celebrity chef with resources I couldn't even imagine. If anyone could have faked a credit card receipt, it was the friendly, charming, and extremely intelligent man in front of me.

I parked the bookmobile in its cozy garage and turned off the engine. "Home, sweet home."

Eddie was too busy napping in Paulette's nest of soft pink to pay attention, but Ivy had already unbuckled her seat belt and was piling up the returned books for hauling over to the library. How this was going to work during the snow-filled days of winter, I wasn't quite sure, but I'd already decided not to worry about it. Things would work out.

Ivy nodded at the contest jar. "Don't forget that we need to recount the candies, to make sure we know how many are left in there."

I made a face. "Thanks. I forgot about that."

"Here." She put down the milk crate she'd picked up. "Let's do it right now. It won't take but a minute with the two of us." Before I could get out a protest, she'd opened the jar and dumped the candies on the computer desk.

"This must be someone's guess." She picked up a slip of paper and handed it to me. "Someone else who couldn't read the directions you so clearly taped to the jar. There's always at least one, isn't . . ." She realized that I wasn't part of the conversation. "Minnie? What's wrong?"

"Nothing." I slipped the paper into my pants pocket. "Let's count those candies."

Ivy gave me a measuring look, but she didn't ask any questions. Which was good, because I wasn't sure how to react to the message on the paper, printed in block letters and now burning hot against my skin. TO THE BOOKMOBILE LADY. STOP ASKING ABOUT CARISSA. OR ELSE.

The note in the candy jar rattled me. I tried to convince myself it wasn't a threat, but I couldn't. Ivy knew something was up, but she must have respected my privacy enough to leave me alone when I said I was fine.

That night I slept poorly. I kept rolling over, trying to find a position that would send me into slumber land, and I eventually rolled enough times that Eddie jumped down and left me alone to my troubled thoughts.

I knew I should take the note to the police. Of course I should. But if I did, they'd know that I was toeing the line between helping a friend and interfering with police business. I would get a lecture that would make me steaming mad, I'd say something to make them mad, and we'd end up with a bunch of angry people, which wouldn't be productive at all.

Sunday dawned with a scattering of clouds and a breeze strong enough to make the edges at the houseboat's aging windows whistle. I spent the morning doing chores; then after a quick lunch I dressed in library clothes and patted Eddie on the head.

"Don't do anything I wouldn't do, okay?"

He lifted his head, blinked, then put his head back down. He was snoring by the time I reached the door.

As was often the case on summer Sundays when the weather wasn't nice enough for water sports, the library was busy. I spent the first two hours helping out at the front desk, then took a stint at the reference desk, answering questions and directing people to the books they wanted.

"Excuse me," a woman asked, "but could you show me where the book on diets and exercise might be?"

I blinked. She was fiftyish and slender enough that she looked like the last person on the planet who needed a book on dieting. She was also Annelise Edel.

"It's Mrs. Edel, isn't it?" I put on a wide smile. "Minnie Hamilton. We met briefly at Crown the other day. I was going out, you were going in?"

"Oh, yes, that's right. How are you?"

It was the polite voice. She clearly didn't remember me, but that was okay. I stood and led her toward the 613 numbers.

"Are you looking for anything specific?" I asked. "Because, honestly, you look great, and if it's because of a particular book I want to know which one it is."

Annelise laughed in a quiet library-appropriate way. "The way I look is due to long walks, a little weight work, lots of swimming, and watching every bite I eat. It's a lot of work, but that's what it takes after you turn fifty. I just want to look through the books here to see if I can learn anything new."

"Fifty?" I shook my head. "No way are you fifty."

She smiled. "Fifty-three, actually."

"Well, I hope your husband appreciates all the work you put into keeping in shape," I said with admiration. "If he doesn't, let me know and I'll tell him."

"Aren't you the sweetest?" She touched my arm. "You should be bottled up and sold to middle-aged women to . . . to . . . oh, dear." She dipped her hand into her purse. "I seem to be . . ." Sniffing, she pulled out a tissue and dabbed at her eyes, which were filling with tears.

Sympathy swelled. "Hugo doesn't appreciate you?"

She kept dabbing, then sighed. "No. He doesn't. And I've been so afraid . . ." She bit her lower lip.

I jumped the conversation ahead. "You're afraid he's having an affair."

She sniffed. "He denied it, said she was a potential customer who happened to be single, but she was so pretty and so . . . so . . ." More tears, more tissue blotting. "Then she died, a horrible thing for the poor girl.

But now I'm wondering about every woman he talks to and it's an awful thing. These days I can't sleep for worry. Can't eat, but I don't mind that so much." She gave a small smile.

"The customer," I said. "Was it Carissa Radle? The woman who was murdered?"

"She was so pretty and cheerful, I could see how Hugo would be attracted. Every man she met wanted to be with her."

"Not quite every man," I said quietly, then decided to put out a rumor. "I hear there was an ex-boyfriend involved."

Annelise's face cleared out to sadness. "Oh, how awful for her. Yes, I see what you mean. At least one person wanted her dead." She looked thoughtful. "Even me, I suppose, on one of those bad nights. But I was at a hotel spa down in Traverse City getting a three-day special treatment."

She darted a glance at me. "You know Hugo, don't you? Please don't mention the spa. I told him I went to Chicago to meet my sister. He thinks spas are a waste of time and money, but this spa specializes in skin revitalization. I know my skin isn't ever going to look like a twenty-five-year-old's, but maybe . . ." She ran her hands over her thin hips. "Maybe if I lose a few more pounds he'll look at me the way he used to."

"I am not a snob," Kristen said.

"What makes you say that?" I looked over at her. She was slumped down in a white metal chair, her long legs sticking out so far that they would have been a tripping hazard to anyone coming near our table if we hadn't chosen the far corner. "You sneer at white zinfandel wine, you won't set foot in a fast-food restaurant, and you practically asphyxiate at the idea of eating anything frozen."

"That's not snobbery," she said, "that's good sense. White zin is nasty, fast food is horrible for you, and no one should have to eat frozen food, not when there's fresh around that can be eaten."

"Yet you're here." I nodded at our surroundings. This included a stupendous view of the deep-blued Torch Lake, the Clam River, and the large deck for which the Dockside Restaurant was famous. Boats laden with young people and old, all reddish from a day on the water, idled up and down the river. It was a peaceful scene punctuated with seagull cries and cries from small children who didn't want their fun to end in spite of the setting sun.

"Hey," Kristen said, "you're the one who wanted to come here, not me."

"Don't forget the malt vinegar." I pushed the tall bottle toward her.

"Right. Good idea." She sprinkled vinegar liberally over her fries. "Man," she said as she got ready to stuff her mouth, "these things are awesome."

"And you're just as much a hypocrite as Trock Farrand." I might have sworn secrecy to not tell anyone about Trock's secret eating habits, but letting Kristen know didn't really count as telling. For one thing, I didn't want to sit here all by myself, and for another, it might do her good to know that her idol had feet of clay.

"I hate you," she muttered as she picked up the saltshaker.

"You do not. You just don't like having reality slap you in the face."

"Who does?" She grinned and tossed another fry into her mouth. "Much nicer to live with rose-colored glasses on, if you ask me. No one would ever accomplish anything if they had to stare at reality all the time."

I thought about this. If you truly understood the odds against success when, say, starting a new restaurant, would you even try? Maybe the only way to accomplish anything significant was to decide you were going to be the one to beat the odds. "You know, I think you're right."

"Well, duh. You're a case in point. Would you ever have started the effort to get the library a bookmobile if you'd known how unlikely it was that you'd get the funding?"

Huh. I'd never thought of it that way.

Kristen laughed. "You never thought of it that way, did you?"

"You two ladies look like you're enjoying yourselves." Our waitress approached. "Is there anything else I can get you?" she asked.

That was my cue. We'd taken this corner table specifically because we'd asked to be seated at one of Whitney's tables, she of the smiley face on Trock's receipt. "Do you watch *Trock's Troubles*, that cooking show?"

Whitney nodded. "Sure. It's not like I have to see it every week, but I've watched it a few times. Say, did you know that that Trock guy has a house up here? Petoskey, I think, or maybe Harbor Springs."

I elbowed Kristen, who was starting to correct her. "That's what I've heard, too. And I heard someone say he was here late on Friday night, three weeks ago. Were you here then? Because I was wondering if he's the same in person as on television."

"Three weeks ago?" She squinted at the sky. "Last week in July, right? The whole weekend was a nutso-busy zoo. I'm not sure I would have noticed if Daniel Radcliffe had been here."

"Who?" Kristen asked.

I elbowed her again. If she didn't know the name of the actor who'd played Harry Potter, now wasn't the time to expand her information base. "So you've never waited on Trock Farrand?"

"Sorry." She shrugged, then smiled. "Of course, you never know who's going to walk in here. Wait a few minutes and he might show up."

The next evening after work and dinner, I decided that what I needed was a long walk. Even though it was a Monday night, all the downtown stores would be open to catch the summer tourist trade. A walk would be an excellent idea. Partly to clear my head, but also to work off all the fried food that I'd snarfed down over the weekend.

"How can something so bad for you taste so good?" I asked Eddie as I refilled his water bowl.

He ignored both me and my water offering. He'd been standoffish ever since the bookmobile lunch where I'd abandoned him. "Hey, I said I was sorry. But fried food is even worse for cats than it is for humans. How about a treat?" I opened an upper kitchen cabinet, took out the small canister of cat treats, and shook it to rattle the contents enticingly.

Eddie's ears twitched, but he didn't move. He still didn't move when I opened the can and rolled small treat bits onto the floor.

"Wow, you really are mad, aren't you?" I hunched

down to pet him. "Hope you get over it soon. I love you—you know that, right?"

He looked away and kept looking away as I walked out the door. As soon as it shut behind me, however, he spun and launched himself on top of the treats. I couldn't decide whether to pull out my hair or to laugh, but since my tummy was still feeling heavy with fried food, I opted for neither and walked away, shaking my head. Maybe Eddie wasn't the strangest cat in the universe, but he had to have a good shot at being the strangest cat in the world.

Or maybe he was a new breed of cat. If breeders could come up with a new cat variety, why couldn't nature? Maybe Eddie was the start of a new species. I tried to remember high school biology class and how scientific nomenclature worked. Kings Play Chess On Friday Golf Saturday. Kingdom Phylum Class Order Family Genus Species. Felis was the cat genus. Felis domesticus, the genus and species for domesticated cats. "Felis Eddicus," I said, then laughed.

Smiling, I looked around. And saw that passersby were moving away from me, pulling their children out of my path. Oh, dear. The laughing cat lady, that's what I was turning into. "Mrs. Eddie," I murmured, sputtering out another laugh. Eddie would like that one. I'd have to—

My humor came to an abrupt end. Detective Inwood was walking toward me. He was deep in conversation with a uniformed officer who looked familiar . . . I snapped my fingers. Wolverson. He was with Deputy Wolverson. And I didn't want to talk to either one of them, not right now.

I dodged sideways into the nearest storefront and

quietly shut the door, keeping my gaze on the street. As soon as they walked past, I'd—

"Oooo, it's beautiful!"

I started at the familiar female voice and looked around. Saw the brightly lit glass cases. Felt the thick carpet under my feet. Heard the soft music.

A jewelry store. Of all the stores in downtown Chilson, I'd ended up in the one in which I had the least interest. Not that there was anything wrong with jewelry stores; I just didn't have the means to purchase anything in one. Besides, pretty much everything in here would just turn into a really expensive cat toy.

"Oh, Quincy!"

I edged farther in, far enough to see around the large display case in the middle of the room. There, throwing her slim arms around Quincy's flushed neck, was Deena, her face wreathed in smiles.

"You like it?" he asked.

"I can't imagine a better engagement ring," she said.

Up until that point, I'd been harboring a teensy-weensy hope that Quincy had bought the ring for someone else, say Paulette, and was only showing it to Deena. The kiss that Deena and Quincy were now sharing, however, with the jeweler beaming in the background, smushed that hope into flat dust. Reality was in front of me, and it was time to get used to it.

I stepped out of my hiding place. "Hey, you two. Congratulations!" After a flurry of hugs and well-wishes, I left the store to face another reality.

There was no detective or deputy in sight, so I walked rapidly in the direction I'd seen them heading. Halfway down the next block, I saw them coming out of an antique store and hurried to catch up.

"Detective Inwood," I called. "Deputy Wolverson. Do you have a minute?"

We adjourned to what the city was calling a pocket park, a narrow passageway between two buildings that had been landscaped with plants and brick pavers. We sat down on benches that faced each other. At least the police officers sat on theirs; I perched on the edge of mine as words spilled out of me.

I told them about the candy jar note. I told them that the bookmobile's door had been left unlocked at the art fair and how that was probably when the note had been left. I told them what I knew about Hugo Edel and Trock Farrand and Greg Plassey. The detective nodded all through this while the deputy took notes. I even mentioned what looked like a post from the killer on Cade's Facebook page and was reassured when they told me their forensic computer analyst was working on tracking back the poster's IP address. But when I told them that an old boyfriend of Carissa's had been following her around, Inwood's face twitched.

"You seem to have been following in our footsteps, Ms. Hamilton. If you'd talked to us, you would have known we've already made most of these inquiries. But please let us know if you learn more about the ex-boyfriend."

That didn't make sense. "But you've already talked to him. It's Randall Moffit."

Deputy Wolverson started to say something but stopped and looked at Inwood. When he nodded, the deputy went on. "He has a solid alibi for the time of the murder."

"Sure, but he could have hired someone else to do that." How, I didn't know, but if he had buddies that would paint their bodies in Tigers blue, maybe he had a friend good enough to commit murder for him. "Moffit must have been the one who was following her around to Crown and Trock's TV set. Did you check his alibi for those days?"

The detective sighed, so I knew they hadn't. "And what about the phone call that lured Cade to Carissa's house?" I persisted. "Did you ever check up on that?"

"I'm sorry, Ms. Hamilton," he said, "but we've found no proof it was ever made."

My mouth went dry. "But maybe it was a landline call. A local one. That doesn't mean it was never made. You can't prove a negative." I could see I was losing the detective's interest and started talking faster. "But local calls do show up somewhere. I mean, they must, right? Every call is routed through computers, and computers keep track of everything. It's just a matter of getting the data."

Inwood stood. "Thanks for your input, Ms. Hamilton. And please drop that note off at the sheriff's office tomorrow morning. Have a good night."

He walked off, the deputy followed, and I was left alone with nothing but my own frightened thoughts to keep me company.

Chapter 17

I pushed away my fears for Cade. There had to be something I could do. I had to find something that the police had missed. Only . . . how? I sat on the quiet bench, thinking hard, watching people walk past and cars drive by.

Cars. I smiled. Got it.

I pulled my cell out of my purse to check the time. If high-end car dealerships kept hours similar to downtown merchants, I had almost half an hour until closing.

Bright lights shone out the windows of Talcott Motors. Half a dozen people wandered about inside the showroom, some obviously potential customers, others just as obviously salespeople. And, through an open doorway, I spotted Jari.

Perfect. I unbuckled my seat belt and was half out of the car, half not, when a *Ring! Ring!* sounded at my left ear.

"Hello, Minnie, dear!" It was Zofia on the rear seat of a bicycle built for two. In the front was a white-haired man who looked vaguely familiar.

Zofia waved gaily, the jewels on her ringed hand flashing in the setting sun. "How nice to see you. Do you know Claude? He has a summer home across the street from your aunt. Claude, this is Minnie, the young lady who drives the bookmobile."

Claude and I nodded at each other and made nice-to-meet-you noises as Zofia talked on. "I've been having so much fun this summer and it's all thanks to your aunt Frances."

"It is?"

Zofia smiled fondly at the man sitting in front of her. "If she didn't live where she did, Claude and I would never have met."

"A tragedy," Claude said, turning to pat her hand. "It would have been a tragedy."

"Oh," I said lamely. Remembering my promise to my aunt, I mustered up one last effort. "Leo will be so disappointed, don't you think?"

Zofia made a rude noise. "Haven't you seen the goo-goo eyes he and Paulette have been giving each other for weeks? Open your eyes, young lady, and you shall see." She flung her arms out, palms up. "A wonderful world is out there, just waiting for us to discover it!"

Laughing, I said, "I hope I can be just like you when I grow up."

"My dear, you can be anything you'd like." Zofia blew me a kiss. "Toodle-oo!"

Smiling, I waved and watched them pedal off, their feet rotating in tandem.

"Minnie?"

I turned. "Hey, Jari." All things come to those who are willing to wait outside in a parking lot for a little while. "Can I talk to you?"

*   *   *

A few minutes later, we were sitting on tall stools at a high table in a local drinking establishment. If I stretched, the tips of my toes brushed the stool's top rung.

"What can I get for you ladies?" asked a long-haired young man with a notepad in his hand. He went away with two drink orders; a cosmopolitan for Jari and a sedate glass of house red for me. I glanced about, knowing there was no possible way that Kristen would be here, but leery that she might have spies out. If she heard I was drinking a house red, she'd try to force me to eat something horrible, like shiitake mushrooms.

Jari and I made idle chat about the weather, the summer crowds, and the upcoming winter until our drinks showed up. "Cheers." Jari held up her glass.

"Cheers." I sipped cautiously at my wine. A little sweet, not much depth, but not too horrible. Thanks to Kristen, I was learning something about wine, but not enough to ruin my enjoyment of a cheap glass of the stuff. The best of both worlds.

Jari took a large swallow of her reddish drink, started to put it down, then took another large swallow. "That's exactly what I needed," she said. "You wouldn't believe the day I've had."

"Brush-off Bob giving you a hard time?"

She blinked. "Who?"

I explained the nickname and she threw her head back and let loose with a huge laugh. "That's perfect," she said, wiping her eyes carefully with a small square napkin. "Just perfect. Do you have names for the other guys?"

"Not yet."

"Maybe I'll try to come up with my own. There's got

to be something good that rhymes with Tim." She sipped at her drink. "What was it you wanted, anyway? Something else about Carissa, I suppose." Her newly lighthearted demeanor slipped a bit.

"I'm afraid so."

Her shoulders heaved; once, then again. Finally she looked up. "Okay. Fire away."

I had a number of things to ask but thought I'd start with an easy one. "Carissa's obituary said she'd gone to Wayne State. Do you know what degree she had?"

"Pharmacy," Jari said. "She'd been a pharmacist ever since she got out of school, but she said she got tired of counting pills and all the insurance hassles. One of the reasons she moved up here was to get away from all that."

"Don't pharmacists make quite a bit of money?" More than librarians, I was sure.

"Yeah, I guess. She'd saved a lot, so probably. I asked her once if she thought she'd ever go back to it, but she said she was having more fun selling cars than she ever had handing out medications, so who knows?" Jari shrugged.

"That big Petoskey stone of hers must have cost a lot of money," I mused out loud, then could have kicked myself. Well, maybe Jari hadn't heard exactly how Carissa was killed.

"Oh, she didn't buy that," Jari said. "Her ex-boyfriend, the Weasel? He gave it to her. She thought it was about the prettiest thing she'd ever seen, so she always had it on the table in her living room."

Which made it an easy choice for a murder weapon. Right there on display, and quieter than a handgun with the bonus of no registration. "And you never knew the Weasel's name?" I asked.

"The police wanted to know that, too, but like I told you before, I never knew it."

"Do you know where he works?" I asked. If I knew where Randall Moffit worked, maybe I could find out who his buddies were and figure out if any of them would be the type to—

"No idea," Jari said. "Downstate is all I know."

Downstate? But Randall lived near Chilson. "Are you sure?"

"You bet. I think half the reason Carissa moved up here was to get away from him." She spun her glass around. "He must have had a good job because she said he gave her lots of nice stuff, but she didn't like the way he tried to control her. Weird, since they only dated for a few weeks. Carissa said she was embarrassed about how stupid she was to go out with a guy like that in the first place, so she didn't tell anyone about him."

"His name wasn't Randall?"

Jari looked up at me. "You mean Randall Moffit? No, he came after the Weasel. That didn't last long, though."

She went on, talking about how Carissa hadn't wanted to hurt Randall's feelings, but my brain was locked in place.

The Weasel and Randall were two different people. There were two ex-boyfriends. Zofia had been right, my eyes truly had been closed. How long had they been that way?

And worse, what else had I been wrong about?

*   *   *

The next evening, after I'd had a determinedly cheerful telephone conversation with Tucker, Eddie and I sat out on the deck. We'd started with me on one chaise longue and him on the other, but he quickly decided that my lap was a better location.

He flopped onto my legs, curled into a large Eddie-ball, and started rumbling out a deep purr.

"So," I said, petting him, "it's time to tell Cade that I've failed completely to clear his name. I'm no closer to figuring out who the killer is now than when I started."

Eddie opened one eye.

"Sad, but true," I told him. "Yes, I know more about Carissa than I did, a lot more, but I still don't know enough."

I knew that she'd fled the traffic of downstate for the open roads of northern Michigan. I knew she'd been a pharmacist who'd left it all behind for selling expensive cars, and I knew she'd changed from the serious adolescent my brother had known to a woman who was intent on having a good time. And I knew she'd left behind at least two ex-boyfriends.

Had it been her bad experience with the Weasel that had made her want to take life less seriously? That she needed to have fun, that life wasn't all work and no play?

Eddie yawned and stretched out, his front claws digging slightly into my skin.

I winced. "Watch it, buddy, those are sharp. Someone should clip them for you." I thought about getting up and finding the clippers, but that would mean moving Eddie, and it just didn't seem right.

"You know what else doesn't seem right?" I asked. "That no one knows the Weasel's name. How can that be?" But maybe it wouldn't have been that hard. If you lived alone in a city, didn't have any neighbors you were friendly with, and weren't good friends with your coworkers, there would be no reason for anyone to know the name of every guy you briefly dated.

"We need to find out who he is," I murmured. Whoever he was, I wanted him to be the killer. I didn't want it to be Greg or Trock or even Hugo. I wanted it to be someone I didn't know.

Eddie's tail flicked around, tickling me something fierce. "You can stop that anytime," I told him, but since he was a cat, he kept flicking.

I tried to catch the end of his tail, but he tipped it out of reach every time. Finally I used both hands to trap it down against my leg. "Ha! Got you . . ."

My voice trailed off.

A trap?

I considered the idea. And found it good.

A trap.

There was only one little problem. How do you set a trap for someone when you don't know where he lives? Or even his name?

I left Eddie with a small handful of treats and a new cat toy—one with bells inside that I'd probably regret giving him come two in the morning—and drove up to the care facility to talk to Cade. About ideas for setting a trap for the killer.

It was long past dinnertime, closing fast on sunset, and the halls were mostly empty. The only things moving were the always-busy staff and the birds in the showcase in the hallway a few doors down from Cade's room.

I stopped to admire the bright colors of their feathers. That, as well as their merry chirping, was enough to lift anyone's spirits. "And what's your name?" I asked a little guy. His head poked out of a tiny nest just long enough to let me see his brilliantly blue plumage. "Let me guess. Blackie. No, Snowflake."

"Sorry. He's Chirpy." A nurse's aide was standing in front of a laptop computer on a cart, tapping away at whatever it is that aides have to tap away at. She hadn't been there thirty seconds ago and I don't know how she'd arrived so silently, but maybe that was something they taught you in the certification class.

"Chirpy?" I asked.

"Yeah, I know, not very original, but we let every resident who wanted to name a bird name it whatever they"—she broke off into a huge yawn—"Sorry. Whatever they wanted."

I glanced at the birdhouse. There were dozens of the little guys in there, and a number of them looked exactly the same to me. "Um, how do you know which one is which?"

She tapped at the computer a few more times, then flipped the laptop shut and turned to me. "Don't," she said, nodding slightly.

I began to see the beauty of the plan. Smiling, I said, "I'm Minnie."

"Heather," she said, and yawned again. "Sorry. I just switched from working midnights and it's taking me a while to get adjusted."

I shuddered. People were meant to be in bed and sleeping from eleven to seven, not on their feet and working. However, I was very grateful there were people who could function on that kind of schedule, and I was even more grateful that I wasn't one of them. "I don't even want to imagine," I said.

"Oh, it's not so bad. Like they say, the only thing you miss working midnights is sleep. I could get to all my kids' concerts and soccer games, no problem. I didn't always stay awake, but I was there." She grinned, and the resulting lines around her mouth made me revise her age up a few years.

"I always thought working midnights would be a little, you know." I hesitated, then said it. "Creepy."

She shook her head. "Not to me. Most everyone is asleep; you can chart without an interruption, practically. The best thing about midnights is that it's quiet. Peaceful, even."

I'd never thought about it that way, and said so.

She nodded. "And the shift differential is nice." She rubbed her thumb across the tips of her fingers. "But the kids are older now, and my husband sleeps better when I'm home, so I switched over. Still, I kind of miss how nice and quiet midnights are. At least most of the time." A darkness shaded her face. "Of course, it's not all puppies and kittens. Sometimes . . ." Her voice trailed off and she glanced over her shoulder. Toward Cade's room.

Inside my head, dawn broke, even if it was almost sunset. This must be the aide who'd told the police that Cade was in bed the night of Carissa's murder. This was the woman whose statement was a critical part of keeping Cade out of jail.

"I stopped by," I said, "to visit Russell McCade."

"You know Cade?" Heather's smile was wide. "I've been a fan for years, since I was a kid. The first real picture I ever bought was one of his prints. I'd love to have one of his real paintings. They're so lifelike they almost jump off the wall. Maybe someday I'll be able to afford a little one."

She looked wistful and I didn't say that if I didn't get something figured out, her wish might come true sooner than she might guess. "He's one of the residents you're assigned to?" I asked.

"I was so lucky. He's such a nice man you wouldn't think that he's such a famous artist. I mean, people all over the world know who he is." Her eyes were wide. "He said he's sold paintings to people in over fifty different countries. I'm not sure I could even name fifty countries."

My new friend seemed a trifle dazzled by Cade's fame. I wondered if she'd act the same way around Trock Farrand. Or Greg Plassey, come to think of it. "He does have a lot of talent," I said.

Heather nodded vigorously. "Tons and tons of it. People like him should be given breaks, don't you think?"

"What do you mean?"

"Don't you think that people with that much talent should be given more leeway than other people?"

I didn't, actually, but the hallway of a medical care facility wasn't really the place to begin that kind of discussion. "Well . . ."

"People like Cade. Sorry, here comes another yawn." She covered her mouth, then went on. "They're not the same as the rest of us, so they shouldn't be held to the same standards, don't you think? I mean, we need to protect their gifts as much as possible, so it's only right to protect them."

"Protect them?" A cold draft brushed at the back of my neck.

"Well, sure. If it takes . . . well, not an outright lie, but just a little lie, to make sure Cade gets back to painting as soon as possible, how could that be wrong?"

I stared at her. No question, Heather had been the aide who'd told the police that Cade was in bed at the time of the murder.

And she'd lied.

"Oh, jeez." She fumbled in her pocket. "There's my beeper. Got to go. Nice meeting you." Off she went, her soft shoes soundless on the carpet.

She'd lied.

Cade hadn't been in his room the night Carissa was killed.

She'd lied.

The two words repeated themselves over and over again in my head, filling my brain and driving out every other thought.

Heartsick and suddenly tired beyond belief, I turned and made my way home.

"Minnie?"

I was sitting at the dining table, halfheartedly working away at a plan for the trap, and jumped at the sound of my name. Eddie jumped, too, mainly because he'd been on my legs and had been forced into jumping when I did or risk being tumbled to the floor in an untidy heap.

"Minnie," Cade said. "I need to talk to you."

I could feel my chin sliding forward to form the expression my mother always called my stubborn look. He might want to talk to me, but I certainly didn't want to talk to him. He'd lied to me. He'd had Heather lie for him. What else had he lied about?

"Minnie, please. I know you're in there and the nice young man from the facility who gave me a ride won't be back for an hour. How much of this do you want your neighbors to overhear?"

None, but my cranky neighbors, the Olsons, were out of town and my nice neighbors, Louisa and Ted, were headed out early the next morning and had said good night half an hour ago, earplugs in their hands. Still, if Chris saw Cade standing on my dock at this time of night, he'd have a new rumor circulating around town by tomorrow noon.

I got up from the dining table, opened the door, and went outside.

"Thank you." Cade was standing on the marina dock, leaning on his cane with his good hand, resting his weak side. "When Heather asked me how long my friend Minnie had stayed, I didn't understand what she was talking about."

I crossed my arms. With the sun long gone, the air had turned chilly.

Cade shifted his grip on the cane. "I said I hadn't seen you in a few days and she was extremely puzzled, said the two of you had had a nice chat just this evening. 'A chat about what?' I asked. Her face turned a lovely shade of scarlet, so I knew I'd been the topic." His mouth twisted up in a sardonic smile. "And there's only one thing she could have said that would make you turn away from me."

I looked straight at him. Opened my mouth. Shut it again, because I didn't know what to say. This man was not a killer. How could he be? The doctor said he lacked the strength to kill Carissa. Then again, if Cade had convinced Heather to lie for him . . .

He shifted again. "I did not ask her to lie for me."

If he could convince Heather to lie, would that make him an expert liar himself? It seemed to follow, but my experience with consummate liars was limited to a college freshman roommate. And a former boyfriend, but I'd vowed never to think about him again.

"I can see you don't believe me." Sighing, Cade leaned against one of the dock pilings. "I'm going to describe exactly what happened that night. When I'm done, you can make your decision."

I nodded for him to go ahead.

"That night was clear, if you'll remember. I'd gone to bed about nine, just before sunset, but I couldn't get to sleep and got up just before eleven to watch the moon as it dropped into the tree line. The way that new moon was looking at me, it felt as if it was trying to tell me something, and I thought maybe a series, each showing a slightly different moon phase from a different location. Blacks and purples and deep blues with an underlying tone of . . ." He wandered off inside his head but came back after a minute.

"That's when I went out," he said. "You've seen the courtyard just outside my room. There's an access door just down the hall. I went outside, sat on a highly uncomfortable bench, and planned a series of paintings."

Even in the dim light cast by the marina's lights, it was easy to detect his wry expression as he looked at his weak hand. I mentally edited his sentence and ended it with "And planned a series of paintings I'm not sure I'll ever be able to complete."

"So Heather did see you at the time of the murder," I said.

"Yes." He shifted again. "I wasn't in bed, that's all."

"So . . ." I didn't understand. "Why did she lie about any of it? What difference does it make if you were in bed or in the courtyard?"

Cade's face quirked up in an uneven smile. "You, obviously, have not spent much time in these types of facilities. Heather had looked into my room, noted that I was outside, and charted on the computer that I was in bed, sleeping. If it had come out that she'd falsified data, she would have been in serious trouble."

I still didn't understand, and said so. "But why did she chart that you were in bed? Why didn't she say where you were?"

He sighed. "Because she'd given me the access code to unlock the courtyard door the day before. She shouldn't have, but she did because I'd asked."

Now, finally, I understood. She'd done him a favor, knowing she was flouting the rules, and if she was found out, she'd be . . . well, who knew what. Reprimanded? Suspended? Fired? None of it was good.

"You believe me?" Cade asked.

I wanted to say yes, and almost did, but held back. "I'll have to check with Heather."

He glanced at his watch. "I assumed as much. In three minutes she'll be on break and will be able to take a phone call."

I went in to fetch my cell phone. When I came back out, I saw him straighten up smartly. "Oh, come inside," I said irritably. "Now, what's her phone number?"

Five minutes later, I'd been reassured by Heather's explanation, which was basically the same as Cade's, only told from the opposite point of view. Thirty seconds after that, I was heating water to brew some warming tea for the both of us.

"Hello there, young fellow."

I turned and saw Cade sitting down to the dining table and stroking Eddie's fur. "Oh, uh . . ." I abandoned the tea preparations and zoomed forward to scurry the papers out of Cade's view. "Let me get those out of your way." As I piled them tidily, the microwave dinged. "Tea time," I said brightly, and made two small strides to the cupboard. "Two mugs and then—"

"Mrrorrww!"

I whipped around and saw Eddie sliding down the pile of papers, sending himself and the papers onto the floor. "Oh, Eddie . . ."

"Not to worry." Cade leaned down to pick up the sheets, piece after piece of paper upon which I'd scribbled ideas for getting Carissa's killer to reveal himself. I'd started with the idea of putting some sort of ad in the local paper and moved up to my last idea of spreading the word that I'd found proof of the killer's identity. That last idea was the one Cade held in his hand.

Frowning, he looked up at me. "Is this what I think it is?"

I reached to yank the papers away from him, but he held them out of my reach. "You're setting a trap for the killer, aren't you?" he asked.

My own frown was just as fierce as his. "None of your business."

"I beg to disagree," he said. "It's because of me that you got involved in this business at all. And this?" He waved the papers. "This is far beyond the pale of what you should be doing."

"It's a little late for that," I said, and then I realized I hadn't told Cade about the note in the candy jar. After I did, he immediately started going all fatherlike on me, saying that he was forbidding me to put myself in any more danger. I ignored him and he eventually got tired of talking. "So," I said, "all we need to do is identify the killer," I said. "If he shows up, I'll take a picture, show it to the police, and let them take it from there."

But Cade was shaking his head. "It's too dangerous. This man has killed once; what will stop him from doing it again?"

I wanted to stamp my foot. Didn't, but wanted to. Badly. "I'll be hiding. He won't even know I'm there."

"It's still . . ." A curious expression crossed Cade's face. "You know, if it's a trap you're setting, what you need is some good bait, and better bait would be best." Cade's eyebrows rose. "Yes?"

Now he was doing *B* words. "Not playing," I said. "And what are you talking about?"

"What if," he asked quietly, "your bait included the person the killer had tried to frame for murder?"

Chapter 18

At sunset the next evening, Cade settled into one of my chaise longues. I took my cell and the binoculars I'd borrowed from Rafe and found a comfortable spot under a corner of a large, leafy shrub next to the marina office.

The night before, we'd put a Facebook post on Cade's page, saying that he was going to be doing some recuperating alone on a friend's houseboat. We knew that the killer had probably looked at Cade's Facebook page before, so we were hoping he'd do it again. And since the killer knew I drove the bookmobile, it was likely that he also knew where I lived.

This creeped me out in a big way, but I tried not to let it show as we sketched out the right words to use. Finally we clicked POST and off it went.

Now I sat cross-legged on a swim towel and checked the batteries on my phone. Powered up and ready for a night of surveillance. "We're on," I whispered, and made myself as comfortable as possible while sitting on the ground half under a shrubbery.

Comfortable was good. It might be a long night.

*   *   *

"A pointless night," I told Eddie when I returned at half past four. Tried to tell him, anyway, since I was doing as much yawning as talking. "Who would ever have expected the Olsons to show up on a Tuesday and have a party?"

It had turned out that Tuesday had been Mrs. Olson's birthday and Gunnar had surprised her with a quick trip north via chartered aircraft large enough to hold their closest friends, of which I now knew there were many.

Cade and I had stayed in place until long past the hour when all the partying people had gone to bed, but our quarry hadn't shown. "The only danger involved was the danger of falling asleep," I murmured sleepily.

My furry friend flicked his tail at me and jumped down. I followed him, still yawning, as he stalked through the kitchen, down the steps, past the bathroom, and into the bedroom, where he jumped up on the spare bed and started rubbing his chin against the bulletin board. I'd installed the magnetic bulletin board a few weeks ago when I discovered that my former cat-free existence had given me habits that did not suit a life with cats. Specifically, how I kept track of my household paperwork.

In the old days, I'd put all my receipts in a tidy pile in the middle of the spare bed until I got around to checking my credit card and bank statements. Now I stuck the small slips of paper to the board and hoped they didn't attract Eddie's attention.

"Not a cat toy," I said, pushing at his hind end and twisting him away from the latest object of his affection. "There's nothing about a magnetic board that should interest you." I started pulling my sweatshirt over my head. "I mean, can't some things be off-limits? For example, I don't eat your cat food, so why do you—"

A small *thunk* set me on pause. So much for asking nicely. I yanked off the sweatshirt and inspected the Eddie damage.

"Not so bad," I said, pulling the small calendar out from underneath the furry black-and-white body and putting it back where it belonged. "Pulling down the receipts would have made a much bigger mess. Better luck next time." I leaned down to kiss the top of his head.

"Mrr," he said.

"I know just what you mean," I said, and gave him another kiss.

For the first time ever, I was glad the next day wasn't a bookmobile day. With my level of fatigue, it was extremely possible that I could have fallen asleep at the wheel, and that wasn't a possibility I wanted to dwell upon at all.

I made it through the morning by pouring copious amounts of coffee down my throat and decided the best way to stay awake through the early part of the afternoon was to take an informal inventory of the reading room. Check on the wear of the magazines, straighten the newspapers, all things to keep me on my feet and conscious.

As I put the copies of *Time* magazine into chronological order, Mitchell's booming voice bounded across the room. "Minnie! Hey, Minnie! Guess what?"

He was grinning and more full of life and energy

than I'd ever seen. I'd been ready to tell him my guess was that he'd decided to enter the world beard and mustache championship, but he looked so happy that I didn't have the heart. "Hey, Mitchell. What's up?"

"I've been thinking," he said. "About what you and Holly and Josh have been saying, and I think maybe you're right. I should get out more. It's good to try new things, right? Keeps the old noggin going, yeah?"

He tapped the side of his head. It made a hollow sound, but that could have been my imagination. "So you know what I'm going to do?" he asked. "I'm going to open my own business. It's going to be great, and I'm sure I'm going to be real busy real soon. I probably won't be hanging around here as much anymore, but I'll stop in every once in a while so you remember my name." He laughed, flashed a dazzling smile, and bounced out.

I stared after him. Mitchell was starting a business? What could it possibly be?

"Well, well, well." Stephen stood in the reading room's doorway, his arms folded on his chest. "Looks like you've finally taken care of The Situation. Excellent work, Minnie. Nicely done." He gave me a nod and strode off.

Excellent work? I hadn't done a thing. And nicely done? I wasn't so sure.

At all.

All that afternoon and through the evening I mentally tossed everything I knew about Carissa into a big pot and tried melting it together.

As I should have known, all that did was make a big muddled soupy mess that gave me no answer in particular and only made my stomach start to hurt. I didn't feel any closer to keeping Cade out of jail now than I'd been the day I vowed to help him.

The next day was a bookmobile day. Being out and about, bringing books and good cheer to the country-side, should have made me feel better, but the black cloud of fear hung on my horizon all day. On the plus side, Thessie had returned, and her chatter about her college visits kept my darkest doubts out of view.

We had a busy stop late in the day, which was our favorite kind of stop. Kids looking for books, teenagers looking for books, adults looking for books. It did my heart good to see the bus so crowded, and when I heard footsteps creak up the stairs, I turned, ready with a wel-coming smile.

"Hello," I said, then stopped. "Hey, Brett." The man, tallish and thinnish, with sandy brown hair, looked at me oddly and I realized it wasn't Greg Plassey's friend at all. It was just someone who resembled him.

"Sorry." I gestured an apology. "I thought you were someone else."

"I get that a lot. Guess I have one of those faces," he said, shrugging. "I was wondering—can I get a library card here or do I have to go into Chilson?"

Happy day! Was there any job better than this? I reached for the forms and a pen. "All you have to do is fill this out. I'll give you a temporary card now and send you a permanent one tomorrow."

He put the paper down on the computer desk, scrib-bled in his name and address, and handed it back. "That's it?" he asked.

"Easier than buying groceries," I said. "If you want, you can go select any books you'd like, and by the time you're done, I'll have you entered in the system and . . ."

In the act of turning away, he paused when I did. "Something wrong?" he asked.

"Your name." I stared at the form.

"Oh. Yeah, sorry about my handwriting. It's Randall," he said. "With two *L*'s. Last name is Moffit, two *F*'s, one *T*."

I looked at the form. Looked at him. "You have a cousin named Faye."

"Sure. She's the one who told me I should try the bookmobile."

"You dated Carissa Radle."

He shifted. "Yeah. Hate that she died, but we'd been over for a couple of years. I'm dating a dental hygienist these days." He smiled, showing bright white teeth.

I pointed him in the direction of the thrillers and watched, thinking, as he browsed through the Stuart Woodses and James Pattersons.

Randall Moffit and Brett Karringer looked enough alike to be brothers. Randall had dated Carissa. And I remembered Jari saying that Carissa had said she needed to break out of her lean build and sandy brown hair boyfriend rut. Jari had said the Weasel lived downstate. Brett lived downstate. Could Brett be the Weasel? Could Brett be the killer? Could Greg's golfing accident have been a murder attempt?

The questions tumbled around in my brain. I needed to find Greg. For the first time ever, I was in a hurry for the bookmobile day to be done.

At long last, the forty-five-minute stop was over. Thessie and I started shooing people in the direction of the door while Eddie surveyed our efforts from his new perch on the dashboard. Finally only Randall was left. As I slid his checked-out books over to him, he handed me a slip of paper. "My guess for the contest," he said, gesturing at the candy jar, whose lid was now firmly taped shut with clear packaging tape.

I glanced at it and my mouth fell open. "This is exactly right. How on earth did you do that?"

"Felt right, I guess. Sometimes you just gotta go with your gut, you know?" He tromped out into the afternoon sunshine without another word.

But I wasn't paying attention to his lack of social niceties. Sometimes you just gotta go with your gut, he'd said. And what had my gut been trying to tell me?

"Mrr," said Eddie, who moved to the passenger's headrest.

I patted his head absentmindedly. What was my gut saying? I really didn't know. I wasn't even sure it was saying anything at all.

When I got home, I let Eddie out of his carrier, made sure his food and water dish were at the required levels, then headed out again.

The screen door to the marina's office banged shut behind me. Chris looked up from the boat parts he had strewn across the countertop. "Hey, Minster. What's up?"

"I'm looking for Greg. Is he around?"

"Oh, man." Chris put down the greasy whatever it was. "You haven't heard?"

"Heard what?"

"Greg's in the Charlevoix Hospital. Just this afternoon, he fell off his roof. Almost got killed, I guess. Broken legs, broken arm, and who knows what happened to his insides . . . Minnie, hey, Minnie!"

But I was already out the door and halfway to my car.

"He said what?" Greg snorted out a laugh. "You got to be kidding."

I smiled. "Well, you know Chris. There's no story he hears that he can't make better by adding a few exaggerations."

"A few?" Greg gestured at his arms and legs. "No broken bones, and no internal injuries. There isn't much he got right."

"Except," Tucker said, "the almost-got-killed part. Because it was a close call, Mr. Plassey."

"I'm fine." Greg moved to sit up but winced and flopped back down. "Well, almost fine."

Tucker looked at him over the top of a clipboard. "You dislocated a shoulder, damaged a number of ribs, and sprained an ankle. I wouldn't call that fine."

"Hey, I been worse." Greg winked at me.

By the time I'd reached the Charlevoix Hospital, Tucker had talked Greg into staying at the hospital overnight and the three of us were a cozy group in Greg's newly assigned hospital room.

"What happened, anyway?" I asked. "Chris said you fell off your roof."

"At least he got that part right." Greg grinned. "I was up there looking at the flashing around the chimney. There's a leak up there somewhere. I been using that wooden ladder of my dad's for years and never thought to check it. My own stupid fault, you know? I leave it out back of the garage—no surprise it fell to bits."

"Did you ever think that someone tampered with it?" My voice sounded loud in the small room.

Greg stared at me, then started laughing. "Oh, right. Who's going to do that? Because I have so many enemies."

Tucker was also looking at me. He opened his mouth but then shut it.

His eyes were so blue I thought I might be looking into pieces of the sky. His smile was so warm I thought I might kiss it. And I suddenly thought that I might be falling in love with him.

"Hello?" Greg said. "Are you two still here?"

Tucker murmured that he'd be back later, gave us nods, and went off to do busy doctor things. I tore my gaze away from Tucker and turned my attention back to the man in the bed.

"How long have you known Brett Karringer?"

"My buddy Brett?" Greg frowned. "Why?"

Excellent question. Unfortunately I didn't have a good answer prepared. "He looks a lot like someone I met the other day. I was wondering if they were related somehow."

"Oh. Well, I only met him a couple months ago. He lives downstate, but he seems okay. A little intense, if you know what I mean, but okay."

"Has he ever dated anyone up here?"

"No idea."

Internally, I cursed the male gender for their stereotypical tendency not to talk about anything of importance. What I needed was a connection from Brett to Carissa, and I didn't have one. Even a vague one would be good, but I had nothing.

"Say," Greg said. "You want to watch the ball game for an inning or two?"

About as much as I wanted to watch grass grow, but

I studied the lines of pain and weariness on his face, smiled, and said, "Sure."

When I got home, I explained Greg's accident to Eddie.

"So, what do you think?" I asked. "Accidental or intentional?"

Eddie, who was sitting on the back of the dining bench, rotated around so that his back faced me.

"Hey, don't be like that. I'm sorry that you had to spend the evening inside, but you know I have to figure this out. The police still think Cade did it and—"

Eddie was paying no attention to my explanation. The newspaper on the dining bench must have suddenly needed scratching, because he jumped off the seat's back and onto the paper and started ripping it to shreds with his clawed feet.

"Hey! Cut that out!" His current paper of choice was a freebie supplement to the Petoskey newspaper. The *Graphic* was a guide to everything fun that was going on in the area, which mostly meant weekends, but there were—

My brain suddenly spun off into a direction it had never gone. Weekends. Greg Plassey had been whacked on the head with that golf ball at a weekend tournament. Trock Farrand had almost been run off the road when? On a weekend. Hugo Edel's boat had blown up on a weekend, and it had been on a weekend, a Friday night, that Carissa had been killed. Okay, Greg's ladder escapade was a weekday event, but the ladder could have been damaged on a weekend.

"Everything happened on a weekend," I said softly. "Do you think it matters?"

Eddie opened his mouth in a silent "Mrr" and

jumped back onto the back of the bench, where he sat and started cleaning his left front paw. To get the newsprint off, no doubt.

"Well," I told him, "since you think it matters, maybe I should call a detective." Eddie had no response to that. I took that as confirmation, found the number for the sheriff's department, and dialed. Since it was getting close to ten at night, of course there was no detective around. I left a message to call.

"Think one of them will?" I asked Eddie. He stared at me, unblinking. "Yeah, I don't think so, either."

Which meant it might be time for another trap.

Chapter 19

A few minutes later, my cell phone rang. "Ms. Hamilton? Detective Devereaux returning your call."

Within the hour? A new record, folks! "Thanks," I said, and launched straight into everything I'd found out, from the visits of Carissa's ex-boyfriend to Crown Yachts and Trock's set. I told him about my suspicions regarding the accidents, and about what had happened yesterday to Greg Plassey.

I told him all that and about the weekends and everything else I could think of and when I was done, the detective said, "Thank you for the information, Ms. Hamilton. And we appreciate that you stopped by to drop off that note you received."

Somewhere in there I heard the warning signs of an upcoming qualifying sentence. "But . . . ?"

"There's been a development in the case against Mr. McCade."

All the muscles in my body tightened. "It's that nurse's aide, isn't it?" I blurted out.

For a moment I heard nothing from the other end of the phone. Then I heard the distant sounds of a file drawer slamming. Devereaux was still there; he just wasn't talking. Which could only mean he didn't know what to say, and to me that could only mean that I was right. They'd discovered that Heather, Cade's aide the night Carissa was murdered, had lied.

"It's not what you think," I said fast. "Really, it's not. See, there was a moon and Cade wanted to sit out in the courtyard and besides, there's no way he could have left that note in the bookmobile and—"

"Thank you, Ms. Hamilton. Please be assured that we're investigating the incident to the fullest extent possible, and don't hesitate to contact us if you have any new information." And he was gone.

Slowly, I put down the phone, my fear for Cade reaching a new level.

It was definitely time for another trap.

Trap number two.

I asked Eddie about the wisdom of setting another trap. "I don't see what else I can do. What I need is proof, but all I have is suppositions and guesses and theories." And redundancy, apparently, but I was so worried about Cade that I cut myself a little slack in the vocabulary department.

Eddie, who was lying on my lap, kneaded it gently with his claws. I wasn't sure what that meant, other than my lap wasn't quite what he wanted it to be, so I kept going.

"The fact that everything happened on a weekend doesn't necessarily mean that it was the Weasel, who-ever he is." Or anyone else from downstate, for that matter. "Maybe the killer was using that as a red herring, or maybe the killer lives up here but has a long commute and only has weekends free."

Eddie rolled partway over, purring and exposing his tummy.

I rubbed his soft belly fur and did some more thinking out loud. "Either way, I think setting up a second trap is the way to go."

"And were you going to do this all alone?"

I twitched, Eddie jumped, and I turned to see Cade standing on the dock, leaning on his cane.

"You might as well check yourself out of Lakeview," I said, "for all the time you spend outside the facility."

He smiled. "I was cleared for all activities of daily living this morning. You are speaking to a man who will sleep in his own bed tonight."

"That's great!" I said. "But where's Barb? Shouldn't you two be out celebrating?"

He nodded in the direction of the parking lot. "She's waiting for me. But we'd like to invite you to dinner next week, since it's mostly due to you and your Eddie that I was able to recover so quickly."

A happy warmth glowed inside me. "You don't need to do that. I was glad I was in the right place at the right time, that's all."

"Ivy will be there, too," he said. "And I would love a chance to see three of my favorite women in the same place at the same time."

I laughed. "Then I accept. Thank you."

"One condition." He shifted his grip on the cane. "This proposal of a second trap. The entire escapade is far too dangerous. This is something best left to the police. They are trained for this sort of work and you are not.

Perhaps they think I killed Carissa, but I didn't, and they will at some point determine who did. Let them do their job."

A sensible person would have agreed, but as many people had told me, I was not always sensible. I held my thumb and index finger an inch apart. "The police are this close to arresting you. Detective Devereaux as good as told me so. If they still think you did it, how hard are they going to look at anyone else?"

He shifted again. Didn't say anything.

"Aren't you the least little bit worried about being convicted for a murder you didn't commit? Sure, we'd all like to believe in the infallibility of our justice system, but we also all know that mistakes are sometimes made."

Cade looked out to the lake. He didn't say anything.

I pressed on. "And how about the value of your paintings? About all the money so many people have spent, purchasing your work for a retirement nest egg? Or aren't you concerned about them anymore?"

A half smile creased his face. "I totally withdraw my objection to Trap Number Two."

We were clearly onto *T* words, but I didn't have one ready. "Good." Though I was going to set the trap no matter how many objections he put up, it was nice to have his tacit approval.

"Tomorrow night, then," he said. "I'll make the Facebook posts."

I nodded, then remembered the long hours we'd spent in the first trap. "And I'll bring snacks."

At sunset the next night, I hauled the picnic basket down from the top of the kitchen cabinets and shoved every kind of quiet snack I could think of into it.

This turned into an interesting exercise, because I quickly realized that most of my favorite snacks were noisy. Or if not the food itself, then the wrapper. It wouldn't do at all to scare away the killer because I was taking the wrapper off a bar of Hershey's Special Dark.

In the end I included water bottles and a number of items in separate, nicely soft zippered plastic bags. Cheese cubes, fudge from the downtown shop, bananas, and grapes. I even remembered to tuck in something upon which to serve the food. Sometimes I was so smart I amazed myself.

Cade and I had figured that if this trap was going to work at all, the killer would surely show up after everyone else in the marina had gone to bed, which on Friday night meant after the weekly party tailed off around two in the morning. I could hear the action in full swing a couple of docks away, so there was oodles of time.

I'd also had time to think about my previous position in the shrubbery. While my phone's camera function was good, I wasn't absolutely certain it was good enough to capture the face of someone on my boat from that distance. This time I was going to be up close and personal.

"Minnie?"

I abandoned the picnic basket and poked my head out the door. "Hey, Cade. Come on in. I was just finishing with the provisions."

He opened the houseboat's gate and, using his cane for assistance, stepped up onto the deck. "The closer this moment comes, the less sure I am you should be doing it."

"Me? What about you?"

"It's my problem and I should never have pulled you in."

I snorted. "As I recall, I pulled myself in. The next big question is, do I take the basket of snacks, or do you?" He started to protest, but I crossed my arms and stuck out my chin, becoming the immovable object. Cade sighed, clearly choosing not to try to be the irresistible force, and lifted the picnic basket off the counter.

The weight almost toppled him. "Goodness, Minnie, we're only going to be out here for a few hours. How much did you pack?"

Since he'd lifted the basket with his weak arm, I didn't want to make fun of him. "Enough to feed a small army. After all, it's better to have and not need than need and not have."

He nodded sagely. "Words of wisdom. Now, where is that Eddie of yours? I'd like to say hello."

"Last I checked, he was napping on my pillow." I made a move toward the back of the boat. "I'll go get him."

"No, don't." Cade held up his hand. "I wouldn't want to wake him."

I blinked. The man, clearly, had never kept company with a cat. "He'll go right back to sleep," I said. "Cats aren't like babies."

But Cade was already shuffling toward the door. "Let's get you settled."

Outside, I propped the ladder I'd borrowed from the marina office up against the side of the cabin and scrambled up. Cade stood a few rungs up, lifted the picnic basket to the roof, and slid it across. I patted the front pocket of my black sweatpants. Phone. I patted the other pocket. My aunt's small digital camera for backup. Set and ready.

"Did you look at the weather?" I asked.

"If you believe weather forecasters"—the chaise squeaked under Cade's weight—"we're in for a mild evening of temperatures in the low sixties, calm wind, and clear skies."

I hunted around in the darkness for the cushion I'd tossed up earlier. "That's a nice forecast. I hope it's true."

Cade chuckled. "You, me, and all the merrymakers over there."

Tonight's marina party was roaring at full throttle. The two docks and multiple boats between us weren't doing much to muffle the music and laughter. I sat cross-legged on the cushion, tempted to reach for the picnic basket, but knowing I shouldn't start down that snack-filled road so early.

Cade and I talked quietly. He told me that he'd always wanted to spend a night in Sweden's ice hotel; I told him that I'd always wanted to watch a horse race at every track Dick Francis had mentioned in his mysteries. Cade said he'd never been able to cook bacon properly and I confessed that I'd never once made a biscuit worth eating.

It might have been an hour later when Cade stood and stretched. "I'm getting downright old," he grumbled. "Can't even—"

Crash!

I knew exactly what had happened. I stuck my head out over the edge of the roof. Now that my eyes had adjusted to the dim light, I could see well enough, or almost. "That's my bucket of rocks," I said. "You must have kicked it over. Leave them for morning. They're just, you know, rocks."

But he was already stooping down to pick them up. "Can't have a mess," he said, glancing sideways, "now, can we?"

He stopped abruptly. With a rock in each hand, he looked straight up at me.

Chapter 20

I stopped breathing. Looked at Cade's taut face. Looked at the stones in his hands. Looked at Cade. Had I been wrong? Had all this been a complicated maneuver to get me in a place where he could kill me and blame it on the ex-boyfriend?

"No!" Cade shouted, and pulled back with his arm, cocking it to throw.

I yanked myself back, shouting who knew what, stunned that I'd been so wrong, angry that Cade was trying to murder me, and pumped full of determination that I'd get out of this situation. Somehow.

"Leave us alone!" Cade shouted, and the rock flew across the boat's deck and crashed against something that went "Oww!"

I lifted my head. Someone was standing on the dock. A male figure, nondescript, not short and not tall, not wide and not thin. He was standing with one foot on the dock and one on my boat, grasping his shoulder where Cade's rock must have hit him nice and square, but it was an awkward look, because the hand doing the grasping was holding a deadly looking handgun with an attachment that every moviegoer knew was a silencer.

"It's him," I gasped, part of me very relieved that it wasn't Trock, or Greg, or Hugo, or even Randall Moffit.

"Stay still," Cade ordered. He reached for another rock, cocked his arm again, and let it fly.

Brett Karringer ducked. Cade's stone hit a piling and splashed harmlessly into the water.

Cade was grabbing stone after stone, throwing, fighting as best he could, but there were only so many rocks in the bucket. All Karringer had to do was wait it out, and then he could come after us with the gun and do . . . well, whatever he'd been planning on doing.

I was yelling, shrieking for help, but the music from the party was drowning me out.

There had to be a way out of this. There *had* to be, but calling 911 wouldn't get the police here anything close to fast enough.

Frantically I looked around for a weapon. I didn't have an accurate aim—I'd always been one of those kids picked dead last for softball teams in gym class—so even if there were more rocks, it wouldn't have done us any good. What we needed was to get that gun away from Karringer. What I needed was something . . . ah.

I lunged for the picnic basket. Sticking out high was the cutting board I'd stuffed in to work as a serving tray. I yanked it free.

"Minnie, call the police!" Cade shouted, still throwing rocks at Karringer.

Rocks weren't going to work much longer and there was no time to hold a committee meeting about this. Karringer's head was down and he was fumbling with the gun, trying to bring it up and around into shooting position.

Though the last thing I wanted to do was approach a guy with a loaded weapon, there wasn't much choice. Well, I could have screamed like a little kid and crumpled into a ball of fear, but that wouldn't be very productive. It wouldn't have helped my self-esteem much, either.

I sucked in a quick breath and, as quickly and as quietly as I could, climbed down the ladder. How close did I have to get? I had absolutely no idea.

With all my heart and might I wished that I'd spent more time in the backyard playing catch with my brother. If only Greg Plassey were here to give me some pointers. Then again, if Greg were here, he would have beaned Karringer in the head with that first rock and I wouldn't have to be doing any of this. An empowerment exercise, that's what this was.

I was aware of the stupidity of the thoughts running through my brain, but I didn't try to stop them. If I stopped them, I might start thinking about how scared I was, and there was no way that could be a good thing.

Closer. I had to get closer . . .

A loud metallic *crash* hit the dock, followed by an odd wooden thumping sound. Cade had run out of rocks. He'd heaved the bucket at Brett and now he had nothing left to throw.

It was up to me.

Karringer lifted the gun in Cade's direction. Time slowed. I saw nothing except the end of that gun, felt nothing, heard nothing except—

"MRRR!" Eddie's yowl came from the roof.

Karringer jumped when Eddie shrieked, and let his gun arm drop.

Perfect, because I knew what had happened. That wooden sound I'd heard. The picnic basket. Eddie had oozed himself into his old cat carrier, hoping he was going to get a ride on the bookmobile. No wonder Cade had said it was heavy. Now Eddie was out and wanting off the roof.

I planted my feet, pulled my arm back across my body, cocked my wrist, and whipped the cutting board at Karringer, Frisbee-style.

"Uhh . . ." Karringer staggered back, his arms flailing.

I'd hit him! From the way he was clutching at his side, I'd skimmed his ribs instead of knocking away the gun, but I'd actually hit him!

Karringer staggered forward, falling against the boat's railing, trying to recover his balance, his arms whirling.

Something long and skinny whizzed past my head. Cade's cane thumped Karringer in the wrist. The gun clattered to the boat's deck and skittered away.

I dashed forward and scooped it up, pulling the lethal thing out of Karringer's reach.

He glared at me, a look full of such malevolence and hate that I took a step back. Librarians are used to many things, but pure unadulterated hatred is not one of them.

"Minnie," Cade said. "Do you . . . ?"

I pointed the business end of the gun straight at Karringer's center mass. "Yes," I said confidently, sliding back the pistol's chamber. "I do." My self-defense classes hadn't just included lessons in close combat. I didn't know if I could actually fire a gun at a human being, but Karringer didn't know that.

He glared at me, glared at Cade, uttered an extremely rude curse, then turned and ran down the dock. For the briefest fraction of a second, I paused. Chase him? Let him go? If I let him go, what were the odds that he'd disappear?

"I'm going after him," I yelled to Cade as I scrambled over the railing. "Call nine-one-one!"

"Minnie, I dropped my phone. I think it's in the water." He stumbled over to his cane and picked it up.

I reached into my pocket and tossed my cell over to him. "That button on the bottom turns it on and—"

"Tell me in the car," he said. "I'm coming with you."

I opened my mouth. Shut it. There wasn't time to argue. "Come on." I glanced up to the roof, but I couldn't even see Eddie. No doubt he'd settled down onto the cushion where I'd been and was already asleep. "Be back soon," I whispered.

Fast as I could, I dodged inside the houseboat. I put the gun's safety on, grabbed my backpack from the dining table, and tossed in the gun, urgency tugging at me hard.

We clattered down to the dock, me first, Cade coming behind me, his stroke-induced limp slowing him down. In what felt like hours, but was probably barely a minute, we were in my car and away.

I braked hard when we reached the road. Which way had he gone? If I was a killer trying to run away from people who could put me in jail, would I turn left, heading toward a road that would take me north and away from towns and houses and anyone who might be able to identify me? Or would I go straight into Chilson, then through and past town, to head downstate and lose myself in the downstate crowds?

"That way." Cade pointed straight.

I squinted and took my foot off the brake, but I didn't see any taillights. "I don't—"

"There was movement. No lights, just movement."

I still didn't see anything, but I trusted Cade's judgment. My right foot smacked the gas pedal down hard, and my little car did its best to roar forward.

"It's white," Cade said. "And . . . there!"

Finally I did see something. The vehicle was small and white and had a single occupant. Karringer was behind the wheel of an electric golf cart.

"No wonder we didn't hear him drive up," I said. Golf carts were a common means of transportation for many people in resort communities, but I'd never once thought that Karringer would have one. How had he . . . ?

I shook my head. Didn't matter. The only thing that mattered was keeping track of him until the police showed up. Which shouldn't be too hard, since even the top speed of even the fastest golf cart was . . . well, whatever it was, it had to be less than what my car could do.

We sped down the street, closing in fast on Karringer. "Call nine-one-one," I told Cade again. "Tell them we'll follow him until someone catches up to us."

Cade pushed at the phone's buttons and soon he was chatting with a helpful young man from dispatch.

"Where are we at this moment?" Cade asked the dispatcher's question out loud and glanced out the window. "Traveling east on Main Street, just passed the Hill Avenue intersection and—Minnie, he's turning left!"

I pounded the steering wheel in frustration. Karringer knew the streets and sidewalks of Chilson better than I'd expected. He'd turned into the narrow park where I'd sat with Detective Inwood and Deputy Wolverson. This end, the downtown end, was relatively flat, but it descended quickly toward a short street that ran along the lake's edge. And though the golf cart's width would easily zip down the sidewalk, there was no way my car would fit between the stonework planters.

The car's brakes screeched as I pushed hard on the pedal. The second we came to a complete stop, I opened my door and was outside.

I was halfway around the car and picking up speed when I heard the passenger door open. "Key's in the ignition," I called. "Drive around to the bottom of the hill. Make sure he doesn't get out."

Cade's voice came through the night. "Take your phone, Minnie. No arguments."

I wanted to argue, of course, but there wasn't time. The dim illumination from the few streetlights wasn't enough to guarantee catching a beach ball if it had been thrown straight at me, so I skidded to a halt, reversed direction, ran back, grabbed the phone from Cade's outstretched hand, and took off running again.

"Be careful," Cade shouted. I lifted one hand in a wave of agreement and kept on going.

What little light there had been up on the road filtered away quickly in the ornamental trees that dotted the sidewalk. Until tonight, I'd always enjoyed this hidden pathway, smiling every time I walked its brick-lined walk that curled around trees and shrubs and landscaped flower beds.

Now, as I pounded a straight path, running over grass, sidewalk, wood chips, and whatever else lay in my way, I hoped a small part of my brain would remember where the big rocks were and implement that memory in such a way that would allow me to avoid running straight into something and hurting myself so badly that, this time, Cade would be the one to take me to the emergency room.

Down the sidewalk, down the hill, down toward Janay Lake. If Karringer made it to the street that lay at the end of the park, he could zoom off in two different directions. And if he made it to the street before we caught up to him, we wouldn't know in which direction he'd gone. We'd lose him, maybe forever.

An insistent squawking noise came from the phone. Right. Cade had been chatting with the 911 dispatcher. But I was running flat out and had no breath to spare for talking. From what Cade had told him, maybe they'd anticipate what was happening. Maybe a police vehicle was already speeding on its way to intercept Karringer.

Nice thought, but I couldn't count on it.

I hurdled a flat rock that, if I remembered correctly, held a bronze marker that dedicated the park to a former mayor of Chilson. The perfectly executed leap boosted my confidence and I found that I hadn't been running as fast as I could. Not quite.

Run, Minnie, run, I told myself. *For Carissa. For Cade.*

I don't know if it was because I'd sped up or if Karringer had slowed, thinking that he'd lost us in his clever turn into the park, but I finally saw the back end of the golf cart. So far ahead, though, that I wasn't sure I'd be able to catch up. I had to stop him . . . but how?

Come on, Cade, I thought.

"Stop!" I yelled, loud as I could. "Stop right now!"

Karringer's head swiveled around and the golf cart

started drifting to the right. I saw his mouth move when he caught sight of me, and it didn't look like a very nice word that he said. He turned back around, but by the time he'd done so, the cart was headed directly toward a large and very solid-looking trash container.

He wrenched the steering wheel around. The cart turned hard. Too hard. In one quick movement, it fell on its side.

Car headlights swept across the scene, pinning Karringer down with its bright beams. My car, since I heard Cade's voice calling, "Minnie! Minnie, are you all right?"

"Fine," I said, waving, and ran to Karringer. His legs were trapped underneath the golf cart.

"I think my ankle's broken," he croaked. "I think it's bleeding. You have to help me."

With great caution, I approached. "You're hurt?" If he was injured, I did need to help him. And if his ankle was broken, he wouldn't be running away. I edged closer, trying to see.

"Minnie!" Cade was limping fast, cane in one hand and the gun in the other. "Stay back! I'm sure he's trying to get you close enough to grab and use as a hostage."

I backpedaled, my eyes wide.

Karringer cursed.

"Thanks," I breathed to Cade as he came up to me. "Sometimes I forget how naïve I am."

"Part of your charm, dear Minnie," he said. "You are all right, aren't you?"

"Pretty as a picture," I said. "You?"

"Fit as a fiddle."

Karringer was still whining about his ankle, and off in the distance, we heard the welcome sound of sirens rushing toward us.

"Well, my dear," Cade said, "I'd say Trap Two is turning out terrifically."

I laughed, and was pleased that only the teensiest bit of it sounded out of control. "Totally."

Karringer made one more try to wriggle out from under the golf cart, but Cade stepped forward, raising the gun. I grabbed a rock from the nearest flower bed and Karringer fell back, giving up.

Trap Two was Tremendous.

Chapter 21

The next morning, I'd given Kristen the short version of the previous evening's events, but she hadn't had time for the full-length story.

"Stupid restaurant," she'd muttered. "Why can't I have a Monday-through-Friday job like everybody else?"

"You did, remember? You hated it."

"Oh, yeah." Her smile came through the phone. "I did, didn't I?"

We scheduled a confab on the marina's patio, and I headed up to the boardinghouse for the last of the big summer breakfasts.

Come Sunday afternoon, Kristen and Eddie and I were comfortably sprawled out in the warm sun. Kristen and her long legs, which were somehow deeply tanned in spite of her long hours at the restaurant, were stretched across two chairs that she'd dragged together. Eddie and I were sharing a glider love seat that, for the first time all summer, was not squeaking on the forward glide. Either Chris had finally remembered to oil it or the people in the closest boat slip had done it themselves.

"Spill," Kristen said lazily, her face lifted to the sun. "Top to bottom."

So I did. She'd known bits of it before, but now I told her everything. I told her about Barb calling me when Cade had been questioned by the police, told her about my promise to Cade, told her about the accidents and the various possible implications, told her about Greg Plassey and Trock Farrand and Hugo Edel and Carissa's friend Jari. I told her about the traps, about the weekends, and about Eddie being on the roof and saving the day. I did not tell her about the rabbits.

Kristen turned toward me and opened one eye. "So it was the Weasel?"

I nodded. "Brett Karringer. After the police got there, he wouldn't stop talking. That Deputy . . ." I paused. "Ash Wolverson, do you know him?"

Kristen shook her head, which meant Wolverson wasn't from Chilson. I felt a small bleat of disappointment; I'd been a little curious about the man. "Anyway, after the police showed up, Brett confessed to everything. It was kind of weird, actually."

It had been very weird. Uncomfortable didn't begin to explain how I'd felt, stuck there until the police gave me permission to go, having to listen to Brett Karringer talk on and on as if he'd never stop.

"I love her so much," he'd said. "It was the worst torture to see her throwing herself at those older guys. She was the love of my life. Maybe she didn't know it, but she would have, I know she would have. All I had to do was show her how much I loved her, that's all."

At that point, Deputy Wolverson had pulled him to his uninjured feet. The effort didn't stop Brett from talking.

"I knew I had to do something after I saw her picture with you on Facebook." He practically spat at Cade. "She was seeing way too much of you. I couldn't let that keep happening."

Cade murmured something indistinguishable and Deputy Wolverson made enough of an encouraging noise that Karringer kept going.

"Yeah, I've been one of her Facebook friends for years, not that she knew it was me," he said, smirking. "I just tracked down a yearbook from her high school, found some guy who wasn't on Facebook, and signed up to be him. She friended me right away, asking if I was still dating Mimi Martin."

He laughed at his own cleverness.

I shivered.

"The way she posted stuff online," Karringer went on, "it was the easiest thing ever to see what she was up to. I can't believe some of the stuff she posted. I mean, if someone was out to get her, it would have been a piece of cake to track her down." He shook his head, then grinned at Cade. "That phone call I made got you to come running, didn't it?"

I glanced over. Cade was staring at Karringer with an expression that I couldn't quite interpret, and wasn't sure I wanted to.

Karringer tried to point at Cade. His movements were now restricted by the handcuffs that the deputy had placed around his wrists. "I'm the one who really loved her. Not you, not Plassey, not Farrand, not Edel, not anyone. Me! I was the one!"

He stopped, blew out a few guttural breaths, then slid into a kind of whine. "I had to take care of all those guys she posted about on Facebook. I thought those accidents would be just the ticket, but none of them worked the way they should have. I knew I'd have to try again, so I got a gun, but I had to lie low after Carissa. Didn't want to make it look too obvious, you know?"

"You did something to Greg's ladder, didn't you?" I asked.

Karringer chuckled. "Big expensive fence he put up doesn't do much good when he gives the code to all his friends. Pretty smart of me to be his friend, huh? I figured that was the way to go after threatening Edel didn't work. Telling Farrand to keep his hands off didn't work, either."

He'd shaken his head. "All those old guys, it didn't make sense for Carissa to be with them. It wasn't right, you know? I had to stop her from wasting her life. I wanted to kill you worst of all." Karringer had nodded at Cade. "But I couldn't work out how, not if I wanted to set you up for Carissa's murder."

"Sorry about that," Cade had said dryly.

"Yeah, me, too." Karringer had shrugged as the deputy guided him into the back of the police car. "Sometimes things just don't work out the way you want."

And sometimes they did. I'd used my cell phone to record every bit of Karringer's confession, and had promptly sent the digital file to Detectives Devereaux and Inwood. Almost as promptly, Detective Inwood had called to thank me, saying it would help build the case against Karringer.

"Really?" I asked.

"Everything helps," Inwood said. "Even if he pleads out, it speeds things up when the bad guy knows he was caught on tape, dead to rights. So, thank you."

"Oh. Well, you're welcome, then."

"How did Wolverson do?" Inwood had asked.

Do what? I'd wondered.

"You knew that Don and I have been training Wolverson up to detective, didn't you?"

Not sure how I could have known that since no one had told me, but whatever. "He did just fine," I'd said.

Inwood had gone on to describe the college courses Wolverson would be taking, and when we hung up, I knew more than I'd thought I ever would about the requirements for becoming a detective in the Tonedagana Sheriff's Office.

Kristen reached out for a potato chip and scooped it deep into the ultrafancy dip I'd slapped together half an hour earlier: dried onion soup mix in a container of sour cream.

While she concentrated on getting all the dip into her mouth without dropping any on her shirt, I thought back to the conversation I'd had yesterday with Cade. The aide who'd lied about his whereabouts the night of the murder had been put on suspension, but Cade had made a stand for her and she would keep her job.

Plus, Cade was going to contact Carissa's family and tell them he'd like to donate a painting to Carissa's favorite charity for a fund-raising auction, and that they could choose any painting currently on display anywhere in the world for the donation.

I told this to Kristen. "What's the charity?" she asked.

"You're not going to believe it."

"Society for the Advancement of Mincemeat?"

"You make the weirdest guesses ever. No, her mother said her favorite thing as a kid was visiting the library. When Cade told her there's a wonderful library in Chilson, she said that would be the perfect memorial." I looked over at Kristen. "Are you crying?"

Kristen sniffed. "Allergies. I get them something fierce this time of year."

She'd never had an allergy in her life, but I smiled and kept my mouth shut.

Coughing and rubbing her eyes, she asked, "So, is the Mitchell Situation resolved?"

"Now, that's an interesting question." I reached into my pocket and handed her the business card Mitchell had handed me the day before, a card inexpertly printed via a home computer and a laser printer.

"Northern Detective Agency," Kristen read out loud. "Mysteries Solved by Mitchell Koyne." She read it again, this time with her voice rising into question marks. "Mysteries solved?" She hooted with laughter. "Watch out, Minnie. This guy might be your new competition for tracking down killers."

"He's welcome to it," I said. Poor Mitchell. He was operating his new business out of his sister's attic, which, as it turned out, was where he was living these days. I wished him the best of luck. And who knew? Maybe this time Mitchell would actually make a success of himself.

Which reminded me. "Say, did I tell you who won the candy contest?"

Randall Moffit had been the only person to guess the correct (averaged) number of candies. I'd called him yesterday and he'd been happy enough to take the candy, but he hadn't cared about the bookmobile coming to his house. I'd suggested that he give the bookmobile prize to young Sheridan, the boy who'd wanted to have it stop at his grandmother's house.

Moffit had agreed, and my ear was still ringing from the squeal Sheridan had made when I called. I'd contacted the grandmother, who was thrilled at the idea of a library coming to her house. We got to talking, and it turned out that Sheridan's grandmother was on the board of Chilson's chamber of commerce. One thing led to another and the bookmobile and I were already booked to be in the town's Christmas parade.

Kristen hopped her chair a little to follow the sun at a slightly better angle. "Soon Eddie's going to have more friends than you do."

I patted Eddie on the head. "He already does. Everyone who sets foot on the bookmobile knows Eddie's name. I bet only half of them know mine. But that's okay. I don't really enjoy being the center of attention."

Kristen yawned. "That's the understatement of the year." She dipped another chip. "So, what's the deal with this furry guy and your doctor guy? Is he really allergic?"

I sighed. "My doctor guy has an appointment with an allergist. We'll know more in a couple of weeks."

"Hey, isn't that Greg Plassey?" Shading her face from the sun with the flat of her hand, Kristen pointed to a large boat cruising past.

It was indeed. Greg had ended up buying the boat that Chris had picked out for him the day I dragged Chris to Crown Yachts. I wasn't sure I believed in fate, but sometimes it was hard not to.

"Forgot to tell you," Kristen said. "The Edels were in the restaurant the other day, celebrating their anniversary. The two of them looked like newlyweds."

If Hugo had been seeing Carissa on the side, maybe her death had made him see how stupid he'd been. I smiled, happy for Annelise. "Was it a special anniversary?"

"Dunno. All I know is Hugo called ahead, asking for that small room, and had the whole place filled with roses." She rolled her eyes. "Nice gesture, I guess, but that rose smell didn't do anything to enhance their dinner."

"You have the sentiment of a soap dish."

She grinned. "Did you know that Trock Farrand's right-hand guy came in the other day? Said you'd talked up my place so much that he had to try it."

"Scruffy?" I went at the dip again. "Are they going to put the Three Seasons on their show?"

"Maybe."

The way she said it made me look up. "What do you mean, maybe?"

"Just what I said. Maybe. Scruffy would like to discuss it over dinner. At the City Park Grill in Petoskey."

The potato chip broke in my hand. "You're going on a date with Scruffy?"

"And I have you to thank for it."

"Huh." I put the chip pieces together. "Aunt Frances is the matchmaker in the family, not me."

"About that. Is it still all messed up?"

I smiled. "Yep. But it's just the way it was meant to be. Aunt Frances had things mixed up a little, is all." I laid out the news I'd heard at breakfast yesterday morning. Some of which I'd known already, of course. Deena and Quincy were engaged, as per the scene in the jewelry store. Paulette and Leo were making plans to move in together, and Zofia and her bicycle partner were making plans to drive Route 66 in October.

"What about that hot kid?" Kristen asked. "You know, what's his name?"

"Harris." I laughed out loud, disturbing Eddie enough to make him pick up his head and move it two inches. "Remember Megan? The girl Josh was dating but dumped because she's a White Sox fan?"

Kristen groaned. "Don't tell me. Harris was born into a White Sox family. His childhood bedroom was decorated with Sox stuff and his first book report ever was on a biography of Whitey Herzog."

"Pretty much."

We ate the bowl of chips down to the bottom, talking about nothing in general, giving Eddie an occasional scritch under the chin as we watched the boats float past and the clouds drift by. Late summer in Chilson with my two best friends. I couldn't think of any place I'd rather be.

"Pretty as a painting," Kristen said lazily. "Speaking of which, how is Cade's recovery coming? Will he . . . you know."

"Ever paint again?" I patted Eddie's head, thumping him just enough to make his head go up and down and up and down. He started purring. "Cade's physical therapist says he should be able to have enough motor control for painting before Christmas. Maybe even Thanksgiving."

"Sweet."

Yes, it was. I'd been worried that the exertions of Friday night had set him back, but it turned out that the clearing of his name had been of more benefit than a month of exercises.

"And it's all due to you," he'd said. "You and your ferocious feline. Thanks to your efforts, the investments of thousands of people are safe and sound. What can I possibly do to repay you?"

I'd protested, saying I didn't need anything, that I'd been glad to do it, that any halfway decent friend would have done the same thing, but he'd insisted. So had Barb and so had Ivy. Eventually we'd hammered out a compromise. He would paint a portrait of Eddie and I'd say thank you when it was delivered.

Kristen looked at me. Looked at Eddie. "You know," she said, "I've been watching him the whole afternoon and it really does seem as if he understands what we're saying. Especially you."

"Don't be silly." I picked him up and turned him around. "What do you think, Eddie? Do you understand a single solitary word of this sentence? If you do, say something. Anything."

Eddie looked me straight in the eye.

And didn't say a word.

Also available from
Laurie Cass

Lending a Paw
A Bookmobile Cat Mystery

Eddie followed Minnie home one day, and now she can't seem to shake her furry little shadow. But in spite of her efforts to contain her new pal, the tabby sneaks out and trails her all the way to the bookmobile on its maiden voyage. Before she knows it, her slinky stowaway becomes her cat co-pilot!

Minnie and Eddie's first day visiting readers around the county seems to pass without trouble—until Eddie darts outside at the last stop and leads her to the body of a local man who's reached his final chapter. Together, Minnie and Eddie will work to find the killer—because a good librarian always knows when justice is overdue.

Available wherever books are sold or at
penguin.com

facebook.com/TheCrimeSceneBooks

M884G101